An Unlikely Blessing

An Unlikely Blessing

ISBN-10: 0-8249-4814-9
ISBN-13: 978-0-8249-4814-6

Published by Guideposts
16 East 34th Street
New York, New York 10016
www.guideposts.com

Distributed by Ideals Publications, a Guideposts company
2630 Elm Hill Pike, Suite 100
Nashville, Tennessee 37214

Library of Congress Cataloging-in-Publication Data

Baer, Judy.
    An unlikely blessing / by Judy Baer.
        p.   cm. – (Forever Hilltop)
        ISBN 978-0-8249-4814-6
1. Clergy – Fiction.   2. Life change events – Fiction.   3. Country life – North
Dakota – Fiction.   4. Adjustment (Psychology) – Fiction.   5. North Dakota –
Fiction.   I. Title.
    PS3552.A33U55   2010
    813′.54–dc22   2010021742

Cover design by Kathleen Lynch
Cover art by Donna Nelson
Interior design by Gretchen Schuler-Dandridge
Typeset by Aptara

Printed and bound in the United States of America
10 9 8 7 6 5 4 3 2 1

An Unlikely Blessing

JUDY BAER

New York, New York

CHAPTER ONE

𝓤ncle Alex! Look out for that...*pig?*"

Jared's voice trailed away as Alex Armstrong applied a heavy foot to the brakes of his aging gray van and came to a screeching halt. A pink pig sat on its backside in the middle of the two-lane highway, its black hooves splayed on the concrete. It turned its head and gave them a baleful stare from one small eye, but made no signs of moving. Alex craned his neck and saw that the porker had company—piglets scurried back and forth across the road, squealing.

"Looks like a truck tipped over." Jared pointed to an old pickup jerry-rigged with a makeshift cage that lay on its side a few yards ahead. The driver of the truck—a thin, spry man who'd seen seventy in his rearview mirror—and several other passersby flapped their arms, but the pigs ignored them.

A man in oil-stained jeans, a denim shirt with a frayed collar, and a billed cap that announced Red's Gas & Garage sauntered over to Alex's van, bent to peer into the driver's side window, and grinned a flashing white smile. "Sorry about the holdup. We'll get them rounded up soon as we can. I *told* Ole that this piece of junk pickup wouldn't move Twinkle Toes, but would he listen? No way. I knew that if the pig and babies all moved to one side, that tin excuse for a truck would topple, and look what happened."

"Twinkle Toes?" Alex stammered.

The fellow gaped at him and shook his head, like Alex had been hiding in the other half of the world. "He's taking her to tonight's petting zoo at the park. It wouldn't be the same without Twinkle Toes." The man nodded as if that explained everything and meandered toward the sow. He pulled the billed cap from his head and yelled, "You pink varmints are blocking traffic!"

"Like that's going to help," Jared muttered, but he never took his gaze from the chaotic scene before him.

The man named Ole, apparent title-holder of the dented pickup, rummaged in his jacket pocket and produced a dark, spotted banana days past its prime. He held it out and peeled it slowly to reveal a brown pillar of mush.

Twinkle Toes gave a soft, almost loving grunt, hoisted herself to her feet and tiptoed toward the gelatinous muck. She reached her owner, opened her mouth, and made the banana vanish, peel and all. In a quick, practiced move, the elderly man slid a homemade halter over her head to trap her.

"If you guys would quit standing around gawking and help me get my pickup righted, I'd get her back in." A strong Norwegian accent frosted Ole's words. "The piglets will follow." The voice sounded familiar to Alex.

By this time the crowd had grown significantly, as traffic piled up in both directions. Alex took a step forward, ready to help. Then he remembered his impractical leather loafers. He wouldn't be able to get enough traction to make a difference moving the truck. Jared, city boy to the core, looked as helpless as Alex felt. Several men stepped up and, with much pushing and grunting, rocked the elderly pickup back onto its tires. Ole hopped into the box like a man half his age, shoved one end of a piece of three-quarter-inch plywood onto the ground, and turned it into a ramp. Twinkle Toes scrambled up the makeshift ramp. The piglets congregated by the back tires and were lifted one by one to join their mother.

Ole used a piece of rope to secure the door on the battered cage, rounded the truck to the cab, revved the engine, and crept off at a snail's pace.

"Ole is batty about that pig."

Startled, Alex jumped. The fellow who'd first spoken to him had returned. "Excuse me?"

"Oh yeah. He does presentations at schools, teaching grade school kids all about pigs. He tells them how pigs sniff out truffles and that they have to wallow in mud to keep cool because they don't have sweat glands."

"Oh." Jared shot Alex a befuddled look. "Weird. I guess you learn something new every day." He turned the crank to roll his window up.

The traffic jam was dispersing now that the excitement was over. One by one, the cars pulled away until Alex's van and the chatty fellow's truck were the only ones left.

"He even compares himself to President Harry Truman, if you can believe it." The man said.

Alex, who was beginning to feel as though he'd fallen through a rabbit hole and ended up in Wonderland, did a double take. "Excuse me?"

"According to Ole, Harry Truman once said that 'no man should be allowed to be President who does not understand hogs.'"

"I didn't know . . ." Alex stammered. How was he supposed to respond to that?

"I'm Dixon Daniels, by the way." The farmer thrust his hand through Alex's open window to shake hands. Before Alex could say more, the stranger wandered back to his own vehicle.

"What *is* this place?" Jared asked, shaking his head.

Alex glanced at the road sign not thirty yards from them.

WELCOME TO GRASSY VALLEY, NORTH DAKOTA.
CITY POPULATION: 1,254.
A PLACE LIKE HOME.

Alex took a deep breath. "Well, Jared, I guess you could say we're home."

⬛⬛⬛⬛⬛⬛⬛⬛

So this was it.

Alex Armstrong pulled his van to the side of the gravel road and stared at the panorama before him. He gazed across gently undulating fields, past a small, glittering azure pond painted brightly with late afternoon sun, and beyond a flock of marsh ducks coming in for a landing. The mallards' glossy-green heads glinted in the sunlight, and a tawny deer streaked from its hiding place near a stand of plump cattails as Alex fixed his gaze on a white outline butted against the horizon.

He squinted slightly and the structure took shape. A rectangle, with concrete steps protruding from the prow and an added-on shanty jutting from the stern, rested atop a slight rise in the prairie. A spire rose upward from the roof near the front of the building and seemed to disappear into heaven but for a wink of metal, a cross, piercing the sky.

"Is that your church, Uncle Alex?" Jared unwound in the passenger seat and stretched until Alex thought the seventeen-year-old might put his foot through the windshield. Sometimes Alex wondered how this lanky beanpole of a kid with feet the size of Volkswagens could possibly be related to his petite, proper sister Carol, but he'd been thankful for the companion-ship Jared had provided on the drive from Chicago.

Jared scraped his fingers through his already-tousled dark hair and peered at the vista before him. "It's like a photo-graph... or a movie set." He dusted tortilla chips from his lap and leaned forward. "It doesn't even look real."

Alex couldn't disagree with that. It didn't feel real either. He was a city boy through and through. What was tangible to him was the ivy-covered Christian college campus where he'd met the woman he'd planned to marry and had taught English for more than twelve years. Taught, that was, until the hand of God—a surprisingly heavy hand in this case—had turned him around and sent him off to seminary to become a pastor. There, he'd felt like an old man in a sea of youth. Most of his classmates were little older than the college seniors he'd taught for so many years.

Now here he was, a tenured professor turned inexperienced minister. His former fiancée married to someone else. Starting over at age forty-two. Gazing helplessly at his first assignment, a tiny, two-church North Dakota parish situated at a sparsely populated bend in the road.

Jared squirmed like an eager puppy in his seat. "Drive to the church. I want to see it up close."

Alex didn't move. Couldn't make himself. He'd known it would be small. He had been warned that this part of North Dakota was rural. But still, somehow, he hadn't expected this. The muscles in Alex's stomach tightened. It was the clench of anxiety he'd been fighting ever since the call had come and he'd been invited, sight unseen, to pastor this congregation. He was out of his element here.

Maybe God hadn't spoken to him at all, Alex thought, a sinking sensation in his stomach. Perhaps in his eagerness to get away from the pain of the break-up, he'd only *imagined* he was following God's will by coming here. Maybe this whole thing was a gross error in judgment on his part.

"Don't be like this. You told Mom and me that God sent you to seminary and brought you here for a purpose." Jared waved his hand toward the pristine white church. "So here it is. Let's take a look at it."

"It doesn't look much like a purpose," Alex muttered as he drove forward and pulled into the tidy churchyard. "It's barely as big as a shoe box." A cemetery with headstones in orderly rows sat off to one side. It must have been recently mowed, and not a blade of grass was out of place.

He'd have to investigate it later. Alex's senses were already tripping into overload. A riot of peonies and beds of petunias greeted them from well-kept flower beds along the foundation of the building. Old-fashioned flowers, he thought. His grandmother had grown peonies.

"Paul Bunyan's shoe box, maybe," Jared corrected him. "It must hold close to a hundred people."

"Sixty could pack in, maybe. Sixty sardines, I mean."

Jared gave his uncle an appraising look, and Alex clamped his mouth shut. His nephew probably thought he was a crotchety old geezer.

"I know, I know," Alex retorted to Jared's unspoken reproach. "I'm living my dream-come-true." Alex parroted his persistently cheerful sister's parting words as they drove away from her house in Elmhurst, outside Chicago.

"Mom says God puts people in situations that seem all wrong but turn out to be great somewhere down the road. Like how I used to hate mowing lawns and now that I have a little summer business doing it I really like it, you know?"

Bless Carol's heart, Alex thought. *She's raising him right.* Of course the kid was still supremely annoying on occasion.

Alex *was* being shaped for something. He had to be. God had asked him to walk by faith. And then God had trotted him here. The sky was so big here, the land so vast—so utterly unlike anything he'd ever known.

"This is cool." Jared opened the car door and jumped out.

Everything was either "awesome" or "cool" to Jared, including hot chocolate, summer days, the Sahara desert, and tanning beds. He ambled loose-jointedly toward the church. When Alex caught up with him, his nephew was staring up at the lofty steeple, head tipped back, squinting into the sun.

"Actually, my dream was more along the lines of an associate pastor position in a church in a mid-sized city," Alex said mildly, trying not to reveal his anxiety even though his heart was tripping like a drum major in the Rose Parade. "Some place offering lots of programs and several services on Sunday morning. My dream would have had an attached preschool and daycare. And, if there was a parsonage at all, it would be within five minutes of a grocery store and post office. *That* was *my* idea of a humble way to start." The worst part was, he'd almost had it. And then Natalie—

"Who needs that stuff? Here you've got pigs, cows, and . . . tractors and . . . wild animals and stuff. . . . "

Jared was trying. Alex had to give him that.

"There's something I don't get," Jared added. "Why is this called Hilltop Community Church? There isn't a hill for miles.

Why isn't it called Grassy Valley Community Church? That's the name of the town we drove through."

"This church isn't located in the town of Grassy Valley. It's out here in the country, in Hilltop Township, hence, the name Hilltop Community Church."

"What's a township?"

"I had to look it up myself," Alex admitted, feeling a little sheepish that he had so much to learn. "It's a subdivision of a county, with a local government that takes care of things like road maintenance—a community within a community, of sorts. The people of Hilltop are tied together by their interest in this particular area, and the church is named after the township."

"Oh," Jared said. He snapped his gum and took the steps to the front door two at a time. He tested the doorknob and the ten-foot-high door glided silently open. "There aren't even any locks." A shadow flitted across Jared's features. "Different from our church at home, isn't it? Mom still talks about the fuss everyone put up when the council decided that we needed to lock the doors when no one was in the church office."

Alex remembered it vividly. He, too, had hated the idea of having someone seek solace in a church and be turned away by bolted doors; but after several acts of vandalism on the property, what else could they do? Theirs was an inner city congregation, a beacon of light in a poor, tough district, a church his family had loved for years in a neighborhood that had aged badly. But here were open doors to welcome anyone who might come.

Alex took a deep breath and followed his nephew into the building. He felt immediately at home in the high-ceilinged vestibule, as if welcomed by the generations who had wor-shipped here. The floor, worn from years of footsteps, was solid beneath their feet and polished to a high shine. Two ropes, one thick and meaty, the other slightly finer, hung straight down from the ceiling.

"Bells!" And before his uncle could stop him, Jared grabbed the thickest rope and tugged. Something grated, and the sound of a clapper striking the inside of a gigantic bell gonged out its song. Alex felt the sound reverberate in his chest.

"Cool." Jared dropped the rope and pushed through a pair of tall, white swinging doors into the body of the church. Alex followed more slowly, soaking in the scents of pine oil and candle wax, feeling as if he were at a precipice, looking upon the sheer drop into which he was about to tumble.

"It's like landing on another planet." Jared said.

"You've got that right," Alex murmured. Planet Hilltop Community Church. "I guess no one will mind if we go in and look around." It was peculiar to feel like an interloper in what was now "his" church.

"Didn't the call committee want to bring you here first?"

So Jared actually *had* been listening when his uncle told him what had transpired prior to being hired. Alex hadn't been sure, plugged in as Jared was to a pair of headphones. He'd been busy listening to music and eating bag after bag of chips all the way across Minnesota.

"Let's take the risk."

The interior looked more like a replica in a museum than a functioning church. Ahead of Alex, Jared followed the ruby carpet runner down the aisle toward the altar, his size-eleven athletic shoes making a squishy sound as he walked. He tipped back his head to stare at the ceiling. "What's that stuff?"

Alex followed the direction of his nephew's pointing index finger. "Embossed tin. The real stuff." He glanced down and paused to run his hand along the back of a pew, a curve of wood with intricate carving. "This is a masterpiece. Every care was taken in building this place. It's incredible."

Thanks to sunlight flowing through the elaborate stained glass windows depicting the highlights of Jesus' time on earth, every bit of the church glistened. It was as if they were standing inside a jewel box. From a painting above the altar, a kindly, loving Jesus with small children scattered at His feet beckoned them forward. *Come to Me, all you that are weary and burdened, and I will give you rest.*

"Are you scared, Unc?" Jared's question hit hard at the queasy pit of Alex's stomach.

"Scared?" He paused. "I'd like to say no, but I suppose I am, a little. This"—he tipped his head toward the church and the fields beyond—"is foreign territory."

Here I am, Lord. You've taken me a long way from home in so many ways. It is *like another universe.* He took a deep breath and opened his eyes.

He put his hand on Jared's bony shoulder. "But I'm sure God will bless it in ways I can't even imagine." He added a silent prayer to the end of his statement: *Please?*

CHAPTER TWO

Alex and Jared swung around at the sound of a small scuffle in the doorway. A tall, athletic, sandy-haired man in denims strode into the church, followed closely by a pretty, pleasant-looking woman with deep auburn hair and vivid blue eyes. Alex and Jared froze where they stood, guilty as children caught with their hands in the cookie jar.

"You rang?" the man said. His hazel eyes shone with amusement. A lock of hair flopped into his eye, and he scraped it back with his fingers.

Alex and Jared stared at him blankly.

"You rang?" he said again, this time tipping his head toward the entryway. "You rang the church bell?"

"Oh . . . sorry. That was me." Jared flushed to the roots of his hair. "I didn't mean to disturb anyone. Out in the country like this," he glanced ruefully at Alex. Jared's cheeks grew ruddy as he scuffed the toe of his foot and lowered his gaze. "I thought that no one would hear."

"But that's the reason you ring the bell, isn't it? So it can be heard."

Alex felt sorry for his impulsive nephew. "We apologize. I hope you didn't drive all the way over here to check it out."

"It isn't exactly a cross-country trip," the sandy-haired man said dryly. He was of medium build but his arms were tanned and sinewy—a man accustomed to outdoor work. "Takes all of three minutes to get here, including turning the key in the ignition. We live on the first farm north." He tipped his head in the direction that was, apparently, north and thrust out his hand. "Mike Carlsen. This is my wife Lauren. And you are . . . ?" He let the question trail into the ether.

Alex took two steps toward the man's wife. "Lauren? From the call committee? I believe we've already met. Via the telephone, at least. I'm Alex Armstrong, and this is my nephew Jared. He kindly agreed to keep me company on the drive out from Chicago."

"*Reverend* Armstrong! So nice to meet you in person!" Lauren gripped his hand in a warm, firm shake. Once she spoke, Alex recognized her as the brisk, cheerful woman with an easy laugh and a rich, refined voice that sounded smooth and inviting as a cup of hot cocoa on a winter's day. That warm husky mocha-laced voice was difficult to forget. "I didn't realize you were coming today."

"Jared and I took a few extra days to drive here. I hadn't spent much time with my nephew recently, so we did some sightseeing along the way." He glanced at Jared, who was once again staring at the church's interior. "I'd planned to call you from the road to tell you I'd be here a day early, but then decided that perhaps I'd do some exploring unannounced first."

"No problem. We're accustomed to early around here." Mike drawled. "No matter what time the church organist gets here to play the prelude on Sunday mornings, there's a gaggle of older people already waiting for the music to start. She suspects they arrive the night before and sleep in the pews just to get her goat."

Jared's jaw dropped and Alex looked startled. Then Lauren's rich, hearty laughter spilled out. "Mike, quit teasing! Don't believe everything you hear, Reverend. Mike's sense of humor sneaks up on you sometimes." She waved him away. "Have you eaten?"

"We ate lunch four or five hours ago, but we still have some bagels in the car. We'll be fine."

Lauren wrinkled her nose. "So you *haven't* eaten. We'll remedy that first thing. While you are looking around the church, I'll go home and fix a little something. Mike, bring them to our place when they're done."

"That's not necessary," Alex protested, "you don't need to bother—"

"You'll soon realize that very little is accomplished around here without a pot of coffee and a plate of goodies," Mike said. "Rule number one is that Hilltop Community Church and plentiful food go hand-in-hand.

"We moved back to my family home to farm after twenty years in Fargo. I'd nearly forgotten how much of a friendship ritual feeding of others is around here." She patted her lean stomach. "But I got the hang of it again very quickly."

She turned to her husband, who was gazing at her affectionately. "Give me twenty minutes." Mike nodded and raised his index finger in the air as his wife turned to leave.

"I'd be happy to give you the tour unless you want to explore the church for yourselves," Mike offered.

"We'd like a tour," Alex said. "I felt like an interloper just walking in."

"That's what churches are for, aren't they? Walking in, sitting down, praying. No one is turned away here." Mike's lip twitched as if he were trying to hold back a smile. "Of course, newcomers do have to endure a lot of curious stares. I suppose it's the price you pay for walking into a place where everyone has known everybody else for a hundred years."

Alex wondered how long it would be until he was no longer considered a newcomer or if that would ever happen.

"When we moved here, I had to go through that rite of passage myself," Mike added, eyes dancing. His even temperament was apparent in his every word. "After all, I was a stranger and I had married a girl from the community. I had to prove myself worthy. Now it's your turn."

Alex swallowed thickly.

"Don't worry about it," Mike assured him. "The people here are eager for you to come. We've been without a pastor for some time. They are ready to love you. We worried that we wouldn't find another pastor for our little two-point parish."

Jared suddenly tuned in to the conversation. "What's a two-point parish?"

"Just a way of saying that I'll be responsible for two individual churches with two separate buildings and two congregations," Alex explained. "Each church is too small to meet the expense of a pastor on its own, but by working together they can afford one. In this case, me."

"Not just anyone wants to come out to a small, isolated spot like this," Mike said. "It's hard to find someone willing to take it on. Podunk USA, that's us. The economy hasn't done us any favors lately what with high gas prices and all."

That, Alex mused, was worrisome.

Seeing Alex's expression, Mike hurried to add, "You see, you really are a gift from God."

An odd feeling settled in the pit of Alex's stomach. He tried to keep his tone casual. "How many pastors did the call committee interview before they chose me?"

Mike's his eyebrows practically disappeared beneath that lock of sandy hair. "How many? Only you. Nobody else would even talk to the committee. Something about the location or some such thing."

Alex and Jared glanced at each other. Jared's face had gone white, and Alex felt the color draining from his own cheeks as well. *No one* would even *talk* to these people?

"Of course, Lauren and the others took that as a really good sign," Mike continued, unaware that he'd shot a dart of terror into Alex's heart.

"A . . . a *good* sign?" Alex wasn't sure he'd heard correctly.

"Sure. We asked God to send us the *perfect* person for Hilltop, and He picked you." Mike had more confidence in his voice than Alex thought warranted.

"Obviously He didn't want our minds muddled with a bunch of choices and opportunities to make a mistake. No, Reverend Alex, you were the only candidate, hand-picked and hand-wrapped by God. I *told* you that you are a gift to us."

"No pressure," Jared said with a grimace as they followed Mike into the basement.

The expectations for him couldn't be higher. It was a recipe for unbridled success or complete disaster. At the moment, he just didn't know which. They'd driven past several ponds on the way to the church. Alex hoped they weren't deep. He was afraid that someone might ask him to walk on water.

They spilled out of the narrow staircase passageway and into a large room filled with long tables, surrounded by metal folding chairs. Sheer lace tablecloths and bud vases holding artificial pink roses softened the hard edges of the room. Simple ruffled valences cozied up the high, narrow windows. Off to the left, through a pass-through, they could see a sparkling kitchen.

"We like to keep things nice," Mike explained. "God's house and all. The community has a lot of fussy housekeepers. No dust gets by them."

Alex imagined an army of women marching, gimlet-eyed, brooms held high, ready to mount a frantic attack on smudges and dust.

Big white enamel coffeepots and gold and black serving carafes were lined in rows on the counter, and although he might have imagined it, Alex thought the aroma of freshly brewed coffee lingered in the air.

"What's that?" Jared pointed to a porcelain sink over which an old-fashioned hand pump loomed.

"There's a well beneath the church that was dug when the building was built."

"You mean there's no running water?" Jared's eyes widened.

Alex recalled the half-hour shower Jared had taken at the hotel that morning.

"That pump isn't hooked up any more. We just left it there when we remodeled the church basement—sentimental, I guess."

The teenager looked dubious. His expression read, *What could be sentimental about a pump?*

"Lauren likes to tell about how her grandmother used to wash dishes after a potluck. She'd pump the water into a kettle, heat it on the stove, and then use it in the sink. More than once she pumped up a little lizard or a garter snake. They just slithered right out. That's why, Lauren says, they carried water from home to make coffee."

"Gross!" Jared shuddered. For once, something wasn't cool.

Funeral bells, hand pumps and snakes, a church kept clean as any five-star restaurant's kitchen, only one candidate for the pastor's position . . .

What else would he find in this strange place?

"We'd better go," Mike said. "Lauren will be waiting. I wish we had time to drive by the Hubbard house. You'd enjoy seeing it. We'll do it another time."

Alex wasn't sure what was so special about the Hubbard house, and Mike didn't seem in any rush to tell him. No matter. He'd find out soon enough.

Mike, Alex and Jared rode together down the long, straight road to the Carlsen farm. The road was flanked by windbreaks made of rows of trees that Mike referred to as shelterbelts. The gravel driveway led into an open area where several buildings circled the working part of the yard. Mike pointed out the old-fashioned wooden granaries, a machine shop, a storage shed, chicken coop, and bunkhouse as well as a shiny cluster of round metal grain bins as they drove up. A red barn loomed large over a fenced-in pasture that, at the moment, was occupied by a caramel-colored Belgian draft horse, a miniature donkey, and two brown-and-white llamas.

"Llamas?" Jared's mouth hung open. "Here?"

"They're Lauren's project." Mike shrugged. "She wants to raise them and use the fiber for weaving. She's always got some new project she's working on." As Mike spoke, a gleaming red rooster perched on the top fence rail fluffed his feathers, stretched to his full height, and crowed a perfectly splendid cock-a-doodle-do.

Jared pointed to a small building on the far side of the yard. "Is that a pig pen? Cool!"

The four square house was old—built in 1909 according
to Mike—but solid and inviting. "There are several houses like
ours throughout the neighborhood," Mike explained. "Sometimes they call this style a Prairie Box. When you used to be
able to order an entire house from the Sears catalogue, these
square houses were easiest to ship. The Hubbard house that I
mentioned earlier wasn't one of those, however. The first
Mrs. Hubbard had very specific ideas about the house she
wanted built."

"What, exactly, is so special about—" Alex began.

"A house from Sears?" Jared interrupted. "Like a kitchen
appliance or pair of shoes?" Jared sounded incredulous.

"Hard to imagine now," Mike said agreeably, "but then it
made sense."

He led them into the house through a side door that entered directly into the kitchen. "Lauren's grandparents always
saved the front door for 'special' occasions," Mike explained,
"And now we always forget it's there."

Cherry cupboards lined the kitchen walls and in the center
of the room was a large wooden dining table set with placemats,
frosty glasses of iced tea, and a plate of sandwiches large
enough to feed a small militia.

"Welcome." Lauren ushered them in. "We've got tuna,
roast beef, and my husband's favorite, fried egg sandwiches."
Lauren gestured them to their places around the table. "There's
leftover macaroni salad too. Sorry I can't offer you more on
such short notice. I took an apple cake out of the oven an hour
ago, so we can have that. I would have cooked more had I
known you'd be here for supper." She paused for a breath. "Or
do you call it dinner? Around here, dinner is usually what's
served at noon and supper comes at six o'clock."

"You can call meals anything you like when they're like this." Alex admired the feast, mouth watering.

Mike winked at him. "We *told* you nothing gets done without food around here."

"You'll be fine here, Reverend Alex," Lauren assured him. "If you like food, you'll be okay. People around here *love* to feed the minister."

Jared studied the food-laden table and muttered, "Awesome." Alex, however, could only imagine his waistline expanding.

"Please, take a place, sit anywhere you like," Lauren encouraged.

Mike was the last to sit up to the table. He looked at Alex expectantly. "Would you like to say grace?"

He was happy to do it. This request would be made of him often from now on, he suspected.

They bowed their heads. "Lord, I am grateful for this opportunity to share this meal with Lauren and Mike, and for their hospitality. Thank You for safe travel and delicious food. Bless the people of Hilltop, Lord, and guide me so that I may become the pastor they are hoping to have. Amen."

And thank You for a fresh start, Lord. Help me to make the most of it.

"Pass the sandwiches," Mike instructed, "And dig in. I never pass up a fried egg sandwich."

Jared took one of the sandwiches, laid it on his plate and peeked tentatively under the top piece of bread. Alex was amused to see that the egg yolk was broken and cooked hard and looked like a big white eyeball with a yellow iris. It was liberally sprinkled with pepper, and both slices of bread were thick with melted butter. This would be very new to his nephew, he knew. He doubted his sister Carol ever made this fare.

Mike took a bite and chewed, a smile on his face. "The only thing better is an onion sandwich, but Lauren won't let me have any of those."

"Onions and what?" Alex asked. He'd never heard of some of the things people ate around here.

"Onions and nothing—except butter and salt."

"Don't you need meat on the sandwich?"

"When you order a roast beef sandwich with raw onions, what do you taste?" Mike asked and helped himself to another egg sandwich.

"Onions mostly, I guess."

"Exactly. Why bother with the meat when you only taste the onions anyway? Sad to say Lauren taught me what an onion sandwich was and then said I couldn't have any."

"Why?" Jared shoved his sandwich into this mouth and took a huge bite. He looked puzzled and his uncle tried to suppress a smile.

"I had to pick between onions and kissing my wife." Mike grinned impishly. "What else could I do?"

"Oh." Jared blushed until he was the color of the barn outside the window. "I get it."

Lauren patted the back of her husband's hand. "He made the right choice."

Alex couldn't stop the smile he felt spreading across his features. He felt a flutter of excitement and a lightness he hadn't experienced of late. At the moment he was feeling sorry for all those other poor fellows who had passed up this opportunity.

"So tell me about your sister church, All Saints Fellowship. I don't know much about them."

Lauren and Mike exchanged a potent glance, and a blush reddened Lauren's neck and rose all the way to her forehead. "I'll apologize in advance for them. All Saints is an ironic name, according to some people. Wags around here think 'All Sinners' might be a better moniker."

Alex laid his sandwich down. "I don't understand."

"Some think the problem boils down to pure jealousy," Lauren said with a sigh. "Although I think it's more complicated than that."

"Jealousy?"

"Hilltop is bigger by half, so it has half again as many offerings in the plate. We put a new roof on our church and shored up the foundation years before All Saints could afford to do it." Lauren spoke as she stacked empty plates. "Then we remodeled the kitchen and laid new carpeting. That ruffled a few feathers too. Our quilting ladies send a lot of quilts to overseas missions each year." She appeared pleased by this bit of information. "We do nearly one hundred layettes and they can barely manage fifty. But the worst of it is that we give three times as much to missions as All Saints, and it's given them an inferiority complex the size of Minnesota. That may be at least part of the issue."

Alex was reminded of the petty jealousies that often haunted competing departments in his college. "How do they know how much your church is giving? Aren't these gifts supposed to be given quietly, without trumpeting numbers to the whole world?"

"When you give alms, do not let your left hand know what your right hand is doing, you mean? The two churches have always shared a treasurer, and those things get out. Of course that doesn't take Alf Nyborg into account. . . . "

The doorbell rang and Lauren sprang up. Before Lauren could reach the door, they heard the screen door slam and heavy footsteps on the stairs.

A small, stocky woman shot into the room like a rocket from a cannon. "We have to kill them all immediately," she announced. "Lauren, you've got to help me!"

CHAPTER THREE

$\mathcal{T}$ he little woman appeared to be a series of squares, from her high cheekbones and square jawline to her blocky shoulders, rectangular body, and stocky legs. She even wore a pair of shoes with broad squared toes.

"Hello, Mattie," Lauren said pleasantly. She didn't seem the least bit concerned about the mayhem the older woman was advocating.

"Poison. We need poison." Mattie's eyes glittered with malicious glee. "Do you think Sam Waters sells anything at the hardware store powerful enough to do them in?"

"Coffee, Mattie?" Mike said mildly. "We're going to have apple cake with ice cream in a minute."

"I'm so upset I couldn't eat a thing, I'm sure." Yet she trotted to the table and sat down with a thud on a spindle-backed chair. She made a lot of noise for a little woman. "Just a sliver, please. And the tiniest dab of ice cream."

Lauren smiled and stood up. "I assume the rest of you want some too?"

Alex and Jared nodded mutely. Alex didn't know quite what else to say.

It was only then that Mattie appeared to notice them. "Company, I see." She looked them over like they were fresh produce at an open air market. "Young man," she said to Jared. "You'd better have a double piece. You need fattening up."

The teenager stared at her, deer in the headlights.

Lauren came back to the table with a slab of cake and put it in front of her newest guest. There were two huge scoops of ice cream on top. Mattie didn't even blink. It seemed that the word "sliver" had an entirely different meaning here.

"This is our new pastor, Alex Armstrong, and his nephew Jared. Alex, this is Matilda or, as we call her, Mattie Olsen. Hers is one of the oldest families in the community."

"Pastor Armstrong!" Mattie patted at her hair, and gray sprouts erupted all over her head. Unfortunately, it made it look worse rather than better. "Welcome to the Hilltop community." Her words were now warm and buttery, and her complexion deepened to a ruddy color not unlike beet juice. "Oh, my, I hope you don't think I was rude. I'm not usually so impolite. It's just that I've been so distressed and we really need to do the killing soon." She nodded as if that explained everything.

Her eagle eye fell again on Jared. "And young man, you really *are* too thin. What if you got sick? You'd have nothing to go on." She patted her own ample mid-section. "Now I, on the other hand . . . I'll have you over for rommegrot one day soon."

"What's—"

She cut Jared off. "It's a pudding made with cream, you know. Very tasty." Alex marveled that she'd gone from murder and mayhem to clogging Jared's arteries without a beat.

Mattie's head spun again, this time toward Mike. Her mouth curled downward and the edges of her brow knit together. "Why wasn't I told they were here? I should have known. I'm an *Olsen!*"

"They arrived less than an hour ago. We found them at the church looking around. Other than us, you're the first to meet them," Lauren said soothingly, obviously accustomed to smoothing this particular bird's feathers.

"Oh, well then. . . . " Mollified, Mattie turned again to Alex. "If you have any questions whatsoever about the church or the community, come to me. I've been here a long time and my grandfather was one of the first pioneers in the area. I'm familiar with everyone and everything."

Alex had no doubt she was. Out loud he said, "Maybe you could start by telling me who you are planning to kill?"

Mattie reddened and put her hands to her cheeks. "Goodness, I didn't make a very proper entrance, did I?" She paused, and her eyes narrowed. "Ants. Armies of ants, multitudes of ants, *legions* of ants. In the back entrance to the church. We've got to do something before we serve the next church dinner or they will be crawling on every counter. I wonder if Sam has enough poison for the job. Who did I hear was going to Minot? They could get more poison there."

Anxiety flooded her features. "I saw a documentary on imported red fire ants. Do you know they swarm? And that their bites are painful? Dreadful little things, ants." She stabbed her cake with her fork.

"That kind of ant doesn't live in these parts, Mattie," Mike said calmly. "Besides, I rather admire the little things. They're hard workers, ants."

Mattie glared at him.

"Why don't you let me take care of the ant traps and you put your energy toward those angel food cakes you do so well?" he offered. Alex liked his calm, pragmatic way of dealing with this obviously excitable woman.

"Mattie can make an angel food higher and lighter than anyone I've ever met," Lauren said, genuine admiration in her voice. She brought the coffeepot to the table, poured it into five mugs, and distributed them around the table. When she set a cup in front of Jared, he made a face. Alex gave the boy a warning look. Apparently everyone around here drank coffee.

"It's in the egg whites and the mixing," Mattie said. "And years of practice."

"No church dinner here is complete without a piece of angel food with whipped cream and berries." Lauren smiled a little as she dealt cake out to the rest. "And some devil's food cake just to balance things out."

"Huh?" Jared choked on his cake.

At least, his uncle thought, he hadn't said "Cool."

"Years ago the church dinner committee decided that people didn't need more than two choices for dessert," Lauren explained. "They decided on cake, white and chocolate. Some jokester concluded that, to represent the battle between good and evil, the cakes should be angel food and devil's food. We've loosened up on the desserts now—there are usually several choices—but there's always angel food and devil's food on hand as a tip of the hat to the past." She blew on her coffee to cool it. "There's a story for everything around here."

"And a lot of hat tipping," Mike added. "Wait and see."

Alex was sure he would see.

After Mattie finished her cake and left in her Chevy Impala—on her way, no doubt, to bugle to the community that the pastor had arrived—they sat at the table in companionable silence. Alex found the big country kitchen both inviting and relaxing. There were half a dozen bird feeders just outside the big picture window by the table, and a bird clock—the kind that chirps a birdsong on the hour—over the door. Quilted place-mats, purple violets with fuzzy green leaves, and a radio softly playing country music in the background all seemed so welcoming and so apt out here. So many people to meet, so much history to learn and, no doubt, a potential mine field or two to scope out, Alex mused. There was always at least one touchy, tricky parishioner who could rile the entire congregation. Who would that be? He was in no hurry to find out.

"You two look exhausted," Lauren said bluntly.

"It has been a long day."

"Why don't you just crash here tonight and start fresh in the morning? The parsonage can wait until tomorrow."

Alex's legs and arms felt heavy with weariness, and he could see Jared was wearing out as well. "It's tempting, but we really should..."

"I'll take that as a 'yes.' Get your bags and bring them upstairs. I'll show you the guest room."

He was too tired to protest, Alex realized.

They retrieved what they needed from the van and followed Lauren up the stairs to a guest room. It held a set of antique dressers, a rocking chair, several studio photos from the 1800s, and an open armoire filled with colorful quilts. The bed was large and inviting.

Both he and Jared were asleep as their heads hit the pillows.

"Are you ready to see the parsonage?" Lauren inquired the next morning after a hearty breakfast of biscuits and sausage gravy. "I'll put some milk, eggs and bread in a bag, so you'll have a little something to eat until you get to the store in Grassy Valley."

She returned with an entire bag of groceries gleaned from her own cupboards including fruit, cereal, caramel rolls and a quarter of the apple cake. She handed the bag to Alex. "The parsonage is just across the slough from the church. Seems to work out pretty well. You can see all the comings and goings from your kitchen window."

"'Slough'?"

"That marshy wet area beside the parking lot."

"The pond, you mean?"

"Those birthing rooms for mosquitoes may be called ponds in the city," Lauren told him, "but here they are definitely sloughs."

The parsonage. His new home. It was twenty-four years ago that he'd moved into his first apartment in Chicago, right near the college. At the time, to a broke college student, it was the Taj Mahal. Alex had eventually graduated into a 'real' house, but had never lived more than a few blocks from campus. He thought he was settled in the Chicago suburbs for life. Of course, he'd thought he'd be married too, but that hadn't gone exactly as planned.

"I hope you'll be patient with me as we learn the ropes out here."

"You will have to be patient with us as well," Lauren assured him. "This is a new dance and we're first-time partners. We're bound to step on each other's toes occasionally, but it doesn't mean we won't enjoy the music."

Alex wiggled his toes inside his shoes, imagining already how many ways they could be trod upon.

$\mathcal{M}$ike walked Alex and Jared from the cool, cosseting interior of the Carlsen house into outside brightness, where split-tailed barn swallows with rusty bellies and blue-black wings reeled overhead. The Carlsens' corrugated steel grain bins glinted sharply in the intense light, and the glare forced them to shade their eyes with their hands.

"It's a beautiful day to move in." As Mike pointed a finger in the direction of the church and beyond, a big black lab with glossy fur and a tongue the color of pink cotton candy padded up to them. Mike automatically bent to scratch him behind one ear. "Hey, Laddie. Good boy." He looked up at Alex. "You know where you're going, right? Hang a right after the church. Then it's the first driveway on the left."

"Aren't you coming?" Alex hesitated. He didn't feel ready to be set free to roam quite yet.

"I thought you might want some time alone first, this being your new home and all."

Alex could see the wisdom in that. He didn't have great hopes for his new digs, considering that they'd been standing empty for some time. It might be better to see the place without an observer from the congregation. That way he could regroup if the house was not what he was expecting. He didn't want to start on the wrong foot.

"Good idea. But feel free to stop over any time," Alex said. Not only did he already feel a kinship with Mike and Lauren, but he suspected it could get lonely here on the prairie, with homes sparsely scattered across thousands of acres of land. Alex was accustomed to keeping the side windows of his house shuttered so that he didn't look directly into his neighbor's kitchen. He didn't know what all this space would do to him. He'd read Rolvaag's *Giants in the Earth* and knew of Beret Hansa's spiral into madness alone on the prairie. It didn't seem quite so unlikely to him anymore.

"Don't worry." Mike laughed. "People around Hilltop don't have any reservations about that. You'll see. By the way, the key to the parsonage is under the front door mat. Around here that's where most people keep their keys."

What, then, was the use of locking one's door? Or was that another formality that could be dispensed with now that he was in Hilltop? Alex imagined hoards of curious onlookers crowding into his home to examine the titles of the books on his shelves and white-glove the tops of his counters.

He'd be sure to pick up a dust cloth. But they'd be disappointed by the books. All he'd brought with him were scholarly tombs—theology, history, and the many he'd collected in his years as an English professor. If they looked in his closets they'd find his extensive collection of running shoes and the obscenely large bags of Tootsie Rolls and Hershey's Kisses that his sister had given him as a going-away present. If he had a secret vice for others to discover, it was chocolate. Bars, drops, eggs, bunnies—he loved chocolate in every form. Pretty benign, Alex decided, but still a secret he wanted to keep. If the single ladies of Hilltop and Grassy Valley discovered he liked chocolate, he'd be smothered in brownies before he knew what hit him.

He and Jared clambered into the van and Alex turned the key in the ignition. He'd left the key in the vehicle with the doors unlocked. He was already losing his city ways. Where he'd come from that was an invitation for someone to take a joy ride in his car. Here, it seemed that the worse that could happen was a low flying bird making its mark on his windshield. Alex backed the car up slowly.

"Cool people, huh, Unc?" Jared leaned forward in his seat as if willing his uncle to go faster. "Lauren's a great cook too."

Spoken like a true bottomless pit of a teenage boy. "Very." Alex drove slowly, unaccustomed to the pull and shift of loose gravel rather than smooth pavement beneath his tires. Fresh gravel, his friend and mentor Edward O'Donnell had told him, was the nuisance of many rural pastors. Usually there was little time to spare between services at one church and another. On gravel, however, there was no speeding without the danger of going into the ditch or having a pebble fly up and crack the windshield. More rocks in the road to negotiate— literally.

They turned off the Carlsens' lane and onto another larger gravel thoroughfare, a county road, according to Mike. Someday the community had hopes that someone, somewhere would come up with enough money to tar or even pave it, he'd said, but things were tight in the road department these days, what with people behind on their taxes and all.

They passed the church, its fresh white paint making it glow in the sunlight, and Alex impulsively turned in the opposite direction of the parsonage.

"What are you doing, Unc?"

"Mike told me that All Saints is this way. I thought we'd just drive by and take a look."

Alex patted his shirt pocket and dug out his sunglasses. The sun was bright and the colors so vivid that it hurt his eyes. The sky, but for a few puffy white clouds, was cerulean blue. The fields were a fresh bright green and the tilled fields, a rich, velvety black. They passed an occasional farm, most of them with large white houses and barn-red outbuildings. Once, a dog raced down the road after them, barking, until they passed the territory it was protecting. Alex felt as though he was driving through a Norman Rockwell painting.

After about twenty minutes, Jared started to squirm in his seat. "Are you sure you got the directions right?"

"Mike said we could see the building from the top of a small rise. I was sure this was . . . " Alex's voice faded as they ascended what could barely be called a hill. "Look! There it is!" He pulled to the side of the road and they stared off into the distance where a small church nestled into the flatness of the countryside. Fields of various shades of green made a patchwork design around it. From here it looked like a postcard scene, so quaint and pristine that it could have been an artist's rendition of the prairie. All Saints Church's shape was similar to that of Hilltop, but the building was much smaller than its sister, and squat rather than soaring.

"Cool!" Jared said. "If we're going to look at it, let's go."

Alex drove cautiously into the churchyard, feeling a little like he was trespassing, but Jared had no such reservations. As the car rolled to a stop, Jared flung open the door and burst out of the vehicle. "Maybe they've got church bells here too."

"Please don't ring them this time," Alex pleaded. "I'd like to announce my presence differently here."

Jared reached the church, grabbed the door handle and pulled. Nothing. The door did not swing open in welcome as it had at Hilltop. This place was locked up tight.

"I thought Mike said churches were for walking into," Jared commented. "So what's up with this?"

"Apparently not everyone agrees with Mike's philosophy," Alex murmured. He saw already that Hilltop and All Saints church were going to be very different.

███ ███ ██ ███

The parsonage was a sturdy two-story structure with a green shingled roof. It was painted bright white, its radiance broken up by deep green shutters surrounding double-hung windows.

Peonies, tiger lilies, hostas, and salvia grew around the concrete block foundation, making the house look as though it had erupted in the midst of a patch of flowers. There were several hanging baskets of petunias and begonias blooming on the front porch, and the grass had been very recently mowed. The windows were partially open, and sheer curtains floated on the gentle breeze. It was as if someone was expecting them.

So this was his new home, the one God had planned for him. The flowers made it look like Eden.

He drove around the circle of gravel that constituted the driveway in front of the house and stopped. The house had large windows and an open porch that invited the sun into the house. His last home had been on a busy street, the sidewalks filled nine months a year with college students. He rarely opened his windows and allowed traffic noise to enter. Instead, he ran his air conditioner all summer long and lived in sterile, climate-controlled comfort. Here, all that would disturb his peace was the sound of chirping birds, hard-headed woodpeckers hammering on the surrounding trees and the scent of flowers.

And were those tomatoes and beans staked up in rows in the black patch of earth nearby? Alex climbed out of the car and walked around to the side of the house. A butterfly garden of black-eyed Susans, daylilies, purple coneflowers, and marigolds grew between the house and the separate single stall garage. The butterflies flitting in the midst of the flowers mimicked the nervous fluttering in his belly.

"Are you *sure* no one lives here?" Jared stared at the flourishing garden. "Maybe we're at the wrong place."

Alex looked out at the empty prairie. He'd followed the directions he'd been given. This was the farmstead closest to the church. "We couldn't be. There's got to be an explanation. Let's look inside."

Jared reluctantly trailed in his uncle's steps.

The skeleton key was under the mat, right where Mike had said it would be, and turned smoothly in the old-fashioned keyhole. Obviously the church didn't want to keep intruders out very badly.

The door glided open, and instead of the musty, closed-up smell he'd expected, he was greeted with the aroma of Pine-Sol and lavender. The entry was cramped but welcoming. A small rocker padded in chintz, a brass floor lamp, a coat rack and a small bookcase took up most of the space. They wiped their feet on the colorful woven rug and moved deeper into the house. Alex stopped abruptly at the kitchen door. What in the world . . .

Jared bumped into his back. "Hey, watch it!" Jared ducked around Alex, peeking into the kitchen, and froze. "Whoa!"

The kitchen had fresh white cupboards, Brazilian black granite countertops, a black-and-white tile checkered floor and pendant lighting. The cozy eating area held an antique pedestal table and six chairs placed just so on a round red rug with roosters crowing around the perimeter. A massive gas range hunkered in a corner.

"They might have gone a little overboard on the remodel. It was just completed last week. What do you think?"

Alex and Jared almost shot out of their shoes at the sound of another voice in the room. They turned in unison to see the fellow they'd met yesterday, at the sight of the piglet spill, still wearing the Red's Gas & Garage cap. He stuck out a grease-stained hand and flashed a pearly smile in a tanned face. His shake was strong and firm, just like the rest of his person.

"Dixon Daniels. We met on the edge of town yesterday when Ole and Twinkle Toes tipped over. Sorry I didn't realize you were the new minister. I could have given you directions or something."

Alex opened his mouth, trying to think of what to say, when Daniels began to answer the flood of questions raging in Alex's head. "Mattie Olsen—with an *e*—called me as soon as she met you at Mike and Lauren's, so I came over here this morning to open the windows and mow the lawn." Seeing the perplexed expression on Alex's face, he added, "People tend to meddle in each other's business around here. You'll get used to it. Why, sometimes word gets out about what I've done before I've even gotten around to doing it."

The man nodded toward a glass vase filled with flowers. "Tried to cozy things up a bit. Hope you like it."

"Like it? It's more than I ever expected." Alex gestured toward a single-serve espresso maker on the counter.

"Lauren led the charge to get the kitchen updated," Daniels explained, the toothpick in his mouth waggling precariously.

"I think she gave you the kitchen she wants for herself, but that's okay. You'll probably be doing a lot of entertaining, right?"

He would? Alex's mouth gaped open but no sound came out. Fortunately, Daniels didn't seem to mind.

"Are you sure nobody's been living here? There's a garden." Jared jumped into the conversational gap. "My mom grows tomatoes," he added as an afterthought.

"Does someone else use the land?" Alex ventured. But he was still thinking about what the man had said about entertaining. His culinary skills revolved around things with "instant" and "precooked" in their labels.

"No, there's plenty of land around here without borrowing someone else's. The garden was Lauren's idea too. The call committee decided to plant one here last spring so that the new pastor would have fresh garden produce when he arrived."

"But you hadn't called anyone yet, had you?"

"No, but Lauren figured the committee was making a statement to the congregation." Daniels looked at the pair of puzzled faces. "You know, reminding them that God will provide. She wanted to encourage everyone to have faith that we'd have a pastor by the time the tomatoes were ripe. You got here just in time."

Alex's head was still spinning when Daniels added, "Of course, it's usually that way with God, isn't it?" He took off his cap and scratched his head. His mop of brown hair appeared to have been cut with a gardening shears. "He's never late, but He's not known for being early either. He's always where He needs to be though, just in the nick of time."

Alex couldn't argue with that. While he was pondering Dixon's comment, Jared poked his nose into a walk-in pantry to the right of the refrigerator and whistled. "Unc! You're set!"

Alex flipped on the light switch beside the door and looked to see what his nephew was staring at. Food, of course. Nothing excited Jared as much as food. But Alex could see why. There were rows and rows of it—pint and quart jars filled with ruby apple rings, pale and luscious pear halves, flawless peaches, and pickles of every kind and size—slices, planks and baby dills—as well as what he could only guess were pickled watermelon rinds. And the tomatoes! Fresh from the garden to the canner—stewed, chunked, pureed and made into salsa— even at the farmer's market he frequented in the city, he'd never seen such a variety of home-canned delicacies. There were clear canisters full of flour; white, powdered and brown sugar; and miles of store-bought canned goods—pork and beans, pineapple rings and cream of mushroom soup, to name a few.

"You won't have to buy groceries for six months," Jared observed. Then he turned a canny eye to his uncle. "And you're going to have to learn to cook."

"It looks like it." God—or the parishioners—were certainly giving him a huge push in that direction.

"This is crazy." Jared methodically opened drawers and cupboards filled with pots and pans, cooking utensils, everyday dishes and flatware. Even the salt and pepper shakers were full. "They really meant it when they said Hilltop was expecting you, Uncle Alex."

Dixon grinned. "I told you so."

A fullness in his throat nearly kept Alex from responding. This quiet yet confident welcome overwhelmed him in ways a lavish party or a marching band could not have. They were his people, caring for him already.

While the foyer, kitchen and dining room took up most of the front of the house, a living room, bath and former bedroom turned office ran across the back. There were large windows in the living room overlooking a lawn that sloped down to the rows and rows of trees that Mike referred to as shelterbelts. A perennial flower bed was filled with salvia and day lilies and an annual bed of nasturtiums, marigolds, petunias, moss roses and other varieties Alex couldn't identify.

"Not bad, Unc!" Jared moved forward to sit in one of two leather recliners in the living room and promptly leaned back to put his feet up. There were more lamps and bookcases and a long floral couch like those that were so popular in a previous decade. The pictures on the walls were predictable— a rendition of the Last Supper, one of Christ praying on the Mount of Olives, several florals, and the traditional Gainesboro Blue Boy painting that seemed to grace all of the homes of a certain era. For a moment Alex was transported back in time to his grandmother's living room.

"There was a committee of ladies who spruced up the parsonage. Edith Bloch, Stoddard's wife—he was on the call committee—and Flossie Kennedy worked hard on this," Dixon informed them.

Alex recalled Stoddard Bloch, a blustery gentleman determined to interject his opinion into the conversation at every opportunity. Alex had thought he might have served better on, say, the building committee, where his comments on "shoring up the foundations of the church," "hammering everything into place" and "sawing off unnecessary expenses" would be more appropriate.

"I remember Mr. Block from my interview. Who is Flossie Kennedy?"

"Flossie is Horace Abel's housekeeper and she lives there with her son Charles, who runs an Internet business."

"That's interesting. Hilltop is very diversified."

"Some people wonder why Charles never moved on but mother and son relationships are complicated. My mother tried to kick me out of the house when I was twelve and she barely puts up with me now."

Dixon's impish grin told Alex that he said it all in fun.

"What kind of trouble are you causing her?"

Dixon laughed. "It makes Ma crazy that I'm not married and neither is my sister Emmy. Mom's itching for grandchildren and no one's very enthusiastic about giving her any." He smiled cheerfully. "Now I'd better finish mowing that last patch of grass behind the garage. See you in a few minutes." He sauntered off, whistling again, his confident easy gait seeming to match his breezy personality. If there was a more likable personality than Dixon, Alex mused, he had yet to meet it.

By this time, Jared had tried out the sofa and every chair and settled on the big leather recliner. He leaned back and stretched out his lanky frame in repose. "This is where you'll sit while you are reading," Jared stated confidently. "I can see it already."

"Am I so predictable?"

Jared nodded slowly. "Totally."

Alex wasn't sure he was flattered. "Well perhaps I'll be less predictable out here. This is as good a place for new beginnings as anywhere."

"Right," Jared said doubtfully.

Alex took it as a challenge. He wasn't a predictable, tedious college professor anymore. And he wasn't engaged anymore. He was a spiritual explorer on a mighty exploit, so he might as well act like one. That would show Jared not to pigeonhole his old uncle too quickly.

Alex stopped dead in his tracks at the door to the former bedroom, which was filled with floor to ceiling bookshelves, a desk even bigger than the one he'd chosen for his home study in Chicago, and a small, realistic-looking electric fireplace with an elaborate mantel.

"This is exactly what I've always wanted in an office—cozy, inviting, a place I can fill with books," Alex finally murmured. "*This* is where I'll be spending my time."

Jared's enthusiasm faltered. "Books give me the creeps."

"You don't mean that," Alex said lightly, even though his nephew's statement had an unfortunate ring of truth.

"You've got a great crib here, Unc," Jared said, putting his stamp of approval on the place. "My mom has got to see this someday."

"You'll have to come together next time," Alex said as they negotiated the steps to the second floor. "A visit from my sister would be most welcome." He and Carol were only a year apart in age. They been raised as if they were twins and the bond between them had never wavered.

They'd barely begun to discuss Jared's next visit when Dixon appeared again. He was sweating from exertion and his hair stood in unruly spikes on his head. His ruddy features gleamed with perspiration and he wiped at his forehead with the back of his shirtsleeve. "Mowing is all done."

"I don't know how to thank you . . . ," Alex began.

"I do." Dixon's white, even teeth flashed in his tanned face. "Mattie Olsen put a container of iced sweet tea in the refrigerator and a plate of cookies in the breadbox. "Some of that would be thanks enough for me."

"Gladly." Alex found the tea and cookies right where Dixon said they would be, and Jared brought out plates and glasses. They sat at the big round table.

"So, Dixon, what can you tell me about this place?" Alex asked, pouring Dixon a second glass of tea. He'd slurped down the first with barely a blink.

"Everything."

Alex started to laugh and then realized Dixon was serious.

"I've lived here all my life. I know this place as well as the back of my hand." Dixon's blue eyes twinkled. "But I'm not going to tell you everything all at once. That would be overload. I'll be glad to dole it out on a need-to-know basis. It would be my pleasure to help you along until you have your footing here."

"Much appreciated," Alex said with relief. "I'll need a guide for a while."

"Happy to oblige. It's a good place, Hilltop. It was settled by Scandinavians—Swedes and Norwegians. There's always been some rivalry between them but they got together long enough to build the church. It's a carryover from 'the old country.' I understand Swedes and Norwegians have always exchanged jabs over their nationalities. The church helped to erase that. And Grassy Valley is a fine little town. We have our issues, of course, but everyone hangs together and we muddle along."

The fondness in Dixon's voice was apparent. A good sign, Alex thought. "Maybe you could start by telling me a little about yourself, Dixon. I think I can handle that much."

"I'm just a simple farm boy, that's all."

Alex doubted that.

"I farm the same farm my great-grandfather did. He homesteaded it in the late 1800s and there have been Daniels here ever since. My great-grandfather and his son, my granddaddy, helped build the church. They came from Illinois. My great-grandfather and Lauren Carlsen's were friends back then, newcomers, all of them." He shoved his hat to the back of his head and stared up at the sky, a signal, Alex was soon to realize, that Dixon had a story to tell.

"In fact, the way my granddad told me—he was only a little boy at the time—his parents came across the prairie in a covered wagon. A storm was brewing in the west about the time they arrived out here and it looked pretty desolate." He gestured toward the tidy rows of shelterbelts that marched between many of the fields. "Most of the trees around here came much later, and my great-grandfather and his wife could see the windstorm rolling in, wheeling and raging across the prairie in a fury."

Alex tried to imagine it, a single, lonely covered wagon on an empty prairie, a sky churning with black clouds, a whipping wind and a storm bearing down. In comparison, it was a little embarrassing to consider his own trepidation at arriving at this new place with a cozy home, a surfeit of food in the cupboards and newly polished windows.

"Anyway, my great-grandfather saw the trouble coming and let the horses loose. He's just gotten his family tucked into a gully when the wind hit and turned the covered wagon upside down. There it sat, wheels spinning, like a big turtle on its back—and him with a wife and five little kids laying in the dirt wondering if they'd been sucked into a nightmare."

"Whoa," Jared's eyes were wide.

"I'm ashamed to say I've never given the trials of the pioneers much thought," Alex admitted, "until just now." It was interesting—and a little sad—how insulated he'd been from the raw beginnings of this country.

"That's okay," Dixon said generously, "you'll be giving it plenty of thought out here."

They sat together at the table in companionable silence for some time before Alex ventured to ask, "How about you, Dixon? It sounds like you come from a long line of family men. Do you want to settle down and have a wife and children someday?"

Dixon's complexion grew ruddy. "Not yet. I've been looking at the ladies, but there are so many pretty ones that I just can't decide who to choose." Then he flashed that winning grin. "Besides, most of the ones around here feel like sisters. One of these days I'll just have to get out of town and look around."

A car's tires crunching on the gravel outside the house cut short Alex's response as he and Dixon both stood to peer out the window.

"Well, look who's here," Dixon murmured.

CHAPTER FIVE

Alex had seen wrecks in his day but this took the cake. The car was as patchwork as the quilt on his bed, every fender a salvaged part of a different color. The doors weren't much better. One of them he deduced—from the tape holding it closed—didn't work at all. Duct tape was the obvious remedy of choice. It appeared on a cracked rear window, the trunk, and the roof and was also used to patch and mend several smaller faults and fractures.

The man who slowly exited the car didn't look much better. He wore thick denim carpenter pants. A pair of pliers peeked from one pocket. Another held a hammer. The tools looked heavy enough to tug the pants right off the scrawny hips of the wearer. All his clothes were too large, including his cotton red and navy plaid work shirt. Over his salt-and-pepper hair, the man wore the traditional headgear of the area, a billed cap advertising Red's Gas & Garage.

Dixon moved to greet the fellow as if they were long-lost brothers. "Jonas Owens! Where have you been keeping yourself?"

"I haven't been getting out much." The man's voice was flat and unenthusiastic.

"Came to see the new pastor, did you?" Dixon gestured in Alex's direction. "Here he is, and his nephew Jared from Chicago."

Jared lifted a hand in greeting. "Hiya."

"Actually, I came looking for a cow. My best milker. She wandered off through a break in the fence."

Jonas stuck out his hand and as they shook, Alex felt the rough calluses of a man accustomed to hard labor.

"Pleased to meet you, Reverend. I'm Jonas Owens. Welcome to Hilltop. It's a good place to live."

"At least it was," Jonas added under his breath.

"Jonas' great-grandfather was another pioneer who came to this area about the same time mine did," Dixon informed Alex. "He built a prosperous wheat farm here." Dixon pointed off in the distance.

"What a long, rich heritage you all have here." Alex hoped this was the right response. "I can see I have a lot to learn."

Now his nephew's head bobbed in agreement.

"I'll say you do," Dixon agreed cheerfully. "Just so you know, it's best to be careful who you talk about around here. It's not like a city full of strangers. I'm sure a preacher wouldn't gossip or anything, but if you did, you'd likely be talking to someone's great uncle or third cousin."

"Whoever belittles another lacks sense but an intelligent person remains silent," Alex murmured, quoting Proverbs.

"You've got that right." Dixon clapped Alex on the back. "I've got to be going now. I've got a tractor torn apart and lying on the shed floor. I should probably put it back together before

I forget where all the parts came from. I'll see you in the office for coffee tomorrow."

"You will? What office?"

"The church office, of course. Didn't they tell you that you had one? We aren't *that* far behind the times out here. It's the cubbyhole past the foyer on the south side of the sanctuary. If you didn't know it was there you might think it was a closet. Yesterday I installed a new coffeepot and put a pound of nice full-bodied Sumatra in the cupboard for you and me. I've got a hard-to-find Indonesian coffee that we can try next. And I make a pretty mean mocha too."

Sumatran and Indonesian coffees? Mochas in the church office?

"And three pounds of Folgers for everyone else. That's what they prefer. I try to introduce them to new things, but they aren't very adventurous around here, at least not with their coffee. Most everybody still prefers egg coffee if they can get it."

Egg coffee? Alex was still puzzling over that when Dixon said his good-byes and pulled out of the yard in his pickup. Jared wandered off in the direction of an unattached garage across the farmstead, leaving Alex and Jonas to stare at each other, each shifting awkwardly from foot to foot.

"So, Jonas," Alex began awkwardly, "I haven't seen your cow, but I'm happy to help you look."

Jonas shrugged. "Come along then."

Alex crawled into the wreck of a car, trying not to disturb the duct tape that held the seat together. He said just a little too heartily, "Tell me a little more about yourself."

Jonas shifted uncomfortably, as if Alex had just asked him to explain black holes. "Like Dixon said, there have been members of the Owens family around here for more than a hundred years." His voice trailed away, as if he'd lost interest in the conversation.

"I'm going to drive out on that lane." He pointed toward some clumps of grass. There was no discernable path that Alex could see but he was beginning to believe that one could inexplicably appear out of nowhere.

"I've found her down here before. There's good grass," Jonas said. "Hang on." He pressed on the gas pedal and the car exploded across the yard and into the field.

Jonas hit the first rut and Alex bounced into the air and came down hard. It was a tooth-rattling ride but at the end was Jonas' cow, a brown-and-white Hereford with a sweet face, placidly chewing a mouth full of grass. She looked up at them with soulful eyes.

"Now how will you get her to move?" Alex asked. The cow didn't appear to be in a hurry to go anywhere.

"I'll send my boys over to herd her home now that I'm sure she's here."

Jonas didn't look particularly happy that he'd found what he'd been looking for, Alex observed. Something more than the wandering animal had to be bothering him. They turned around and Jonas drove slowly back to the yard.

"Thanks for the ride, Jonas," Alex said as he opened the car door. "Next time she's missing, just call me and I'll go out and see if she's there." Alex paused before adding, "Is there anything else?" Alex asked softly. "Something I could do for you?"

Jonas' forehead creased and a look of melancholy shaded his features. "Could you pray for me and my family, Pastor Alex? I'd sure appreciate it."

"Consider it done. Is there something special . . . ?"

Jonas shook his head. "Just pray. God will know what it's about. And welcome again. It's good to have you here." Without another word, Jonas shifted his miserable excuse for a car into gear, and with some grating noises and a few gunshotlike backfires, he drove out of the yard.

Whatever Jonas Owens' problems were, Alex would find out eventually. Until then he'd do just what he'd promised. Pray.

Jared popped his head out of the old garage. "Hey, Unc," he yelled. "There's a lot of cool stuff in here, come and see this."

Alex crossed the newly mowed lawn and stepped into the dimness of the old building. There were dozens of North Dakota and Minnesota license plates hammered to the walls in tidy roles and a veritable art gallery of oil-streaked old calendars—1957, 1958, 1959—and all the way to the present. Many had obviously been distributed by the ubiquitous Red's Gas & Garage. Some of them had penciled notations about the daily activities of their former owners—things like "pick up baby chicks at railroad depot" and "State Fair begins." One notation said "See banker." Some things, Alex realized, never change, especially troubles.

Mike had said things were tight in the road department because people were behind on their taxes. And there was Jonas Owens' down-and-out appearance and demeanor, not to mention the trouble at All Saints. Beneath the pastoral beauty here was an undercoat of financial, emotional and spiritual concerns that he did not yet understand.

The garage smelled of grease and oil and reminded Alex of his Uncle Bert's auto repair shop in Naperville. He'd spent many a pleasant afternoon there in the perfume of motor oil, surrounded by tool benches, car bays and the jokes and jibes the three repairmen shot back and forth like lightning bolts.

His uncle was considered a fine mechanic and was never lacking customers. People always need oil and filters changed, tires rotated, or fluids checked. Here, it appeared that he would be expected to do that himself. A farmer was a jack of all trades, Alex was learning, and independent in ways that were difficult for city folks like Alex to comprehend.

Alex was growing to appreciate the pioneer spirit that lingered here.

Nostalgia hit him like an ocean wave. He longed to become a part of this tight-knit place someday. He would make time to study this wall of calendars and to discover more about the people who'd lived here before him. And he would go to Red's and pick up his own calendar so that, at the end of the year, he too could contribute to this wall.

There were old wooden boxes the size of steamer trunks lining the back wall. Some had ancient cast-iron padlocks with keys still hanging in the undone locks. Other, newer padlocks' shackles dangled open, all inviting exploration. That would have to wait for another day, however.

"I'd like to look more right now, Jared, but I'd better have you help me carry my things into the house. I promised your mother I'd put you on the train back to Chicago tonight."

"I don't want to go yet." Jared's lips turned downward and the light in his eyes dimmed. "It's not as lame here as I thought it would be." Then he looked up at his uncle with a more cheerful light in his eyes and a smile on his face. "I should stay here for a while. I don't want you to be here all alone."

Alex shook his head. "Your mother will be waiting for you, and she won't be happy if I don't send you home on time." And, Alex thought to himself, if what he'd seen so far was a hint, he wouldn't be by himself for long. There'd probably be a caravan of neighbors parading through the church parking lot tomorrow to check him out.

He had brought enough boxes for a family of four, Alex decided as he toted the last of them into the house, and most of them were books, papers and music. His clothing took up two large suitcases and there were household things and more clothing his sister was storing for him, which she would send later. It didn't look as if he'd need most of it, however.

Alex carried an armful of papers into the office, where Jared had just set down a box of books—fiction, biographies, autobiographies and books on spiritual matters. Jared looked up as Alex entered.

"Hey, Unc. When are you planning to do all this reading?"

"Most of these I've already read and will use for reference." Alex lifted a leather-bound volume by one of his favorite theologians. "And the rest? I suppose there will be some long quiet nights around here, especially this winter."

Jared's eyes narrowed slyly. "Maybe you'll meet a nice lady out here. There must be some single women around. I wouldn't mind having a new aunt. . . . "

Alex glared at his nephew until Jared's voice trailed off. "Now you sound like your mother. 'Alex, find a nice woman and settle down,' 'Alex, you don't want to spend the rest of your life alone. . . . '"

"My favorite is 'Find yourself a wife so I don't have to take care of you in your old age,'" Jared offered unhelpfully.

"My sister Carol has been trying to boss me around since the day I was born. It rarely works. I wonder why she persists." Alex sighed and plowed into a box of books that had not yet been arranged on shelves.

Carol had disapproved of the women he'd dated in college, deeming them all shallow. She was probably right—who wasn't a little shallow at eighteen or twenty? They were all like steel, only partially tempered. People needed a little more time in the fire to develop into the people they were to become.

But he'd expected more of Natalie, a sociology professor at the college at which he'd taught. He'd expected loyalty, love . . . and faithfulness. Alex had been badly disappointed on all counts.

He should have listened to Carol. Life might have turned out differently.

At five o'clock Jared announced "I'm hungry. What's for supper? A pizza, maybe?"

Alex heard his own stomach growl. Or was it tires crunching on gravel outside? He walked into the kitchen to look out the window that overlooked the circular driveway. A gray 1987 Buick Regal in mint condition pulled up slowly to the house. When it had come to a complete stop, the passenger door opened and a small, timorous-looking woman in a navy skirt and pale green blouse emerged. In her hand was a quilted dish carrier. A portly, gray-haired gentleman exited the driver's side. He rummaged in the back seat for a moment and emerged with a large tin cake pan with a metal cover. The kind, Alex thought, that his grandmother used to use.

Hesitantly, the pair started toward the house.

"Looks like we have company, Jared, and they brought food."

Jared popped out of the back room like a Jack-in-the-box. His sandy-colored hair was in disarray and sweat beaded on his forehead. He looked flushed and warm from exertion. "Food? I'm starving."

Alex couldn't agree more. Hopefully this was some of the country hospitality others had assured him he'd see here. He hurried to the door before his visitors could knock and threw it open. "Hello, come in. I'm Alex Armstrong and you are . . ."

"I'm Clarence Olson—with an *o*—and this is Lydia. She thought you might like some supper brought in, considering it's your first night here and all." Clarence wore a pair of dark navy trousers, a bright pink shirt with a white collar and Italian knock-off black loafers with silver horse-bit detailing. He was the peacock to Lydia's pea hen.

"That's very kind of you. My nephew Jared and I were just discussing what to have for dinner and here you are."

Lydia looked disappointed. "Dinner? I'd hoped you'd eat it tonight . . . for supper."

He had to remember that dinner was the noon meal here and supper was eaten in the evening or he'd confuse everyone.

"Absolutely. Will you join us?"

"Don't worry about it. Lydia made the same meal for Jacob and me," Clarence said. "It's in the oven at home right now. You just sit down and eat if you're hungry."

Alex could see Jared's head bobbing and he was eagerly rubbing his stomach. "Will you stay and visit if we do?"

The man tapped a finger with grease embedded under his nail on the nine-by-thirteen-inch pan. "That's Lydia's special German chocolate cake. I'd join you for a slice of that."

Clarence took a seat at one end of the table and sat there contentedly while Jared filled glasses with ice and water and Lydia scurried about serving massive portions of tater tot hot dish. Alex had the impression that if he'd first met them in their own home, it would have played out the same way, with Clarence being served and Lydia doing the serving.

"Can I say grace, Uncle Alex?" Jared asked, igniting an approving smile on Clarence's and Lydia's faces. "Dear God, " he began in the same conversational tone he used with the rest of his family, "thanks for this great food, which looks awesome. Love those tater tots. Thanks, too, for this cool place my uncle will be living. You really take care of him, God. Take care of all of us . . . please? In Your name, Amen."

"Why that was lovely!" Lydia burst out. "So . . . cozy and genuine." She appeared more at ease than she had moments earlier.

"So, Clarence," Alex wasn't sure how to phrase this. "I noticed that when you introduced yourself you said your name was Olson—with an *o*—and Mattie Olsen said her name was Olsen—with an *e*. What exactly does that mean?" Alex asked.

"Traditionally, because of the Danish influence on Norway, the Norwegian surname Olsen is spelled with an *e*. When it is spelled with an *o*, it's usually Swedish. Olsen—Olson." Clarence appeared proud to impart this bit of information. "Mattie's heritage is Swedish and ours is Norwegian. It's as simple as that."

Simple? Hardly. Alex dug into his food. He would need energy to keep all this straight in his head.

Finally he came up for air. "This is a great meal, Lydia. This was the perfect welcome for us. Thank you so much." He laid down his fork. "I wish I could cook like that. I'd open a restaurant."

Lydia's laughter pealed throughout the room, a pleasant, unexpected sound. "Then you'll have to have some lessons. There are a lot of good cooks around Hilltop and Grassy Valley."

Alex turned to Clarence. "And what do you do, Clarence?"

"I'm a retired diesel mechanic. I worked for the implement dealer in Grassy Valley for years. And we farm a little and have a few cattle." He crossed his hands over his stomach. The buttons and buttonholes of the pink shirt were sorely strained by the size of his belly.

"You mentioned a Jacob. Is that your son?"

Lydia choked on a sip of water and Clarence's face turned red. "Lydia and I aren't married. We're brother and sister. Jacob is our other brother."

Now it was Alex's turn to flush. "I'm sorry, I shouldn't be making assumptions. Maybe I'd better study the church directory before I embarrass myself more."

"It's quite all right," Clarence said generously. "The three of us have lived together on the farm ever since our parents died. Our father went in 1975 and Mother in '86. We get along just fine, Jacob, Lydia and me."

Alex caught a brief movement from the corner of his eye. Had Lydia flinched?

CHAPTER SIX

Alex watched Lydia drop her gaze to her plate.

"Tell me about yourself, Lydia," he encouraged, hoping to draw her out and not simply defer to her brother on every issue.

"There's not that much to tell. I enjoy cooking, of course." She flushed a little. "And my jams and jellies usually win blue ribbons at the county fair."

"No kidding? That's great." Alex sat back and crossed his arms over his chest. "I haven't been to a county fair since I was a kid and my grandparents took me."

"I'm planning to enter my strawberry-rhubarb jam this year. My rhubarb plants were exceptional this year." Her voice grew animated as she described the large leafy plants with edible red and green stalks, but the light in her pale eyes dimmed when Clarence interrupted to impart information about the spring's weather. As he talked right over her, Lydia's soft, round features hardened into a scowl. It occurred to Alex that Clarence's obliviousness to his sister's feeling's might easily churn up a rebellious spirit in the mild-mannered Lydia.

"Liddy is the youngest in the family," Clarence informed Alex, "born when our mother was in her late forties. At the time, it seemed like a calamity, an embarrassment, you know, having a child at such a late age, but it turned out to be a blessing." He turned a fond eye on his sister, who was blushing pink as the single peony Alex had picked for the table.

Alex wondered what it would be like to be considered the family "calamity."

"But Liddy here took care of both our parents until they passed away, and now she's invaluable to Jacob and me. Quite the little cook and housekeeper, that's our Lydia."

Alex felt a little sorry for Lydia, caretaker first for her parents and now her brothers. Before he could comment further, the conversation veered into territory more pertinent to Alex himself.

"Have you met the Holmquists yet?" Clarence asked as he took a bite of his cake.

"Not yet."

"You'll like Mildred and Chester," Lydia assured him.

"Mildred was quite a looker in her day," Clarence added.

Lydia sent him a disapproving look.

"She's in her eighties now, but I remember her when I was a boy. Our father told us that every single man between the ages of six and sixty wanted Mildred for his wife, but once she met Winchester Holmquist, that was it for everyone else. She never looked at another man."

"He was a handsome fellow too," Lydia added. "And polite! I've never met another man with such lovely manners." She flushed. "But you have lovely manners too, I'm sure, Pastor." Lydia folded her hands in her lap and sighed. "Such a nice love story. So romantic."

"Romance!" Clarence erupted. "Lydia, you're a perfectly good woman if you'd keep your head out of the clouds."

Lydia pursed her lips and ignored her brother. That was probably what had kept her sane all these years with him under the same roof—ignoring him.

"Has anyone told you about the Bruuns yet?" Clarence inquired. "One of them is a little"—he put his finger to his temple and made a circular motion—"crazy."

"And those Packard kids that run wild around here! Let me tell you . . . "

"What about your brother Jacob?" Alex urged, eager to get the train of conversation on an alternate track. "You haven't said much about him."

Lydia and Clarence exchanged a quick glance that Alex couldn't decipher. The garrulous Clarence became suddenly secretive.

"Oh, Jacob is a homebody. There's not much to say about him," Clarence said dismissively. "Is there, Lydia?"

"Jacob is a little shy," Lydia explained. "He's a hard worker but doesn't leave the farm much." She flushed a little. "And he's a big fan of my pies, especially the crème ones and my lemon meringue."

Clarence snorted derisively. "You spoil him, Lydia."

She straightened and thrust her chin forward. Alex could see the faintest flicker of fire in her eyes. Her diminutive frame seemed to gather volume, and her mousey brown hair fairly bristled with indignation. "You don't seem to complain about my strawberry-rhubarb crunch or sour cream–raisin pie, Clarence. Or the cakes, cookies and those orange scones I serve with cream. . . . "

Jared coughed into his elbow to hide a smile. Alex used sheer willpower to suppress his. If Lydia *were* ever to decide to resist Clarence's brotherly bullying, it might be an interesting match to watch.

Lydia insisted on washing the dishes while the men had seconds of her tender chocolate cake.

"You don't have to do that, Lydia," Alex said, but she was already scrubbing at the casserole dish vigorously, putting her whole body into it. There were damp curls at the base of her neck. "Relax with us. It will give me a chance to try out the new dishwasher later."

Lydia opened her mouth to speak, but Clarence beat her to it. "She doesn't mind. Our Liddy has her hands in dishwater three times a day. She's used to it."

"Yes, Clarence," she said meekly, but rolled her eyes at Alex.

A portrait of the Olsons was coming into view. So far there were just hints of the officious Clarence, the quiet Lydia with her deeply buried feisty streak, and the mysterious Jacob. Lydia, most likely, was the glue that held their household together. But she was underappreciated and, like a good adhesive, nearly invisible, only noticed when it came unbonded and no longer worked.

"Have you got plans for the evening, Reverend?" Clarence inquired, readying himself to settle in and entertain the new pastor for the rest of the night.

"My nephew is leaving on the train for Chicago in a few hours." Alex glanced at Jared, who looked away. "How far, exactly, is the drive to the depot?"

"I'd plan for more than an hour. It's better to be there earlier rather than later. The train pulls in and out again so fast it barely stops."

"Oh my, we'd best be going." Lydia placed her dish back into its carrier. "We don't want you to be late." With a hearty round of handshaking and good wishes, Clarence and Lydia made their way to the car.

As they stood on the front step waving them away, Alex turned to Jared and asked, "Well, what do you think?"

Jared chewed on his upper lip for a moment. "I'm glad I won't be around when Lydia Olson finally gives her brother what's coming to him."

Out of the mouths of babes.

The Olsons' taillights disappeared over a slight rise in the road, and Jared turned to his uncle. "I'm sorry I have to go home," he admitted a little sheepishly. "I'd like to find out how this all turns out."

Alex picked up the broom leaning against the wall. "What do you mean?"

"This place is full of stories." Jared's brow furrowed. "The people we've met— Lauren and Mike, Dixon, that sad-looking man Jonas, and now the people who just left—they've all got stories, and we've only had time to experience the first page of each of them."

His nephew was right. Hilltop was a veritable library of reading material. Alex would have to peruse and eventually understand it all.

"You'd better put your stuff in the car," Alex called to Jared. "Since I don't know exactly where the station is, I'd like to start a little early."

Jared's head popped out the door that led to the bathroom, a toothbrush in his mouth, and nodded. He disappeared again, and Alex heard the sound of running water. Shortly he reappeared, grooming evidently complete. "Are you sure we have to go already? I wish we'd come straight here rather than spending time at the water park and sightseeing."

Alex recalled how much talking he'd had to do to convince his nephew to make this trip with him to "beyond nowhere," as Jared had so succinctly put it. He clapped his nephew on the shoulder. "Then we should discuss when you're coming back."

Jared's shoulders sagged. "Talk to my mom. She's got this thing about missing school. She won't let me do it. I'd stay away from school entirely if she'd let me."

On their trip, his nephew had made several comments in the same vein, Alex observed. "I wasn't suggesting that. You'll have school breaks, and there's always next summer. Why don't you look at your school calendar and call me with some dates?" Before Alex could pursue it further, he heard a vehicle pull into the yard.

He moved aside the curtain to peer out. It was Dixon Daniels again, this time in a pair of khaki trousers and an indigo knit shirt that emphasized the blue sparkle of his eyes.

Alex opened the screen door, and Dixon sauntered to the door and stepped over the threshold. "How do you like your new place?"

"Great, so far. Lydia and Clarence Olson were here with an amazing supper. We're beginning to feel right at home." He turned to his nephew. "Right, Jared?"

"Yeah." The boy's face was long and gloomy.

"You don't look all that happy about it," Dixon commented. "I saw another guy recently with that very same expression on his face. 'Course, a horse had just stepped on his foot."

"Jared's not ready to leave," Alex confided. "I don't want him to go either, but we'll both have to answer to my sister if he doesn't show up at the train station tomorrow."

"Leave a sock under the bed," Dixon advised the teen.

Jared cocked an eyebrow. "Why?"

"Seed. Whenever my family went somewhere, we always 'accidentally' left something behind—a piece of clothing, a pair of reading glasses, a toy. My mother said it was seed for another visit because we'd have to come back to pick it up."

Jared brightened. "Maybe I'll leave the iPod. It belongs to mom, and she'd be out here in a heartbeat if I left it behind."

"Don't press your luck," Dixon advised. "I'd recommend a jacket or maybe a belt."

"Gotcha." Jared glanced at his watch. "I suppose I'd better check to see if I've left anything behind."

He disappeared up the flight of stairs three steps at a time, and Alex turned to Dixon. "To what do we owe the pleasure of this visit?"

"I just washed my truck," Dixon said, "so I thought I'd volunteer to give you and Jared a ride to the station. It will be a long drive home, especially when you're anticipating your first night at the parsonage."

A load lightened in his chest, one he hadn't even known was there. This place with its wide open spaces, sparse trees and endless horizon left him feeling exposed and a little vulnerable. He knew how to maneuver himself about in a seedy neighborhood, but this . . .

"That's very nice of you."

"No problem. I just have to make one stop to drop off a chain saw that I borrowed from one of your neighbors. His name is Mark Nash. I'll introduce you. You'll like him. Mark's a good guy."

"I believe God provided me with a very human guardian angel, Dixon—you. I needed someone with whom to navigate this first bumpy patch as I learn my way around Hilltop Township."

Dixon looked startled and then amused. "I hope I'm not an angel. There's no room under my shirt for wings."

They put Jared's dufflebag in Dixon's truck and set out. Dixon pulled out of the yard and drove the two and a half miles to another farmyard. A man was in the yard, his head under the hood of an old Jeep. A lanky dog sat at his feet. The animal, skinny and long legged, looked to be part greyhound, but had fur the pale silvery gray of a Weimaraner. She had a white head and a dusky ring around one eye like the dog in *The Little Rascals*. She looked like she had been put together by a committee with opposing visions. Her long, straight ears perked up when Dixon's pickup entered the yard.

"That's Dixie," Dixon said, pointing at the dog. "Mark picked her up at a flea market when she was a pup. Kinda looks like she came from a rummage sale, doesn't she, a little bit of this and a little bit of that?"

Indeed she did. But her tail began to wag in a slow, fanning fashion that indicated welcome.

"Good dog, Dixie. Smarter than a whip. She knows every car and truck in the township and only barks at strange ones. Don't be offended if she barks at you the first time you bring that van down the road. She'll soon learn who you are, and then she'll be silent as a lamb."

Alex remembered his Uncle Bert's dog, Wally. Wally had had as questionable a lineage as this mutt but, also like this one, was intelligent and sensitive. Alex had pleaded for a dog many times in his childhood, but his apartment building didn't allow pets, so his pleas had always fallen on deaf ears.

"Do you have dogs?" Alex asked.

"Hunting dogs. Labs. Willie and Wonka. They're pretty rowdy, so I don't usually bring them with me in the truck." A faint blush crept over Dixon's features. "They're more like pets than most hunting dogs. Don't tell anyone, but they sleep in my bed at night. It's great in the winter. We have plenty of two-dog nights."

Seeing the confusion on Alex's face, he continued. "You don't know about dog nights? In Alaska, mushers bring their sled dogs into bed with them to stay warm. If it's really cold, you might need four or five dogs. Most people are familiar with a three-dog night, but that might have something to do with the fact that there's also a rock group by that name. Like I said, a two-dog night usually works for me."

"Of course. Why didn't I think of that?" Alex murmured. Chicago seemed farther away by the minute.

Alex catalogued that bit of canine information, opened the door and slid to the ground. He would have to find a more polished way to get out of these high vehicles. The seats must be three feet off the ground. Long-legged Jared leaped out far more gracefully.

Mark's head appeared around the hood of the Jeep. He was a man familiar with hard work, Alex guessed. His eyes were sharp with intelligence and his expression good natured.

He sauntered toward them, wiping his hands on an oily rag that had seen better days, but somehow he'd avoided getting any grease on himself. He wore his jeans and denim shirt like they were business attire. He looked nothing like the farmer in bib overalls Alex had imagined before he'd arrived in Hilltop.

"Hello, Dixon," Mark's voice sounded cultivated and refined. "Who have you got here?"

"This is the pastor, Alex Armstrong, and his nephew Jared. I'm driving them to the train station so Jared can go back to Chicago. I thought I'd return your chain saw on the way." He gestured toward a building behind the house. "I'll put in the shop."

"Pleased to meet you, Reverend, and you too, Jared. Welcome to Hilltop." He studied them with sharp eyes, and Alex felt a little as though he was being run through an X-ray machine. Dixie, the dog, was staring at them in exactly the same way, sizing them up.

Then her tail started to fan wildly. Soon her whole rump was involved in the welcome. Alex and Jared had been approved.

"We've spoken on the phone once," Mark said. "I was part of the call committee." Before Alex could respond, he turned to Jared. "Do you know much about engines?"

Jared brightened. "A little."

That was an understatement. His uncle knew that he'd taken the family vacuum cleaner, sewing machine and lawn mower apart by the time he was six.

"Take a look under the hood. I've been tightening belts."

Jared darted forward and disappeared under the Jeep's hood. "The fan belt is fine, but your alternator belt is still a little loose. Mind if I tighten it?"

"Here's a nine-sixteenth wrench." Mark put the tool in Jared's open hand.

With Jared occupied, Mark turned again to Dixon and Alex. "How's Hilltop so far?"

"Good." Alex shrugged. "The church, the parsonage, the people . . . all wonderful."

"Mark's great-grandfather homesteaded here in the late 1800s, like everyone else," Dixon explained. "He came from the 'old country' like most of the Norwegians and Swedes who settled around here. The original house is gone. Burned in a fire. Still, this is the family place." Dixon moved his hand in a grand gesture that encompassed the tidily mowed grass, the newer ranch-style house and lush fields.

"So you've lived here all your life?" Alex nodded to Mark.

"Off and on." Mark slid the rag into his pocket. "I went to college, spent some time in New York working as a stock broker, saw the error of my ways and came back to farm a few years ago. One of the smartest moves I've ever made." He laughed. "I decided that if I was going to be involved with bulls and bears, they'd be of the Angus and grizzly kind."

"I don't have the stomach for the ups and downs of the market," Alex said. "People's emotional highs and lows are one thing. The financial ones are quite another."

Mark smiled knowingly.

Alex had always been diligent about money, not for his own gain, but for pet missions and charities that he'd given to for years and that needed support now more than ever. "I admire people with financial savvy. You're on the board of trustees for the church, I hope."

Mark and Dixon laughed out loud.

"He's going to be good, I can already tell," Dixon said. "He's already trying to put people on committees."

"Just so you don't put me on the potluck dinner committee. My mother was in charge of it for years. She said she didn't know how the ladies did it, but some years almost everyone would bring desserts, and another it was all salads. She started buying hams to have in the refrigerator in case all that came in was Jell-O and buns."

"I'm anxious to experience my first potluck at Hilltop."

"You'll enjoy it," Mark assured him. "Once Hilltop gets a look at you, you'll be fed quite nicely, I'm sure."

Dixon sniggered and dug his hands deeper into the pockets of his khakis.

"What do you mean?"

"You're single. As soon as the ladies around here think there's someone without a wife who needs feeding, they'll be right on it. You can expect two or three casseroles a week, I'd wager."

"Yeah, and that's only from the married ones," Dixon added. "The single ones are even more attentive." He grinned. "Mark and I should know."

A sense of foreboding shimmered at the edge of Alex's consciousness. The last thing he needed right now was romantic involvement. Only months before his wedding, Natalie had announced she was in love with someone else. If Alex had had his way, he never would have even heard of Hilltop, but now he was here. God had given him what he had needed—a fresh start—and he wasn't going to mess that up just yet.

"Until the single ladies know if you are a *serious* bachelor or could possibly be husband material, they'll keep feeding you. There aren't many new men moving to the area, so every eye will be on you. Trust me, Mark and I have been through it."

"And you are *serious* bachelors, I take it?"

"That's the public face," Dixon said cheerfully. "Otherwise we'd have so much attention that we'd be like pigs fattened for slaughter right now."

"Thanks for the word of caution."

Dixon clapped a hand around Alex's shoulders. "The Three Musketeers, that's us. Our motto will be theirs, 'All for one and one for all.'"

Athos, Porthos and Aramis. The inseparable friends from Dumas' French novel *Les Trois Mousquetairs*. Alex felt warmed and welcomed by the idea.

"Hey, Unc," Jared called, emerging from under the hood. "What time does the train leave?" He wiped his hands on a rag on the roof of the car.

Dixon and Alex simultaneously looked at their watches. "We'd better get going," Dixon suggested.

They said their good-byes, and Dixon peeled out of the yard, gravel flying from beneath his wheels. Alex sat back, feeling pleased that he'd met two men who could become good friends. He'd worry about the concerned women of the church later. For now, it was a start.

CHAPTER SEVEN

"I wish I didn't have to leave," Jared said as he slumped in the back seat of the extended cab pickup.

"Your mother says you've got some work to finish at home. Besides, the start of school is only five weeks off." Alex's sister and her husband had scrimped and saved for years so that Jared could attend The Academy, a fine private school with an excellent reputation.

"I like the social stuff," Jared said vaguely, refusing to look Alex in the eye, "but not the rest." He obviously didn't want to talk about it.

Dixon pulled off the highway and into a town called Wheatville that Alex vaguely recalled from their trip out. It was large enough to have two fast-food restaurants, a big-box store, a truck stop, an implement dealership and, apparently, a train station. Dixon drove directly to a picturesque but aging brick depot with a two-story central tower and a covered platform supported by columns and trusses. It was a veritable historic jewel.

They walked inside, and Alex discovered that the inside was even more charming, with high oak wainscoting, plastered walls, arched ceiling and maple floors. Dixon immediately sat down in the waiting room and began to rummage through two-year-old magazines.

Jared looked around, his eyebrow raised. "Why's it so empty?"

"When these depots were built, they were very busy. Now depots have very little staff and are open only when a train is about to arrive. I figure, though, that high gas prices will wake people up sooner or later and they'll start using the train again."

A train whistle in the distance cut into Dixon's speech. Jared grabbed his duffle bag and headed outside to the platform. As the train approached, Alex threw his arms around his nephew.

"I'll let you say your good-byes without me," Dixon said and headed toward the pickup, leaving Alex and Jared alone on the platform as a searing bright light bore down upon them, accompanied by the roar of an engine. The wheels screeched as the train came to a stop.

"I'll be back as soon as I can, Uncle Alex."

"Next time, you'll stay longer. By then I'll be better acquainted. We'll have some fun, okay?"

The conductor waved at Jared, the only passenger boarding. With a quick look back, Jared stepped on the small stool the conductor had put on the ground and into the silver train. Alex watched him wave from inside as the train's heavy door closed in front of him. Then the train jerked to a start and was gone.

Alex stood alone on the stone paving outside the quaint brick-and-mortar depot, watching the receding train. The station manager turned out the lights one by one. Finally, only the uncovered incandescent bulb over the station door remained lit.

Alex felt an unexpectedly lonely feeling in his gut, and he felt a rush of gratitude that Dixon was waiting for him in the pickup, no doubt twiddling with the radio dials. But how many radio stations could there be out here? How much of *anything* could be out here, even radio signals?

He'd remained calm and assured until his nephew boarded the train, but now the butterflies in his stomach were reproducing at an alarming rate. Why, he wondered, had he thought it a good idea to give up the security and familiarity of a tenured teaching position for this?

Because he'd had to, he reminded himself. Although the door to marriage had closed, God had graciously opened a window on a new life. Alex had put Him in charge, and he wasn't going to pull away now. Though his contract with Hilltop was open-ended, Alex had promised to stay at least two years. Twenty-four months—what would he be thinking then?

When he returned to the pickup, Dixon was leaning back in his seat and using a pen to direct the invisible orchestra playing on public radio.

When he jumped into the car, Dixon dropped the pen into the middle console. "Don't mind me. I played a tuba in the band and never quite recovered from it."

Another surprise . . . a fellow with a bent toward classical music. Alex filed the bit of information in his head, which felt very full already. Before he could comment out loud, Dixon's pickup roared to life and they left Wheatville as quickly as they'd come.

"It's very dark," Alex commented as the miles sped by. There was no way to tell how much ground they had covered because there was little in the countryside beyond the headlights of the pickup by which to judge their speed. A few distant yard lights glowed dimly. They passed very few cars.

"Blacker than a black cat in a coal bin," Dixon agreed. "But look at the stars!"

Alex rolled down his window and tipped his head out to look at the sky, his dark, short cropped hair ruffled by the wind. "It's like the planetarium back home. We never see stars like this in the city. There is too much light from streetlights, signs, buildings and cars to see more than the very brightest ones. Here it feels as if you could reach up and touch them."

"I can't imagine living without stars."

"I can't either—now. I was shortchanged." Alex enjoyed the cool, damp smell of the night air. "Even our family vacations were spent in cities. My mother wasn't much for green grass and the crawling critters that come with it. My grandparents had a cabin on Lake Michigan, but it was a very populated area so it almost felt like a small city as well."

"Can you see the Big Dipper?"

Alex craned his neck to see the distinct grouping of seven stars that created a rough outline of a large ladle-like dipper. "I can. There's the North Star. Polaris," he added, recalling his many visits to the planetarium as a child. "But what's that over there?" He pointed to the north, along what he knew to be the curve of the earth where an undulating curtain of pale iridescent green shimmered east to west across the sky. "It's beautiful."

"Aurora borealis," Dixon said. "Northern lights."

"Astounding." Alex was mesmerized by the ghostly presence of the shifting, flickering striations. He wished Jared were here to see this.

"Their visibility increases with your proximity to the North Pole. During the winter we often think we *are* at the pole. Only thing missing is polar bears and penguins. We have long nights in the winter, which you'll learn for yourself soon enough. The lights are most visible then."

The diffuse glow was riveting, mysterious, like God's window curtains floating on a heavenly breeze. Alex didn't want to shift his gaze. "What causes it?"

"It's an interaction between Earth's magnetic field and solar wind." Dixon hesitated and then chuckled. "It's a little like what happens at Hilltop sometimes. Some people are magnets and others are wind. When they collide, something always happens that lights up the sky. Fireworks."

Alex closed his eyes. Now he couldn't even look at the sky without being reminded of the vast responsibilities of his new job.

Finally his curiosity got the best of him. "Are you going to tell me who you mean when you talk about magnets and wind?"

"Don't you want to find out for yourself?" Dixon's voice was teasing and his eyes glinted impishly in the greenish glow of the dashboard. "I'd imagine there will be quite a thrill in the discovery. Like a puzzle—who tends to get under everyone's skin, who the local troublemakers are, who's the queen bee in the church kitchen. . . . "

Alex heard himself sigh. "I'm not a twentysomething pastor, and I want to make it work. With God's help I want to make this experience a blessing for everyone—even me."

"Music to my ears, Reverend. Frankly, I wasn't sure we'd ever get a pastor like you—still youthful and enthusiastic about growing the church. I thought we'd get someone shaken out of the blankets of retirement."

"Young and passionate? Dixon, you have a silver tongue."

The rest of their ride seemed like eons to Alex. They drove through inky blackness cut only by the beam of Dixon's headlights. They discussed the weather, which Dixon assured him was glorious in the summer and fall and tundra-like in the winter, and conversed about the crops grown in the area—wheat, barley, oats, peas, corn and sunflowers.

"It's a tightrope we walk," Dixon commented. "Too much rain can be as bad for farmers as too little. It's a balancing act with nature."

"It must take nerves of steel to plant a crop and wait months to see if there's a return or not."

"Farmers are betting men. We're always rolling nature's dice, gambling on the weather and holding our collective breaths until the last grain is in the bin. Only then do we know if we've won or lost."

It was after one in the morning when Dixon pulled the Jeep up next to the steps to the parsonage. "Here you are, Reverend. You should sleep fast, because your day will start hot and heavy tomorrow. I figure you'll get at least one breakfast quiche and a pan of fresh sweet rolls by 8:00 AM. Put the coffeepot on early."

Alex was glad he'd left a light on. As he came inside, he shed his shoes on the rag rug in the front entry and headed for the kitchen. There were no streetlights, and the darkness on the prairie was like nothing he'd ever experienced. Lydia had left the German chocolate cake on the counter, wrapped in foil, and he wasn't about to let it go to waste. He poured a huge glass of milk, cut a slice of cake almost the size of the salad plate he was using and ate it standing up.

When he had cleaned his plate, he took the stairs two at a time, and without undressing, lay down on the bed. He was asleep almost before his head hit the pillow.

Unfortunately, his night's sleep was fraught with dreams of Mattie Olsen on a murderous rampage, ants the size of mice invading the parsonage, Dixon and Mark building a barricade at the end of the driveway to stop the flow of quiches, and a long train whisking his nephew into the night.

On Wednesday morning he woke up exhausted.

He peered out the window to make sure that there were no gargantuan ants or a quiche-proof barricade. When he was sure everything he'd experienced last night was truly a dream, he showered, shaved and chose his clothing carefully.

What did one wear to work on the first day of being a pastor? A suit seemed too formal, and denim impossibly casual, so he settled on a pair of light colored khakis, a blue and white plaid shirt, and a navy tie. Approachable, friendly and professional, he hoped, attire that sent a signal that said he was here to work and to be available to those who had hired him.

Then he sat down on the corner of the bed, shoulders sagging, hands clasped limply between his knees. For a moment, feelings of insufficiency nipped at him. But only for a moment.

"I won't stand for this," he announced into the silence and rose to his full six-foot height. "The *Lord* is my shepherd!" he reminded himself. He had that to claim no matter how much doubt and fear assailed him.

Alex walked into the kitchen. The sun was shining across the walls and the black-and-white kitchen floor, and Alex looked around with satisfaction and a little trepidation. The kitchen was so beautiful and professional looking that he felt a sense of obligation settling around his shoulders. No more Pop Tarts and black coffee for breakfast. This was a new, fresh start. Suddenly he craved a bowl of steel cut oatmeal and a banana.

He settled for a homemade, individually wrapped cinnamon roll from the freezer, an apple left over from his cross-country trip with Jared and a vow to do better nutritionally tomorrow.

He felt a little silly driving his van to the church, considering it was less than a mile from the house, but the property between the two structures was low and swampy.

Alex pulled into the churchyard and noticed something sitting behind the church that he'd somehow missed in his first tour—two tidy outhouses sitting side by side. He moved forward slowly, a little unsure about the etiquette for approaching an outdoor toilet. The doors for these intriguing structures were on opposite sides, which Alex could see would provide privacy, and crescent moons carved in the eaves provided vents and light. They were little different from the portable toilets provided for concerts and sports events in the city, Alex thought. He knocked lightly on one of the doors and pushed it open. It was dusky, and motes of dust danced in the light seeping through the crescent moon opening. It was a two-holer, with a third, smaller hole meant for a child. The paper was kept in three-pound coffee cans, he noted; and, oddly, there were framed pictures from a Sears catalogue hanging on the wall.

Alex backed out of the small space. Impressive. It was as tidy and well cared for as everything else he'd seen. Even in the details, Hilltop did not disappoint.

He walked toward the small but immaculately manicured cemetery. It was rimmed with an ornamental black steel fence, the top of which was a series of extended spear-pointed pickets. Headstones of varying colors and shades of granite marched in neat rows across the pristinely mowed grass.

An unsightly plastic bag was caught on the fence in the far corner, so Alex walked the outside rim of the fence, pulled

the bag down, crumpled it up in his hand and headed back in
the way he had come. He glanced back over his shoulder and
slowed his step. There was a large rectangle of dirt covered
with weeds and crab grass that had sunk a few inches beneath
the level of the ground around it. A grave? He retraced his
steps and stared over the fence at the rough, patchy ground,
reminding himself to ask someone why this relatively fresh
grave had no apparent marker.

Stepping into the church was like stepping into a cool,
silent womb. In the foyer, he turned to the right, through
the pair of open doors to the nave, and felt his breath catch
in his throat. The sun was doing dazzling things to and
through the stained glass windows. Ruby, scarlet, emerald,
cobalt, amber, yellow, purple, orange and pink, the windows
looked like bright gems. The light splashed through them
and across the walls and floor. It was like being inside a
kaleidoscope.

He dropped into the last pew and stared at the window
depicting Jesus and the little children. Beneath the window on
a brass plate read the words *Let the little children come to Me:
do not stop them; for it is to such as these that the kingdom
of God belongs. Truly I tell you, whoever does not receive the
kingdom of God as a little child will never enter it.*

Alex loved children. Not so long ago he'd anticipated starting a family. He and Natalie had discussed it often. She'd been
as anxious as he to have children. Not anymore, apparently.

No use dwelling on the past, Alex told himself grimly. It
was time to meet the day.

He ventured into the back, and discovered that his office
was little more than a large walk-in closet that had been created
by simply building one room inside another. The larger room,
Mike had told him, was once used for Sunday school and

overflow crowds at weddings and funerals. It was now home to a series of coat racks, stacks of folding chairs, extra boxes of mouse poison, Christmas greenery and Alex's office. Two outside windows in the back wall of his space let in a pleasant amount of light.

A narrow desk ran parallel to the back wall. Alex was glad for that. He didn't relish being a vast desk's width away from people he counseled. There was so much to be read in a person's eyes, so many unintended flickers of emotion, that he wanted to be close to read the messages there. Off to the right sat a small desk that looked as though it had seen many students through high school before being donated here. It held a phone, a series of neatly laid out pens, and a large photo of a golden retriever. The dog's big licorice-drop nose and lolling red tongue were so well captured that they appear to press against the glass of the frame.

A rolling computer stand and a dented beige file cabinet stood like sentinels on either side of a coffee cart. Alex found both caffeinated and decaf in the drawer of the cart, as well as an assortment of what his grandmother referred to as "store bought" cookies—Pecan Sandies, Fig Newtons, shortbread, Nutter Butters and frosted lemon cookies.

The room was painted an innocuous pale gold color and the carpet was a mousy brown Berber, the kind of rug practical people bought because it "didn't show dirt." There were bookshelves lining available walls, all crowded with old hymnals and the detritus of pastors past.

"I can live with this," Alex said out loud. It was certainly no worse than his office at the college, which he'd shared with two colleagues, a monolith of a copy machine, and a steam cleaner for carpets that had appeared one day and never been retrieved.

Next he dug around in a plastic box on the bottom shelf of the tea cart for coffee filters. Dixon's Sumatra was there, just as he had promised.

He trotted to the basement kitchen to get water, and as soon as the coffee was brewing, Alex sat down behind his desk to try it on for size. The chair fit like a well-worn pair of shoes and he settled into it with a contented sigh. He was ready to work. But his flock must have smelled the coffee brewing. He might as well have made an announcement over a loudspeaker, because people began to arrive.

CHAPTER EIGHT

A blonde woman with hair as wiry as a Brillo pad poked her nose through the office door. She sneezed.

"Allergies?" he asked sympathetically, having been sensitive to ragweed his entire life.

"Pollens, molds, dust mites, dogs, cats. Don't mind me." She put a large box of tissues and her purse on the smaller desk. "It's that time of year. Once the snow comes, I'll be fine. Sorry to be a little late. I had to drive my husband to work. His truck wasn't working and he has to be in early on Wednesdays."

She was slim, energetic looking, and of indeterminate age. Alex guessed her to be somewhere between forty and fifty, but he'd been wrong before. It was difficult to tell from the lumpy pink sweater and multicolored beaded necklace she wore or to see beyond the dramatic sweep of thick brown eyeliner circling each eye. With makeup that was more subtle, she could be quite attractive.

She noticed him studying her and her hands flew to her head. "Don't look at my hair!" she pleaded. "My hairdresser said it would grow out in six months. I'm never letting my sister-in-law touch my hair again, I'm telling you. It's a wonder that we're still speaking. I should have learned after that time she accidently colored it orange. Turning the other cheek should not apply to perms and color treatments."

Without giving him time to respond, she thrust out her hand in greeting. "You must be the new pastor. I'm Gabriella Andrea Dunn, your church secretary. People just call me Gandy, for short."

Alex took a deep breath, hoping Ms. Dunn had not sucked all the air out of the room with her introductory speech. "Alex Armstrong. It's nice to meet you, Ms. Dunn."

She scrunched her brows together. "It's Gandy. We aren't terribly formal here in Hilltop. We're all God's children, right? That makes us siblings. None of *my* siblings call me 'Ms. Dunn.'"

"Very well, then, Gandy." He rather liked her reference to being siblings in God. He hadn't thought of it quite that way before, but he relished the idea. "But you have a picture of a dog on your desk. If you have allergies . . . "

Gandy looked as him as if he were three bales short of a load. "I have allergies but I also have *priorities*, and dogs are *priorities*."

Alex cleared his throat. She was a woman who knew her mind. And Alex suspected she might know a whole lot about how things were done around this church. "Gandy, I have a question. . . . "

"Ask me anything. If I know the answer I'll give it to you. If I don't, I'll find it for you."

"I was looking around outside and noticed the outhouses. . . . "

"They're kept nicely, aren't they," Gandy asked with a note of pride in her voice. "Since we got the fire-breather, we've talked about tearing them down, but folks like them, especially in the summer months."

"The fire-breather?" Alex already regretted his inquiry.

"We don't have sewage or septic out here, so we've installed what's called a waterless incinerating toilet. When you flush, it ignites and burns up the . . . you know. It runs on propane. Works great, and we like an indoor biffy in the winter, but it's nice to get outside the rest of the time. Besides, it's a little alarming to flush a toilet and hear something give a roar and burst into flames right where you were sitting." She looked up at him expectantly. "Anything else you need to know?"

It took a moment for him to regain his composure. "About those pictures in the outhouse. . . . "

"The ones taken from an old Sears, Roebuck catalogue? That was Inga Sorenson's idea. She thought it would be cute to have a memento of the past so she framed those pages. Get it?"

Gandy read the confusion on Alex's features and forged on. "Catalogues are what they used to use before toilet paper came along."

The light dawned. "Oh." Alex quickly changed the subject. "So how did you know I'd arrived? Or do you come in every day?"

"Mattie Olsen told me you were here, so I called Dixon to get the scoop."

Somehow that didn't surprise Alex. Word traveled as fast here as it did on the Internet.

"Then I'm sure you know more about me than I do about you. I wasn't even sure the church provided a secretary."

She snorted in a very unladylike fashion. "They don't provide one. Just me."

"But I thought you were . . . "

"I'm the church secretary all right," Gandy said amiably. "I'm just not paid to do it."

"We should see to that immediately!" It was a horrible oversight.

She waved her hands. "No, no! You don't understand. I'm a permanent volunteer, that's all. Money is tight around our house and most of what we have goes toward living expenses. I work at the church as my tithe, giving to God from what I have. In this case it's my work. We figure out what we earn a year and take ten percent of that. From that I determine how many hours I'll need to work in order for it to be our tithe. You should pray my husband gets a raise—then I'll be full time." She grinned happily and Alex saw that there was a bone deep cheerfulness about the woman. Hardscrabble as her life might be, she'd taken lemons and made lemonade.

"Where do you live, Gandy? Near the church?"

"No, I live on the edge of Grassy Valley. My husband Mac drives a fuel truck for Red's. I feel like I'm part of Hilltop, though. I grew up here on Jonas Owens's place. Obadiah Owens was my grandfather. You'll meet my brother sooner or later." A shadow slipped fleetingly across her features like a cloud briefly obscuring the sun.

"I already did. He stopped by the parsonage."

"Really. Hmmmm." The garrulous Gandy was suddenly subdued.

Before he could formulate a question about Gandy's brother, she pulled a plastic sandwich bag out of her purse. It was filled with small brown lumps dusted with something white that looked like chalk powder. She thrust it at him proudly. "Here, I brought you a treat—puppy chow."

He looked at the bag now in this hand. "But I don't have a dog."

Surprise and then amusement, spread over Gandy's sharp features and she laughed out loud. "It's for you, pastor, not your dog!"

"But puppy chow . . . ?"

"Taste it first, decide later." Gandy sat on the edge of the desk with an air of anticipation. Her thin body quivered with expectancy as she watched him cautiously study the bag.

Alex opened the bag and sniffed. The aroma of chocolate filled his nostrils. His eyes widened. "Is this what I think it is?"

"Try it, you'll like it." Gandy had her hands pressed together in suppressed excitement, obviously delighted to flabbergast the new pastor right off the bat.

Trust in the Lord with all your heart, and do not rely on your own insight. Reluctantly, Alex stuck his hand in the bag and pulled out a chunk of the light, airy stuff. Slowly he put it into his mouth and bit down. Then his eyes lit. "It *is* chocolate!"

"Crispy rice cereal squares, butter, melted chocolate, peanut butter and powdered sugar," Gandy told him. "It's my kids' favorite snack. I made a whole container just for you." She reached into the voluminous bag she'd put on the floor and brought out the treasure.

"It's delicious. Thank you." He dusted powdered sugar off his hands and the front of his shirt. "Do you give out your recipes? My nephew Jared would love this. I'd like to surprise him with it on his next visit."

Gandy looked him up and down like a meat inspector examining a hanging carcass. "You won't have to cook for yourself for a long while, I expect. There will be a lot of people wanting to help you put meat on those bones. By the way, there's a quiche on the back pew that Lolly Roscoe brought by. Do you want me to put it in the church refrigerator, or will you run it to the parsonage yourself?"

Alex was always grateful for his slim physique. He kept it
that way by running and working out. His blood pressure rarely
varied from 120/70, and he had a cholesterol level worth crowing about. He could see that he was a good physical specimen
destined to become a fatted calf.

She turned away and busied herself scrawling something
in longhand on a sheet of paper. Then, with a flourish, Gandy
put the paper into Alex's hand.

"There you have it. Enjoy."

PUPPY CHOW
FROM THE KITCHEN OF GANDY DUNN

- 1/2 cup butter (some people leave this out)
- I cup creamy peanut butter
- 2 cups chocolate chips (sometimes I use semisweet chocolate, which is good too)
- Crispy rice or corn cereal squares (9 cups or a box worth)
- I pound powdered confectioner's sugar (experiment—you
  can probably use a little less)

Melt the butter, peanut butter and chocolate in a saucepan.
Pour it over the cereal, tossing it gently until it is well coated.
(Hint: I put the chocolate-coated cereal in a large paper bag,
seal it and then shake it.)

* It's hard to ruin, Reverend, and I'd be surprised if you
could do it.

This was his first recipe for his new kitchen. It pleased him
more than he could have predicted. Maybe he would become a
cook out here among so many good ones. Then he could knock
his sister's socks off when she came to visit. But he'd have to
collect more recipes than one. He made a mental note to ask

Lydia for her German chocolate cake recipe. And another to learn to cook things that weren't chocolate.

Gandy clapped a hand across her mouth and her blue eyes grew large. "I'll bet I interrupted something important when I handed you that puppy chow. You were probably writing your sermon for Sunday. Don't pay attention to me. Just hand me the Bible readings and hymn numbers when you're ready for me to put them in the bulletin." She plopped down at her desk, took the plastic cover off the keyboard to her computer—an elderly machine that had been purchased in the dark ages of the computer era—and busied herself booting it up.

Alex felt like a slacker because the idea of writing his sermon hadn't entered his mind yet. He retreated guiltily to his own desk and turned to his own computer, which was considerably newer than Gandy's. What would he say on Sunday?

It probably wasn't wise to mention that he felt like he'd landed on another planet when he'd arrived. Was it only a couple days ago? It seemed like a lifetime already. He'd tell them how God called him into ministry and to Hilltop, and share his dreams for the church. This was his formal introduction to the church family, after all. He wanted people to know what they were getting.

For the moment, he would busy himself with reading a few past bulletins to see how things had been done. He would take the church directory home with him to study the faces and names he would soon encounter.

It was barely eleven o'clock when Alex felt his stomach growl and imagined that he smelled the aroma of cooking food. He looked up to ask Gandy a question and saw a trim woman standing in the office doorway holding a large casserole wrapped in a white dishtowel. The sun was at her back and Alex had to squint to get a look at her face.

And what a face it was. The woman was painted within an inch of her life. Her skin was a flawless mask of color topped off by smooth, peachy cheeks. Her eyelids were burnished copper and the mascara she was wearing made her lashes look long as palm fronds. Her lips reminded Alex of the ice at his local hockey arena after the Zamboni had gone by—multilayered and glistening. Only unlike ice, they were an orange color he'd seen only in a Caribbean sunset.

Michelangelo, Alex thought wryly, probably hadn't used much more paint than this on the Sistine Chapel. She trotted into the small office and, had he been standing, Alex might have been knocked off his feet by the scent of citrus and spice. Her perfume was stronger than the cleansers under his sink.

"Hello, Lilly, been cooking, I see." Gandy smiled at the woman. "Don't you look pretty? Been at one of those home makeup parties you give? You smell nice."

"It's Citrus Sunshine. Unfortunately I'm unable to get it any more. I've quit selling makeup. Haven't you heard?" Lilly set the casserole on Alex's desk. "I've started selling jewelry. Going anywhere special, Gandy? Need anything new? How about gifts? Christmas will be coming eventually, you know."

Then the woman seemed to remember where she was and why she'd come. She turned to Alex. "Hello, Pastor, I'm Lilly Sumptner. I stopped to say welcome to Hilltop and brought you something for supper. I'll just tuck it in the refrigerator in the church kitchen. When you get home, just heat at three hundred fifty degrees until it cooks up again. An hour should be plenty."

"Hello, Lilly, this is a lovely gesture." Alex stood up to shake her hand, which was decorated with artificial nails that reminded him of bloodied dragon's teeth.

"My husband Chuck and I will have you over for dinner sometime soon," Lilly promised as she glanced at her watch. "Gotta run. I'm doing a jewelry party in Grassy Valley today and I can't be late. Very unprofessional." She took Alex's hand in her own. "We're glad you're here, Pastor. So very glad."

With that, Lilly Sumptner turned and left on a breeze of Citrus Sunshine.

Neither Alex nor Gandy spoke until the sound of Lilly's car disappeared in the distance.

"She's the party lady," Gandy said finally. "Always selling something. One day it's makeup, the next jewelry. No one knows what she'll sell next."

"Why does she keep changing products?" Alex shook his head. "That's not how it's usually done, is it?"

"She sells something until she runs out of customers. Then she starts selling something else. There aren't that many of us in the area, so she has to do that in order to keep us buying."

"I see," he said. That was unique marketing. "So rather than go outside the area and sell to a wider audience, she changes the product instead?"

"You could say that. It looks like she's using up her makeup inventory on herself, though. It was a little heavy-handed today. Lilly has a good heart, when she can get her head off business."

Buying and selling, marketing plans and product selection. Lilly would probably have done well in business in Chicago, Alex mused, but instead she'd bloomed where she was planted, right here in Hilltop.

Lilly Sumpter's perfume had not yet dissipated when another visitor arrived at the church office. A small woman
walked in carrying a jar of jam. When he first glanced up, Alex
guessed her to be in her eighties, and she too was heavy-handed
in the makeup department. She must attend Lilly's parties.
Then he got a good look at her face. She had wrinkles like a
topography map. Even with her trim figure in a bright blue
housedress and her red lipstick and liberally rouged cheeks,
she couldn't have been a day under seventy. And that was
being generous.

"Rhubarb," she said as she plunked a pint jar with a Mason
lid onto his desk. "I grow it in my backyard. I'll fill it for you
again."

"Thank you. And you are . . . ?" He gave the jar back and
leaned forward, towering over the little woman.

She didn't seem to mind. "Tillie Tanner. Welcome, Pastor.
We're glad you're here."

"You're right about that, Tillie!" Gandy chimed. "He's an
answer to prayer."

Alex felt himself redden under the appraising eyes of the
two women and was thankful when Tillie tapped the face of
the large, man's wristwatch on her wrist. "Almost time for my
soap opera. I'd better go. See you on Sunday, Pastor." Shoulders
square and head held high, Tillie walked out the front door and
down the steps to a car that didn't look a day younger than its
driver.

Gandy glanced at the white-faced clock on the wall, leapt
to her feet with a little squawk and grabbed her purse. "I almost
forgot Debbie. You'll have to excuse me, Pastor, I have to take
my daughter to the clinic for her allergy shot. I'll be back
tomorrow to finish the bulletin." She eyed his desk for a list

of hymns or readings for the Sunday service, but the desk was still bare.

"There's a medical facility in Grassy Valley?"

She snorted again. The sound, Alex began to realize, was her response to many things, usually those she held in low esteem. "There's a 'satellite clinic' staffed by the Wheatville Physicians Group, but it's not going to be revolving around here very long. Doc Ambros is making noises about retirement, and he's afraid that the Wheatville clinic isn't making plans to fill his position. He's afraid they'll close the satellite in Grassy Valley and we'll have no doctor at all. It's a shame. That will put us more than fifty miles from medical help. That's a long drive if you have an injured child or someone with chest pains. I'd like those doctors to break a leg out here and ride in a car for fifty miles to get it set!" She left the office, head high and back stiff.

Alex couldn't blame her. That was another thing he'd taken for granted. In Chicago, Urgent Care Centers were located throughout the city, while here there was one elderly doctor for an entire community.

After Gandy was gone, Alex wandered into the nave and sat down in the last pew. *Am I doing this right, Lord?* As he sat there, a remarkable peace spread over him. He willed himself to remain still, not wanting this moment to slip away. He began to pray.

An hour later he looked up to find Dixon towering over him. He smiled at his new friend. "Have a seat, Dixon, I was just in conversation with the Lord."

"I don't want to interrupt any chat with the Big Guy," Dixon said. "I'll come back later."

"Please stay. I'm ready to get back to work. Is there anything I can help you with?"

"Not really, I just came to see if any quiche had arrived yet."

He got his answer when Alex flushed. "You called it right, Dixon. One arrived this morning."

"I told you so." Dixon's expression danced with mischief. "I hope you know that old saying isn't true."

"What old saying is that?"

"That real men don't eat quiche. They eat it, all right. They just don't *admit* it to anyone."

CHAPTER NINE

After Dixon left, Alex continued to study the stained glass windows in the church. They depicted moments in the life of Christ—Jesus multiplying the loaves and fishes, surrounded by little children, shepherding His lambs. Christ's baptism was depicted with a white dove descending. There was a beautiful stained glass rendering of Jesus praying in the garden and, Alex's favorite, Jesus walking on water as a sinking Peter reached out to Him.

Alex had always identified closely with Peter's weakness, and was comforted by Christ's love for his flawed disciple. It encouraged him, weak as he was sometimes, to carry on. He was so engrossed in studying the windows and what they represented that Alex didn't hear the soft footsteps behind him. A cool, bony hand fell gently on his bare forearm. His heart leapt, and a frisson of panic shot through him.. He spun around to find someone behind him. Bony wrists protruded from his shirtsleeves and his cheeks appeared sunken.

The lanky man jumped back at Alex's reaction, almost as startled as Alex had been. "Sorry, Reverend, I didn't mean to alarm you."

"It's quite all right, Jonas." Alex stammered, his breathing returning to normal. "I was so engrossed in these beautiful windows that you could have driven an entire truck into the church and I might not have heard it."

"I'm here looking for my sister Gandy."

Alex took in the weary slouch of Jonas' shoulders and the hang-dog look on his face and felt yet another pang of sympathy for the man. Alex could see the resemblance between him and Gandy, especially the same pointed nose, rosy at the tip. Their personalities were where the two diverged. Gandy was chipper and upbeat, while her brother carried the weight of the world on his shoulders.

"I'm afraid that your sister has left for the day. Something about her daughter and an allergy shot."

Jonas looked more dejected than ever. "I forgot all about that. I'll have to catch her at home later. I just had some . . . questions." His face was shuttered from all expression.

"Tell me about your family, Jonas." Alex patted the pew next to him. "We didn't visit much on that hunt for your cow."

A faint smile twitched at the corners of Jonas' mouth, and he lowered himself down.

"My wife's name is Barbara. She used to be a hairdresser in Grassy Valley before she started raising kids. She still works a day or two a week."

Alex remembered Gandy's Brillo-pad hair.

"Joe Jr. just graduated. Brett is fifteen. And Crissie, our tagalong, is eight."

"I hear your family has owned land here for a long time."

"In Hilltop Township everyone has been here since the beginning."

"Pardon me?" Alex didn't know what to make of this.

"Hilltop is the only township in the area in which the original families of the men who pioneered the land still own it. Every farm is owned by the grandson or great-grandson of the men and women who put down stakes here in the 1800s."

Seeing Alex's blank look, Jonas continued. "Congress passed the Homestead Act in 1862. For a small fee, a US citizen could claim 160 acres of public land, and a married couple could get 320 acres. Once the claim was made, they had to live on the land for five years, build living quarters and cultivate the land. Then it became their own. No land in this township has ever been sold. People around here are pretty proud of that heritage. Even my kids think it's interesting, and you know how kids are."

"What do you grow on your farm?" Alex asked.

"Wheat, barley, peas, whatever everyone else grows. The only difference is that I never get the yield everyone else does around here."

"You don't?"

"I don't use any chemicals on my crops. I summer fallow my fields, for example. I don't crop them every year, to preserve nutrients in the soil. Old-fashioned, I know, but it's the way my father and grandfather did it.

"Fascinating. Thanks for telling me. And," Alex added, "I hope to meet your family."

"Better meet them soon then," Jonas muttered, "before we aren't here anymore."

Jonas stood to leave, but Alex put a hand on his forearm. "Jonas?"

"Don't mind me, Reverend, I'm just down today."

"Want to talk about it?"

Jonas studied him appraisingly. "Let's just say things haven't been easy the past few years. Crop prices have been up and down. Three years ago I planted too early and my crop got washed out so I had to reseed. The next year I lost it all to hail. Last year my wife had appendicitis and ended up with peritonitis. She was in the hospital a long time and we didn't have very good insurance. Since she couldn't work, she had to close her hair salon. Guess you'd say we had a run of bad luck." A grimness settled about him that was almost palpable.

"That's tough," Alex murmured sympathetically.

"You don't know the half of it."

He turned and lifted a hand to wave back over his shoulder. "Nice to see you, Reverend. You'll like Hilltop. It's a good place to call home." There was sadness in his eyes as he turned to go.

He would walk to the church occasionally, Alex decided as he got into his aging van at five o'clock to return to the parsonage. It would be good to give his heart a little exercise other than being startled by people creeping up on him in the church. It would also provide an opportunity to pray his way into the day before Gandy greeted him at the door, and it would provide him a chance to consider all that he was learning in these first days at Hilltop.

Jonas Owens stuck in his craw—a phrase he'd learned from Dixon. Or perhaps it was more like peanut butter stuck to the roof of his mouth. He couldn't get the man off his mind.

God is our refuge and strength, a very present help in trouble, therefore we will not fear, Alex reminded himself. He would pray that Jonas experienced God's help in his trouble.

As he was about to pull out of the churchyard, he caught a movement from the corner of his eye. Something had scooted around the side of the small shed where, according to Gandy, the lawn mower and snowblower were kept.

Odd. Though he'd only gotten a glimpse of a form in that brief second, he guessed the figure was human rather than animal. While he had no interest in coming face to face with a fox, coyote, deer or moose, all of which Dixon said inhabited the area, a human was an entirely different matter. He turned his van around and drove slowly toward the shed.

The grass was matted around the building but Alex could see no discernable footsteps, at least not from a distance. He slipped out of the van to walk around the building on foot.

After circling the shed, he paused at the door to check the lock. It seemed fine at first glance. A simple affair held closed by a padlock. Alex turned away, chastising himself for a case of overactive imagination, but turned back when he heard an odd rustling sound, like that of large wings, emanating from the shed. A sliver of cold slithered along his spine, and the hairs stood at the nape of his neck. A single line from high school English popped into his mind. *Quoth the Raven, 'Nevermore.'*

Get a grip, Armstrong, he told himself. Here he was, a grown man, acting like a kid listening to spooky stories around a campfire. He looked at the lock again, more closely this time, and swallowed thickly. He poked at the padlock with his finger and it flipped open and dangled there. It only *appeared* to be intact. The building was actually unlocked.

Before he could consider it further, Alex swept the open lock aside and threw open the door.

The flap of wings echoed in his ears as a pair of glowing orange talons lifted from a roost and headed straight for his eyes. These were followed by a blur of blue-black feathers and an inhuman shriek that chilled his core. Alex threw himself sideways, and the creature landed on the ground where he had been standing. Screeching and complaining, the enormous black rooster with glossy feathers, rosy red wattle, and lousy personality fluffed itself into a huge feathery ball and ran off, squawking angrily. Then a small red-haired boy emerged, shooting out of the dimness of the shed, nearly knocking Alex to the ground.

"Now look what you done!" the child yelled, every bit as irate as the rooster. Hands on scrawny hips, the boy watched the bird sprint out of the churchyard, across the road and into a plowed field where the dark earth camouflaged all but the orange legs and bright wattle.

The little boy, who looked to be between eight and ten, spun around and glared at Alex indignantly. "What did you do that for?" the child demanded, rusty freckles standing out across the bridge of his nose. "Are you trying to ruin everything?"

Alex blinked, surprised to be put on the offensive. He spoke calmly into the furious little face. "I don't want to 'ruin' anything, but I have to ask, what were you and a rooster doing in the church storage barn?"

"What's it to you? You ain't the preacher or nothin'." The boy bristled indignantly. He had obviously claimed this as his own personal territory.

"As a matter of fact, I am the preacher." He stuck out a hand. "Reverend Alex Armstrong, at your service. And you are . . . ?"

The boy's Adam's apple bounced in his throat as he swallowed. He was observably startled by this unexpected bit of news. "I didn't know they'd found a sucker . . . I mean pastor yet. My pa said they'd never find anyone stupid enough to come here where everybody is in financial trouble and he probably wouldn't get paid."

This was a new perspective, Alex thought, unsure how to take this bit of information. Finally he said, "That's in God's hands, not mine. But you *do* happen to have been in the church's shed, that bit is clear."

The child kicked his foot backward like a recalcitrant pony, managing to close the door with one swipe. "I'm not in there now." Then he scuttled sideways to get around Alex and make a run for it.

The teacher in Alex knew exactly what to do. "Young man, stay right where you are."

The boy recognized the authority in that voice and stopped.

"You'd better tell me your name. After all, you know mine." Alex felt his sense of humor returning as he looked at the boy who appeared to be a cross between Huck Finn and Jared as a small boy.

"Willard Martin Packard, but everybody calls me Will."

Packard? He'd heard that name somewhere before. It took a moment but then he recalled Clarence Olson sitting in the kitchen with a scowl on his face saying, "those Packard kids that run wild around here . . . "

"Nice to meet you, Will. Now I think we should look in the shed and see if that rooster did any damage." To Alex's surprise, the boy's remarkable pale blue eyes grew round with horror.

"He didn't do nothin', I'm sure of it." The child wasn't so cocky now.

"But *I'm* not sure. Would you open the door for me, please?" Alex was having a hard time keeping a straight face, but it wouldn't do to allow the boy to think that breaking and entering—even a shed—was acceptable.

"We knew it was almost empty." Words began to spill out of Will's mouth. "And they say churches are supposed to do good deeds, so we thought nobody would mind if we did a good deed in the shed. My ma always says God made humankind." He screwed up his face in thought. "And let them have dominion over the fish of the sea, and over the birds of the air, and over the cattle, and over all the wild animals of the earth, and over every creeping thing that creeps upon the earth, so we thought it had to be all right."

The little fellow could quote from Genesis! Alex's curiosity got the best of him. "Who taught you that verse?"

"Ma. So's we wouldn't pull the wings off flies or nothin'."

"I see." Alex steeled himself for what might be inside the shed. He was beginning to have a very bad feeling about this.

Will opened the door slowly, and it groaned agonizingly on its unoiled hinges, making almost as much noise as the rooster had.

Alex took a deep breath and stepped in. The small but dusty windows let in a modicum of light, and it took a moment for his eyes to adjust. When they did, he realized that he was looking at something that was a cross between a pet shop and an animal shelter. There was another chicken, much smaller than the first, black but with more white in its feathers, roosting on a cross-beam. In a cage that had been recently supplied with fresh water and food was a gold and white cat with a nasty but healing gash in its side. Beside it slept two small gold kittens. In the final cage was—Alex swallowed thickly and backed away—an enormous black-and-white skunk.

"Don't worry about Rose," Will said, staring up at Alex. "My uncle took her stink bag out when she was little. She's a pet. I brung her in here to keep the others company. They're friends."

With friends like that, one didn't need enemies, Alex thought. "I think you have some explaining to do, Will. Why are these creatures in the storage barn?"

Will pointed at the cat and her kittens. "My brother and sister and I found her bleeding and half dead by Bucky Chadwick's place. We figure he kicked her or set a dog on her. He does stuff like that. Says it's fun. He doesn't deserve any cats," Will said earnestly, his small face pinched. "Ma won't let us have any more pets at home, so we figured we'd start our own hoomain shelter right here."

"Hoomain . . . ah yes, humane shelter."

"We found the hen and rooster wandering by the side of the road and figured they fell off a truck or something so we brought them here too. We already found a home for the kittens, soon as they're big enough to take away from their mama."

Alex didn't know whether to laugh or cry. The child's earnestness was genuine, and the animals did look well cared for. The shed was relatively neat except for the droppings beneath the roosting area. No other damage had been done except to the broken padlock. It couldn't go on, of course, but what would they do about it?

"I'm afraid they can't be left in here indefinitely. And you know, I'm sure, that it was wrong to break into this building." Alex watched the boy's reaction. "First, we'll have to find a different . . . hoomain . . . shelter for you. Second, we're going to have to figure out how you'll pay for a new lock for the building and apologize to whoever mows the church property."

"*Awww*." Will's freckled nose wrinkled in distaste but he didn't argue. It was apparent he thought he'd gotten off easy. Alex had a hunch that this boy was accustomed to being in trouble. Still, a lesson could be learned with gentleness as well as harshness; that was his theory. And though he didn't say it out loud, he admired the boy for trying to do something about a creature in pain.

When he turned around, he cleared his throat. "Did you break the lock, Will, or did one of them?"

"Me." Will's voice grew small.

"Then it is your responsibility to pay."

"I don't have any money. I spent all my money on cat food. But maybe I could borrow some from my big brother Andy. Andy and Katie always save their money. The others can't hang onto a dime. Andy says he's saving up to run away from home and my sister Katie says she's going to college. I'll bet she'll be a hunnert years old before she gets there at the rate she's going. They said she was too immature to go to school and held her back in first grade. If that keeps happening, she'll be an old lady before she gets out of that place."

Alex turned his head slightly until he could control the smile creeping across his face.

"Don't tell my pa, okay? He'd probably get out the hairbrush."

"We'll cross that bridge later," Alex said firmly, reminding himself to find out more about the Packard family dynamics. "Do you have a job?"

"Me? I'm only nine! Nobody thinks I'm good for anything yet."

"Well, I do," Alex said firmly. "I think you are good for plenty. Come to the church office tomorrow. I noticed some tarnished silver candlesticks in a closet at the church. I think you could earn a new lock by polishing them for me. What do you say?"

Will brightened. "That's it? No hollering or sending me to bed without supper?"

"Not this time," Alex said with a warning in his voice, "but if it happens again . . . "

The child studied him with eyes so blue and intense that he could have been running lasers over Alex. "You ain't so bad. I'm glad you came even if my pa thinks yer crazy."

"Thank you, I think." Alex made a mental note to have a conversation with Lauren, Mike or Dixon to find out more about Will's father and mother.

Alex watched the boy scamper into the ditch and come up again pushing a much used bicycle. He flung his leg over the seat and took off, peddling hard in the gravel. The sun glinted off the boy's red hair and made it look like flames. Then he lifted one hand off the handlebar and waved backward over his shoulder.

That had gone fairly well, Alex told himself, considering it was the first time he'd ever seen a skunk close up and personal.

"You've got a *what* in the church shed? And Will's already been over to polish the silver?" Lauren Carlsen's musical laughter rang over the telephone line like a crystal wind chime. "Those Packards! I should have warned you about them. You've just barely scratched the surface of that clan with Will. There are several more of them, a pack of redheaded, freckle-faced, angelic-looking but uncontrollable scamps. The Packard children are known to be unruly, wild, rowdy and boisterous. Plus every single one has the energy of the Energizer Bunny. They're intelligent too, in a street-smart sort of way. Good luck, Alex. You'll need it with the Packard children."

"What about their parents? Where do they fit into the picture?"

"Minnie Packard is a sweet, shy, over-run wisp of a woman. Her husband Earl is . . . well, let's just say he has problems with authority, alcohol and preachers."

"Will told me his father thinks I'm crazy to have come here."

There was a long silence on Lauren's end of the line. "Mr. Packard has opinions, not many of which I agree with."

"I see," Alex interpreted her hesitation. "A conversation for another time. My mission right now is to do something with the animals in the shed." He was beginning to feel a little overwhelmed.

"Don't worry about that. I'll send Mike over to pick them up. I wouldn't mind another cat, especially a good mouser, and the hen and rooster will fit right in with the batch I already have. If the roosters fight, I'm sure we can find another home for them." She chuckled again. "The whole thing is rather cute, if you don't consider the breaking and entering."

Alex laughed. "Do you have any recommendations about how to approach the parents about this?"

Lauren was silent far too long before speaking. "I'm not sure what to tell you there. The kids can be awful behavior problems, but it isn't something that can be solved with a spanking. It goes deeper than that. I'd better add Earl to my prayer list. If he ever came around, it would probably do miracles for the kids. Poor Minnie can't do it all alone. She's got a good, faithful heart and comes to church all she can. Earl makes it difficult for her sometimes, though. There's a man who has hardened his heart. A good sermon is to him like pearls before swine."

Alex was thoughtful after he hung up the phone. Should he wait, as Lauren had suggested, to speak to Will's father? If *he* were a father, Alex mused, he'd like to know what his child was up to. Slowly he picked up the slender phone book that held the numbers of several of the small communities in the area. He found the Packard number and dialed.

"Yeah? Whadaya want?"

The man's voice was hoarse, belligerent and slurred. Alex realized at once that Will's father had been drinking. Not sure what else to do, he lowered the receiver to its cradle without speaking. After hearing that menacing tone Alex realized he had to think this through. He didn't want to place Will in a situation that either of them would regret.

Jonas Owens, Will and Earl Packard—how long would his prayer list for those in need grow before he was done?

Chapter Ten

Alex was surprised to reach the church before Gandy. He'd taken time to sit on the porch a little longer today, enjoying the morning. Even after just a couple days of being around her, he knew that Gandy was a gem. In all his years in academia, he'd never seen such an enthusiastic, dedicated worker. When he'd complimented her on her work habits, she'd quoted 1 Corinthians 10:31. *Whatever you do, do everything for the glory of God.* If everyone did that, she'd added, the world would be a far better place. He vowed to make a conscious effort to do just that today.

Then he stepped into an apple pie.

It was sitting just outside the door to his office, lurking in the shadows of stored folding chairs and a bevy of mops. And now it was all over his foot. He hopped on his left foot, removed the right shoe, and then jumped awkwardly to the front door of the church just in time to meet Gandy, hair flying around her head in a yellow halo. She was carrying a thermal coffee mug and a baggie containing what she'd told him was her favorite lunch, a mayonnaise sandwich.

"What are you up to so early in the morning?" she asked as she watched him beat his shoe against a concrete step and cause apple slices to fly hither and yon.

"I came in to have some prayer time. I was about to unlock the office door when I stepped into a pie someone had left there."

"*Ahh.*" Gandy ducked into the church to put down her things and returned to pick up an envelope that was covered with sugary pie filling. The imprint of a foot was stamped on it. "It's from Irene Collins. Too bad you stepped in it. She makes some of the best pies in the county. If she'd baked banana bread there'd be less mess to clean up."

Gandy took everything in stride. She would be a good role model for him, Alex realized. This wasn't the first treat that had been left for him. He'd found monster cookies loaded with peanut butter, chocolate candies, and nuts and a note of welcome from Cherry Taylor on the seat of his car, and a package of Hilda Aadland's butter cookies on his front steps.

"I've started to write down the names of my benefactors so I can write them each a thank you note," he said to Gandy. "If things continue like this, I may get nothing else done. Not that I'm complaining, mind you, just overwhelmed with people's generosity and kindness."

"I'll do it. Where's the list?"

Alex pulled it out of his pocket and handed it to her. Gandy stared at it intently, took a pencil out of her hair and added the apple pie to the list. Then she sat back and muttered, "*Hmm . . .*"

"Why do you sound like Sherlock Holmes?" Alex asked. "There's no mystery about who delivered this pie."

"Every bit of this food was brought to you by women."

"What's mysterious about that? I gather Hilltop's women are all fabulous cooks."

"That's true, but there are several single women on the list, ages twenty-seven through eighty-two. The unmarrieds have come out of the woodwork for you: Brunie Bruun, Irene Collins, Tillie Tanner and Lolly Roscoe, to name a few. Some are from Hilltop Township and a few are from Grassy Valley. If this continues we'll have a jump in our church membership. I wonder if the call committee even considered that. If they did, they're craftier than I gave them credit for being."

"You mean they hired me as bait?" Alex wasn't sure if she was joking or not.

"When you put it that way . . . " she scratched her chin. "Nah, they couldn't have."

"Well, I'm glad you've settled that. You had me frightened for a moment."

"You've got to realize, Reverend Alex, that this was bound to happen. There aren't many single men around here, and the ones that are, aren't too interesting."

"Why not?" He was intrigued by Gandy's kangaroo logic and the way it kept jumping around.

"Most of them think a debate about the merits of a John Deere versus a Massey-Ferguson or a New Holland is scintillating, for one thing. And a discussion of what crops to plant next year can go on for weeks. Then there's the weather—too much rain, too little rain, rain in the wrong places . . . "

"I see what you mean."

"Mark Nash and Dixon Daniels were the prime targets until you came along." Gandy shook her head. "I'm glad I fell in love with my high school sweetheart and married him first thing. Sure saved me a lot of time and effort."

"If everyone keeps bringing me food, I'll weigh a ton. No one will think I'm a good catch then," he said hopefully.

"They'll switch to vegetarian casseroles and low-calorie dishes." Gandy grinned up at him. "You can only hope that another single man moves into the area soon and takes some of the pressure off you."

After a futile half hour of trying to polish his first sermon, Alex wandered over to where Gandy was putting together bulletins. "I think I'll take a drive over to All Saints today." He'd left the outside door open so that he could gaze at a tabletop-flat field over which birds were wheeling and diving.

Gandy searched for a pencil in the blonde frizz of her hair. She'd begun keeping them there when she realized that the curl in her hair was good for keeping writing utensils off her desk, where they tended to disappear. "Now you're running off. I shouldn't have told you that stuff about being an eligible bachelor. Nobody is going to trap you unless you want to be trapped, you know."

"I'm hardly running away. I want to get to know more about it before I appear in their pulpit next Sunday."

"Suit yourself. They aren't a friendly bunch. You may have noticed that no one has come to greet you with open arms."

"I had a nice visit with the church janitor yesterday. He said it's pretty quiet at the church during the summer. I also met the organist who was there practicing for the Sunday service." They'd both been pleasant enough.

Alex leaned against the doorjamb, and his long, lean body relaxed, but he was still feeling perplexed. "What happened between these two congregations to put them at odds?" *Now I appeal to you, brothers and sisters, by the name of our Lord Jesus Christ, that all of you be in agreement and that there be no divisions among you, but that you be united in the same mind and the same purpose.*

"Nothing happened on this side of the fence that I know of." Now Gandy searched in her Harpo Marx hair for her reading glasses. "They stirred it up all by themselves. Them and Alf Nyborg."

"Who's Alf?"

"Alf Nyborg is a bit of a sourpuss and hasn't liked Hilltop for years. He's been president of All Saints since Eisenhower was president. Or maybe it was Ford. I'm not much on US history, but my son has it in school, so I imagine I'll learn it when I help him study for his tests. Do you know the names of all the presidents in order? There's Washington, of course, but that's a no brainer. . . . "

Gandy had a charming—and highly annoying—way of wandering off topic. Alex felt like he was always pulling on her rope, dragging her back to shore.

"How long has this been going on?"

"I told you. Since Eisenhower was president or maybe Ford."

"So this isn't so much about the congregation as it is one man?"

"That was true in the beginning, but I can't say if it's so anymore. He's probably brainwashed them all by now." Gandy plucked the tea bag out of her cup and dangled it there to drip dry.

"All Saints is just far enough away from Hilltop that people have never done much as a larger group other than share a pastor. Too bad too. Both churches are losing young people. If they can't find jobs near home and leave to find work, our congregations will shrink faster than wool in hot water. We could use each other, you know."

"I'm sorry to pump you for information, Gandy, but I'd like to understand the situation before I visit. I don't want to put my foot in my mouth and make relations even more difficult. I'd like to understand what motivates Mr. Nyborg."

"Pure meanness, probably. He lost his first wife and child in a house fire many years ago. He's remarried, but I don't think he's trusted God or anyone else since. The people from Hilltop tried to gather around him during that time, but he told everyone he wanted to be left alone. Ever after, he's said that we aren't Christian because we didn't help him in his time of need. Funny about that. He chased my father-in-law off his property with a shotgun during that 'time of need' for bringing over a basket of baked goods the church ladies had prepared. We kept trying but gave up after six months or a year. Seemed prudent not to get one of our own shot if we could help it."

"The man must have been mad with grief."

"And now he's still mad," Gandy agreed. "He pulled himself together, remarried and continued to be on the church council at All Saints, but a trickle of evil got into him somehow and now it's a toxic spill, plain and simple."

A trickle of evil. One that turned into a toxic spill.

Alex sat down and opened the Bible on his desk. He felt a desperate need to pray.

Some time later he was glad to see Mark Nash saunter through the office doors.

"Hi, Reverend," Mark greeted him. "Do you have time for lunch? I'm going to town for a belt for my tractor and I thought I'd eat in Grassy Valley."

Alex looked at Gandy who made a brushing motion with her hand as if to say *"Get out of here."*

"It seems I am. I'd like to go very much. I haven't spent any time in town other than driving through and seeing that pig spill on the highway."

"That was a pretty big day in Grassy Valley," Mark said with a laugh. "I hope you aren't disappointed today."

Alex hiked himself into the cab of Mark's pickup. Every man in the area seemed to have one. Alex had never been concerned with having a new car even though he was long overdue for one. Out here, it seemed a pickup was a status symbol, like a Lexus or Mercedes was in the city. The interior was soft leather. Copies of books by several theologians lay on the seat.

"You and Dixon are both full of surprises," Alex said as he picked up the one of the tomes.

"I guess you just can't stereotype anyone around here," Mark said cheerfully as he navigated the road to town.

Even to Alex's inexperienced eye, the crops looked green and healthy . . . and quite beautiful. He hadn't expected the prairie to have so much variety and personality. Already he was beginning to appreciate the subtle landmarks he wouldn't even have noticed in the city—a craggy rock, a clump of saplings, a dilapidated shed left to be consumed by the elements.

"Sometimes the richest men wear the shabbiest work clothes and drive the oldest beaters. That's how they got so rich. And just because we're isolated here doesn't mean we aren't world-savvy. Lots of people travel in the winter to get away from the cold. Some of them end up in rather exotic places. Mike and Lauren were on a cruise through the Panama Canal last winter, and the Mediterranean the year before."

"How about you, Mark, where have you been? Other than your time as a stockbroker in New York, I mean."

The drive to town passed quickly as they discussed South America, Norway, England and a half dozen other places Mark had traveled.

They were pulling into a parking place when an idea occurred to Alex. "When did you complete the remodel of the parsonage?"

"It must have been close to a month ago. Lauren was on a rampage to have it done before you arrived."

"So not everyone in the congregations has seen it yet?"

"A very few from Hilltop have. No one from All Saints has been over to visit it that I know of. You could ask Gandy. She knows everything."

"I've been wondering how to open a door, get the two congregations together for a common cause."

"Good luck with that."

"Why don't we have an open house at the parsonage so that people can come and see how their hard-earned dollars were spent on the renovation? If the Ladies Aid wouldn't mind providing a few cookies and some coffee..."

"That's no problem," Mark assured him. "But why...?"

"There's been something on my mind lately, something I think God put there."

"And what's that?"

He thought of the enmity between the two churches, the chasm between his old life and this brand-new one. There was even the awkward, unsettled way he and Natalie had left things. "Reconciliation. Resolution. We need to settle these things between the two churches. A good way to start might be an invitation to both congregations for . . . oh, I don't know, an ice cream social at the parsonage, perhaps."

Mark studied him silently. "You might be right, Alex. No one around here has ever been very optimistic about that, but we should try. I'll talk to the council and we'll get it set up. Once we find a date, we'll get in the church bulletins. The least we can do is give it a try."

CHAPTER ELEVEN

They pulled up to a large, low-slung building that was part garage, part showroom and sales, and part coffee shop. Three large repair bays were open; each held a dismantled tractor. In the salesroom window was a huge John Deere that Mark said was a Series 9030—what that implied, Alex had no idea—and a small fleet of lawn tractors.

Tucked in the corner behind the big machines was a large round table with a host of chairs. A long counter held a thirty-cup coffeepot, a hot plate with two pots of hot water, an assortment of fruit leathers and snack bars, and a popcorn machine.

Mark headed for the popcorn. "Want some?" He filled a bag and salted it liberally.

"No thanks, I'll wait for the restaurant."

"Suit yourself." Mark wandered up the counter where a lean fellow in grease-stained clothes nodded laconically at him. "Hey, Roger."

"Hi, Mark. What can I do for you?"

"I need a couple belts." Mark handed the technician a scrap of paper containing the information. The fellow behind the counter nodded and disappeared into one of the long aisles that held rows of equipment parts and appeared minutes later with what Mark had requested.

Alex tried to recall the last time he'd had his own head under the hood of a car. High school or college, maybe. He'd not been one for tearing cars apart and putting them back together like some of his friends. The moment he'd earned his first paycheck he'd taken his old beater to his uncle's garage and had the oil changed by someone who knew what they were doing. That fish-out-of-water feeling was dogging him again.

Mark tipped his head in acknowledgment to Roger, and he and Alex strolled out of the shop. Less than a hundred words had been exchanged between Mark and the parts man, but they'd appeared to communicate perfectly.

"Don't you have to pay him?" Alex matched his stride to Mark's.

"Nah, he'll put it on my bill."

"You certainly didn't talk much."

"He knew what I wanted and got it. Roger's a man of few words. He's worked here ever since he graduated from high school. A lot of people reared in Grassy Valley have never left. You'll discover that for yourself, of course."

"I have a lot to discover," Alex murmured.

Mark laughed and clapped him on the back before swinging himself back into his truck. "I'm going to take you on a brief tour of Grassy Valley, and then you're about to discover the best hot beef sandwich, mashed potatoes and pie ever made."

On Main Street they passed a small building with a red-and-white barber's pole out front. "That's the ice cream parlor," Mark said.

"With a barber's pole?" Then Alex read the sign. Cowlicks Peppermint Sticks—Candy and Barber Shop.

"Our barber got the idea because his pole looks like a candy cane. He cuts hair, and his wife makes the candy."

"Of course," Alex said weakly. "Why not?"

It became quickly apparent that for Grassy Valley businesses, efficiency and cooperation were paramount. The single attorney, Alex noted by his sign, was also an auctioneer. Good Finds; Good Flowers was a combination antique and floral shop.

"There's the lumberyard." Mark pointed to a large, low building with high doors and wood stacked high around its perimeter. "You can go there for all your building needs. The fellow that owns it is also an electrician. His sister is a plumber, and his father is a carpenter. They can build you a house without going outside the family."

"And if you ever need pencils, a CD, a goldfish or a sewing needle, go to More for Less. It's our version of a dime store and has a little of everything. Oh, yes, there are good burgers at the Hasty Tasty Drive-in too. Just don't order the Grassy Valley special. For some reason they put *radishes* on it."

Mark slowed the truck as they went past a large, sprawling truck stop. "That's Red's."

"That I'm familiar with. His name is on every cap in the county."

"That's because everybody in the county has reason to go there at one time or another. He sells gas and is a great mechanic, but every time he sees something that people need, he adds it. There's a nice little Laundromat in the back, a car wash, TV repair and the local insurance agent offices out of there too. One-stop shopping, I guess you'd say."

GOOD EATS HERE the red neon sign proclaimed as they neared The Cozy Corner Cafe. A blue neon arrow pointed to the door of the small café. It was painted white, with red and blue trim, decorated with window boxes full of red geraniums, and bright blue flowers Alex couldn't identify. Through the multi-paned windows Alex could see an inviting café with maple tables and chairs, a row of red and blue vinyl-covered booths, and huge woven rugs smattered across a battered hardwood floor. The waitresses inside, most of whom were on the far side of sixty, wore ruffled white aprons and carried blue-and-white spatterware cowboy coffeepots.

As they were about to enter, Jonas Owens came out of the dry-goods store across the street. Mark lifted a hand to wave him over.

"We're going to have lunch. Want to join us?"

"For coffee, maybe. I have to go to the hardware store first. I'll come over when I get done."

Mark and Alex went inside and walked to a table in the back corner. A woman with bleached-blonde hair and a face that must have once been pretty flipped over two of the white coffee mugs already at the table and began to pour. "The usual?" she said.

Mark nodded. "And the same for my friend. Mazie, this is the new pastor at Hilltop Community Church, Alex Armstrong. Alex, this is Mazie Torson."

"So you got one after all," Mazie turned to study Alex. "I'll have to bring Wally out to hear you speak. My husband always uses the excuse that the preacher is a poor speaker to stay home from church. Maybe you can put a stick of dynamite under the old guy and bring him back on Sunday mornings."

"I can't, but God can," Alex said, passing the responsibility onto broader shoulders than his own.

"Okay, then. We'll give you a try." She smiled and Alex saw the beauty she had once been. "Dinner will be right up."

Almost before they could taste their coffee, Mazie returned bearing two plates mounded high with mashed potatoes and roast beef sandwiches smothered in beef gravy. Carrot medallions provided the only other color to the meal, but steam was still coming off the plate and the aroma made Alex's taste buds quiver.

"You say the grace, Reverend."

Alex bowed his head. "I'm overcome with gratitude, Lord. For the people, the beauty, the opportunities in this place and for the food, Lord. Thank you for so many unexpected, unlikely blessings. May it sustain our bodies so we can do Your work. Amen."

Mark nodded appreciatively and without another word tucked into his meal.

As he ate, Alex gazed around the room, studying the Cozy Corner's patrons. There were two women dressed in matching blazers and name tags—bank employees, no doubt—and a table full of men in work clothes at the far back. It seemed to be a gathering place for solo diners, since chairs would empty and fill again as the others were eating. Two young mothers with toddlers were trying to have soup and pie, but their restless children kept slipping out of their grasps and running to bang plastic toys on the front of an old juke box nearby. Two booths held older women in vivid purple clothing and bright red hats. Their laughter just about drowned out any chance of conversation in the booths on either side.

Alex decided to get right down to business. "Mark, I'm concerned about Jonas. Can you tell me anything about him that I should know?"

Mazie came by and filled their coffee cups and Mark waited until she left to speak.

"Jonas' family has been here from the beginning, pioneers." Mark tapped his fork on the edge of the plate. "Jonas and his sister Gandy are very different. Gandy looks on the bright side of things and makes the best of situations."

"I know. She told me why she works at the church . . . it's her way of tithing. I feel a little guilty about it. If she weren't working there, she could be earning some extra money for her family."

"There aren't that many jobs to be had around Grassy Valley," Mark said. "Besides, Gandy is an expert seamstress. She makes quilt samples for a fabric store in Wheatville. They display them and sell fabric kits for the quilt, and then they sell the quilt itself. I think she makes pretty good money, and she can be home evenings with her family.

"Jonas has always been quieter and more somber, even melancholy. He takes his farming very seriously and has always tried to keep the family farm a showplace." A flicker of some emotion passed over Mark's face.

"And?" Alex prodded. "What's the problem?"

"There's talk that he took out some big loans he hasn't been able to repay and that he could possibly lose the family farm."

"So he feels he's letting down his family and his ancestors?"

"No, it's worse than that." Mark swirled the mashed potatoes on his plate. "He has the idea that he's let down the whole community of Hilltop."

"What do you mean?" Alex accepted another cup of coffee from the very solicitous Mazie, reminding himself to switch to decaf the next time around.

"Jonas believes it would be letting the entire township down if he had to sell out. It would be the first farm ever sold here. That hurts for a man like Jonas. And where would they go? He's only known farming his entire life. He has kids still in school. I doubt Jonas has ever been outside the borders of this state. It has to be tearing him apart, but Jonas never says much, and none of us knows how to help him."

"You talk as if this is practically a done deal," Alex observed. "Is it only a matter of time?"

"Rumor has it that someone has offered Jonas a good price for the land, and he's considering taking it. He's been approached by a group of outside investors who are hoping to make some money growing corn for ethanol because it's in big demand right now. It has to gall Jonas that he might have to sell out to someone so blatantly disinterested in history and so obscenely interested in money."

"Can't he sell his own corn?"

"The bank wants its money back immediately, and he's already sold the corn he grew last year. Farmers sell off crops throughout the year. If he can't make the payments or afford the cost of putting a crop in the ground next year, what's he going to do?"

Alex stared blankly at his friend. He had nothing to say. He knew plenty of people who'd fallen behind on house payments only to lose their homes. That was a tragedy. But hundreds of acres of land pioneered by one's great-grandfather? No wonder Jonas had seemed so discouraged.

At that moment the door opened and Jonas entered. He crossed the room to join them. Alex moved over so Jonas could slide into the booth next to him.

Mazie brought a menu to the table but Jonas waved her away.

"We're about to have dessert, Jonas, what do you think? I'm buying," Alex added.

They were half done with the slabs of apple pie a la mode when the bell over the café door clanged again. Jonas glanced up and blanched pale when he saw who'd come through the door.

Mark and Alex turned to see what had made Jonas react as he had.

Two men in business suits had entered. Pausing in the doorway, they looked from diner to diner until their gazes settled on Jonas. They made a beeline in his direction.

"Mr. Owens. We're sorry to interrupt, but if we could have a few minutes . . . "

Jonas glowered at the man who spoke.

"This is important, Mr. Owens." The taller of the two men spoke. He was a dark-haired fellow with a large nose and black eyebrows that looked like tiny wings. "You've had plenty of time to consider our offer. We need an answer. If you agree to sell the land, and I can't see why you wouldn't, we'd like to take possession as soon as possible."

"An Owens put the first spade to that soil," Jonas retorted.

"History, Mr. Owens, is all about the past," the man said in a tone that told Jonas he was beginning to try his patience. "Our offer is about the present."

"You won't even agree to leave the farmstead intact," Jonas growled. "I don't want my family homestead tilled up for cropland. If I sell it to you, there won't even be a homestead to remember my family by. You'll till it fence post to fence post."

The shorter man had pale blond hair combed straight back off his face. He put a business card on the table. "What's past, is past. We, Mr. Owens, are your future. We'll be waiting to hear from you." The men walked out of the diner without another word.

No one at the table spoke. Jonas groaned and put his head in his hands.

"Is there anything we can do?" Alex understood that being a part of Hilltop meant what happened to the community happened to him as well. And this was intolerable. His mind whirled. There must be some way, *something* someone could do.

"I'm sorry you saw that," Jonas finally murmured. "They know they've got me over a barrel, and they want the farm. They're buying land all over the tri-county area. Those guys have nothing but dollar signs in their eyes."

Mark and Jonas began to talk in low tones. Alex excused himself, and Jonas stood so that he could get by to pay the bill.

This was a case only God could solve. He'd pray about it as Jonas had asked. Bigger problems had been resolved when God was invited into the picture.

He laid his money on the counter by the cash register and looked into the eyes of a plain, pleasant woman in her early forties. To his amazement, she *winked* at him.

"Did you like the pie I delivered to the church, Reverend?" she asked, a blush staining her cheeks. "Fresh this morning. I bake all the pies for the Cozy Corner."

So this is where it had come from! Alex felt himself reddening as well. "I've never come across a finer pie," he said, wanting to be truthful without admitting that most of the delicacy had gone into the garbage. He had, however, even in the face of Gandy's disapproving expression, tasted the untouched parts. "It's even better than my grandmother used to make. She always swore by Granny Smith apples, which I thought were a little tart."

Irene Collins—her name was prominently indicated on her nametag—beamed like a lighthouse. "I use two Granny Smiths, two Macintosh and two Honey Crisps. Of course, if all I have is Galas or even Red Delicious, that's fine too. The secret is to use more than one kind of apple. It makes a more interesting combination of flavors." She lowered her voice. "I'd even share my recipe with you if you like."

"Excellent! Thank you so much" Alex said jovially and backed out the door of the restaurant and out of sight of the glowing woman.

Mark followed him outside wearing a huge grin. Even Jonas was smiling.

"What's so funny?" Alex grumbled. "I almost put my foot in it back there." His cheeks twitched. "Actually I *did* put my foot in it." And he told the men about stepping into the pie in the dark this morning.

Mark burst out laughing. "Irene gave me a blueberry pie, and Dixon got cherry. It's one of the perks of being single around here."

"She seemed like a nice woman," Alex said. "Is she . . . ?"

"Looking for a husband? I wouldn't go that far, but she probably wouldn't mind if one of her pies fished in a live one. Irene Collins is good-hearted woman. Everyone new to town gets a casserole except the single men. I guess she wants us to feel extra special."

"How have you managed to stay single?" Alex asked.

"Fancy footwork, mostly. I love the people around here. I just haven't found one of them I want to marry."

"Well, trust me, seminary didn't warn me about any of this."

Jonas turned to leave and Alex followed him. He cleared his throat. "I know you don't know me very well, Jonas, but if there's anything I can do . . . "

"Thanks. I wish I could let you go to the bank today in my place," he said grimly.

"I can't take your place, but I can go with you if you like."

Alex glanced at Mark, who gave him an almost imperceptible nod. "You two go ahead. I'm going to stop in the hardware store. I'll meet you at the truck in forty-five minutes."

Jonas looked surprised. "You'd do that?"

"I don't want to interfere, but if it would help you to have impartial backup . . . "

Alex was afraid he might have gone too far but when Jonas spoke, he said, "It might be okay, I guess. I've been feeling pretty alone with this. It upsets my wife too much. I've wanted her to come with me, but she just can't handle it. Sometimes I'm afraid all this trouble will drive her off."

"Then let's go."

The bank was not large, and it appeared to have been caught in a time warp, with wood-paneled walls, a patterned carpet in gold and rust, vinyl-covered office chairs, and artwork that had been new in the 1980s. The air conditioning blasting from vents around the room made Alex wish for a jacket. There were three tellers, and they all looked up from their stations to study the newcomers as Alex and Jonas walked in.

Before Alex could figure out where to go, a portly man in a dark brown suit burst out of one of the offices that ran along one wall. "Jonas, come on in."

Alex followed, noting the sign on the man's desk: DONALD KRAMER, PRESIDENT.

"This is our new pastor," Jonas said by way of introduction. "I needed some moral support."

The banker frowned and Alex saw genuine concern on his features. "Jonas, I've worked the numbers up and down, and frankly, I can't help you anymore. It's not that I don't want you to have the land, but these are tough economic times. You know that as well as anyone."

As Alex listened he felt a sinking sensation in his gut. Jonas had been telling the unvarnished truth. If anything, he'd *understated* his predicament. Sell or be foreclosed on. Now.

By the time they left the bank, Alex supporting Jonas' arm and mumbling helpless platitudes as Jonas wilted in defeat, Alex knew that only a miracle would help this man now.

Mark was waiting in the truck, just as he said he would be, when Alex returned. "How'd it go?"

Alex swung himself into the truck and sighed. "I hate to say it, Mark, but I think Jonas might be out of options." Alex ran his fingers through his hair, his gut in a knot. "The banker was as helpful as he could be, but the fact is, it's as bad as Jonas says it is. The history of Hilltop is about to change . . . and not for the better."

CHAPTER TWELVE

W hat's your plan for the rest of the day, Reverend?" Mark draped a wrist over the steering wheel and looked at Alex.

Alex leaned back in the seat and tried to relax. His experience with Jonas had strung taut every nerve and fiber of his body. He didn't know how Jonas withstood the pressure.

"I'd thought about going to All Saints. The organist said she'd meet with me to go over my music choices. She is also the one who prints the Sunday bulletins, so we can cover that at the same time. She told me she planned to be at the church until three."

Mark nodded and backed out of his parking place. As they drove, they passed tall grain elevators that punched into the cerulean sky. They were country skyscrapers that towered above every other building and sat in stark relief to a sky so blue that if he'd seen it in an oil painting he would have called it overdone and unrealistic. After a mile or two, Mark turned north onto a gravel road that cut through the countryside.

"Where are we going?" Alex asked when he realized that they were leaving Grassy Valley by a new route, one that headed away from Hilltop rather than toward it.

"All Saints. This is a back way. Maybe we'll even run into Alf Nyborg. He spends a lot of time over there mowing and doing repairs."

Alex nodded and noticed out the window a massive gray barn and elaborately ornamented Victorian that was equally void of paint. "Is that place empty?" A hand painted No TRESPASSING—KEEP OUT sign sat crookedly at the end of the drive.

"No, it just hasn't seen a coat of paint in twenty years," Mark said. "That's the Bruun place. Brunie and her sister Bessie have spent their entire lives there. Never married, either one of them. Now Brunie takes care of her sister. Bessie hasn't been well for years. The sign is Bessie's handiwork. She's not much for having company."

Alex took it all in and watched the countryside go by.

"Gandy told me about Alf. According to her, Alf eats, sleeps and breathes All Saints' business, and probably isn't much interested in my input."

"It's true." Mark slid his sunglasses into place and gave Alex a brief smile. "He isn't partial to teamwork. Are you worried?"

"I've spent most of my adult life dealing with students— some of them recalcitrant, others just not interested in learning. That never stopped me in the classroom, and it shouldn't here. I've always made it a policy to treat my students with respect, firmness and love. I'll treat Alf and everyone I meet the same way whether they like me or not."

"I think you've got it, Reverend. He's an unhappy man who sometimes takes it out on others. If anyone ever needed respect, firmness and love it's Alf Nyborg. If you can make peace with him, you'll be halfway to home base."

Alex could see a church spire in the distance, thrusting its way upward toward the sky, when Mark slammed on the brakes. Alex caught himself on the dash, glad he was wearing a seat belt. He'd expected sudden traffic stops in Chicago, but here . . .

"Sorry about that. There's a moving party going on."

Alex looked out the window to see a gray-and-black mother tabby carrying a tiny kitten across the road by the scruff of its neck. She disappeared into the long grass at the side of the road and then rapidly reappeared without the baby. She ran back across the road, went into the grass on that side and emerged shortly with another kitten.

"She's relocating her family," Mark explained. "Mama cats do that sometimes if they decide their babies are in danger. I had a cat birth a litter on the seat of my tractor once. Next time I looked she'd moved them somewhere safer. It turned out to be inside a pair of Carharts I'd left lying on the floor."

Mark laughed at Alex's confused expression. "She'd left them inside the work clothes I use when it's particularly cold. I was glad those kittens grew up before bad weather set in."

"This place is a mass of little miracles," Alex said, feeling oddly sentimental. "I see now that all those years in academia took me too far away from nature. I'd forgotten that milk comes from cows and bread exists because of kernels of wheat."

"Well, if you consider those things miracles, hang on, because you're in for a lot of them." Mark put his foot on the gas pedal and nodded toward the horizon. "Here we are."

A half dozen cars were parked around the church, and the front doors stood wide open.

"Something is going on." Alex said. "It's nice to see the doors open."

Mark turned onto the drive that circled the church and parked. "Do you want me to come with you or would you rather meet your flock alone?"

"Come, of course, the more the merrier." What Alex didn't say was that he was feeling the need for a second calm head and clear mind. But maybe he was growing mountains out of molehills. Just because he'd heard very little positive about the situation at All Saints, that didn't mean it wasn't there.

"One would hope," Mark muttered as he pulled the key from the ignition and swung his long legs out of the pickup.

The front door opened onto a foyer lined with coat hooks. Beyond it was a nave considerable smaller than Hilltop's, and there were no stained glass windows, which changed the atmosphere entirely. The light was sharp and piercing, creating an almost sterile mood. A small but beautiful altar graced the front of the church, and short pews lined either side of the aisle. An elaborately hand-carved pulpit hovered majestically to the right of the altar.

"That's a beautiful piece," Alex said admiringly.

"Alf Nyborg's grandfather carved that pulpit."

"Really?" Alex was impressed. "It's a masterpiece." The panels circling the platform depicted scriptural scenes in much the same way as the windows of Hilltop did.

"Hello, can I help you?"

Neither of them had heard the small woman ascend the stairs from the basement until she literally popped up in front of them.

"Hello, my name is Alex Armstrong, and I'm your new pastor. It's good to meet . . ."

The small woman, who appeared to be in her mid- to late thirties, stared at him wide-eyed. "You?"

Slightly disconcerted by the greeting—or lack of it—Alex plowed on. "Yes. And your name is?"

For a moment she seemed to debate whether or not to reveal it to him. Then she came down on the side of politeness. "Amy Clayborn. Welcome, Reverend Armstrong." Her head swiveled from side to side as if she were looking for someone. "Mr. Nyborg isn't here right now. He's probably the one you should be talking to. I could call him."

Did he speak for everyone? Alex wondered wearily.

"No need. I'm sure we'll meet soon enough. We noticed several cars outside. Am I interrupting something? Or could I introduce myself to those who are here?"

There was that deer-in-the-headlights look again. Then Amy blinked, met his eyes and smiled. "It's just our quilting ladies. We meet every week, sometimes twice."

Ah, yes, Gandy had mentioned a quilt competition, Alex thought. It wasn't easy to recall everything she chattered about.

"I would be delighted to meet them."

"Come then." Amy turned and started down the steep stairs to the basement. "Mind that you don't knock yourself silly on the ceiling."

Alex immediately saw what she meant. Just like the steps at Hilltop, the stairs appeared to have been built for people less than five feet high. An outcropping of wood midway down the stairs would injure anyone who inadvertently ran into it. He hunkered down and followed Amy's receding back. When he didn't hear a clunk or a yell, he assumed Mark had navigated the passage as well.

Laughter filtered up from the basement and cheerful chatter that seemed to focus on someone's upcoming wedding. But when Alex arrived at the bottom of the stairs, he was met with seven pairs of curious eyes . . . and complete silence.

As he scanned the room he took a census. The youngest woman appeared to be in her twenties; the oldest, deep into her eighties.

Suddenly, he felt like he was walking in knee-deep mud.

CHAPTER THIRTEEN

The silence was as awkward as anything Alex had ever experienced.

Finally, the eldest of the group—a woman with thinning white hair pulled into a knot at the nape of her neck, rheumy blue eyes and a face seamed with wrinkles—smiled at him.

"Welcome," she said, "it is good you're here." Then she added, "We need help."

The others stared at her with shocked expressions, as if she'd just violated some unspoken law.

Finding one non-hostile face was opening enough for Alex, and he moved forward to shake hands and introduce himself.

It was like shaking warm, limp fish, as halfhearted as those handshakes were, but he pasted a smile on his face and behaved as if they'd welcomed him with a marching band.

"So this is the quilting group."

Silence.

"May I see what you're making?" He moved forward and all but the elderly woman who had greeted him shrank back in their seats. Who, exactly, did they think he was?

Amy obviously felt some obligation to act as hostess. "We're tying quilts. We've run out of fabric and will have to start collecting again so we can make more. We'll send them off to missions in the fall."

"Very nice." Alex hefted one of the quilts and found it substantial yet airy. He could imagine the joy such a gift might bring. "I'm sure they are much appreciated."

"We don't do as many as Hilltop does," a jowly, heavyset woman with a permanent crease between her brows said with a scowl.

"It's not the number that counts; it's the spirit in which it's given. Remember the poor widow who gave her last penny? What's important is that it is given out of gratitude and generosity. God knows your hearts."

They all stared at him warily. Awkward silence filled the room once again.

"So . . . " Alex swung his arms a bit and backed toward the bottom of the stairs where Mark had remained. "I don't want to interrupt your work. I hope to see you all on Sunday. God bless." And he quickly turned and raced up the stairs on Mark's heels, barely missing the rafter that threatened to knock off the top of his head.

"Well, that went well," Mark said, sounding amused, once they were back in his pickup truck.

"Very funny." Alex noticed his hands trembling a little, so disconcerted was he by the non-welcome he'd received.

"No, I mean it. Granted, you didn't get asked to stay for coffee, but it's a start. You don't realize how insular that group has become. It's odd that a church body would close in on themselves like that, but they've come to depend on Alf to take care of everything for them, from roof repair to the collection plate. Since Alf is a mainstay in their church and he has a bone to pick with Hilltop, the All Saints congregation has lined up behind him. We haven't been able to make amends for the perceived infraction. But you're new and fresh. They might give you a chance."

"It's going to be an uphill battle."

"One thing at a time. Now you've been there. Next time will be easier. No one can spend a lot of time around Alf Nyborg without getting a little paranoid. No doubt he's already been expressing his doubts about Hilltop's choice of a new pastor."

"But he was on the call committee too," Alex said, climbing into Mark's truck.

"True, but he stayed neutral intentionally. Now if you don't work out, it will be *our* fault, not his."

"How can two churches have such dissimilar personalities, Mark? I've experienced nothing but warmth and welcome at Hilltop. And at All Saints, if today is any indicator . . . "

"That's part of the reason you're here," Mark told him calmly. He started the engine and pulled out onto the road. "To bring us together. To ferret out the problems and to resolve them. We don't like it any better than you. The feeling is that if All Saints could pay for their own minister and not have to share the cost with Hilltop, they would have left us long ago. But I'm confident you can bring us back together. Like Lauren says, God wouldn't have sent you if you couldn't."

There was that bit of overconfidence in him again. Listening to Mark, Alex realized that if he had to make a choice between dividing loaves and fishes to feed the masses or finding resolution between All Saints and Hilltop, the loaves and fishes gig might be easier.

Mark dropped Alex off to pick up his van at the church, and they arrived at the parsonage just as Dixon and Lauren pulled into the yard in their separate vehicles.

"Hey!" Dixon said by way of greeting through the open window of his truck. "We've got something for you, Reverend."

Lauren jumped lithely out of her car and opened the trunk.

Alex felt cheered immediately. Here, at least, were welcoming faces. "You've given me too much already. I don't need another thing."

Lauren walked toward him, her arms full of parcels wrapped in thick, white butcher's paper. "If everybody carries a load we can get this into the freezer immediately."

Alex took a few icy packages out of her hands. "What is it?"

"Venison. Mike got a deer last fall and there's no way we'll eat it all before he goes hunting again. I called Dixon and asked him to help me deliver it."

"I don't know how to cook venison," Alex ventured, not wanting to admit that he didn't know how to cook much of anything at all.

"I'll teach you. Or one of the guys will. There are also a few packages of frozen peaches. It makes fabulous cobbler. Do you have a recipe?"

"No, can't say I do." He didn't even have a cookbook. His normal dessert was something from his stash of chocolate candy bars. When he did decide to cook something, he'd always depended on the Internet for directions. Alex had a hunch that it just wasn't done that way in Hilltop. He clutched his icy parcels to his chest and hurried after Lauren.

"Where did you say we'll store this?"

"There's a small deep freeze in the basement. You probably didn't notice it behind the pile of Christmas decorations. This will keep you from starving until at least the first of the year."

"I hadn't really worried about starving," Alex said with a chuckle. "So far the food is flowing in faster than I can eat it." He felt a little like the widow of Zarephath—his jar of meal would not empty, nor his jug of oil fail.

"Another reason to have a freezer."

Arms full, Alex, Dixon and Mark followed Lauren into the basement, where she pushed aside boxes of greenery and a plastic outdoor Nativity set. With a practiced hand, she packed the small rectangular chest freezer, even leaving room for some of those seemingly endless casseroles that kept arriving.

"There." She wiped her hands on her jeans and smiled. "I have fresh doughnuts in a container on my front seat. How about some coffee?"

There was no delayed response this time. Mark hustled to her car to get the doughnuts while Alex brewed coffee. Dixon and Lauren set out cups and napkins. The kitchen had a warm, familial feel that Alex relished. It was particularly welcome after his visit to All Saints. It was as if he'd been given two families, one healthy and the other dysfunctional. He'd be on his knees a lot over All Saints in the next few weeks.

"By the way," Mark said as Lauren dug for paper plates in the cupboard, "what would you think about having an open house for Alex? We were just talking about . . . "

Lauren stared at him. "Great minds must think alike. It's already in the works. The Ladies Aid is debating about the date; but as soon as it's set, we're ready to roll. I love the idea of hosting All Saints, reaching a friendly hand across the border, so to speak."

"That was easy enough," Mark said with a laugh.

"What did you guys do today?" Dixon mumbled, a dough-nut already in his mouth. There was granulated sugar all over his lips, which he laid waste with a swig of coffee.

Alex and Mark filled them in on their trip into town, but kept Jonas out of it, other than saying he'd joined them for a piece of pie and coffee at the café.

Dixon leaned back in his chair with a contented sigh. "You make the best doughnuts in seven counties *and* even trump the Cozy Corner Café, Lauren. Maybe you could relieve Lila Mason of the task of bringing doughnuts to me."

"Lila brings you doughnuts?" Alex asked, astounded. "Why?"

"She's adopted me as a son," Dixon said with a smile. "I fix her roof, she gives me doughnuts. I stop the toilet from running twenty-four hours a day, she gives me doughnuts. I—"

"I get the picture."

"Unfortunately, I doubt Lila has two pennies to rub together, so she gets the day-olds or the ones they are about to throw out at the grocery store. Then she makes coffee that resembles dishwater and makes me eat a half dozen at her table." Dixon shuddered. "It's enough to make me consider retiring from the fix-it business at Lila's."

This discovery about Dixon and Lila pleased Alex inordinately, both because it proved his initial reading about Dixon's good nature and thoughtfulness, and because it meant that Lila was not completely alone in this world.

"Since you're discussing eccentrics, I have news on a couple more," Lauren said. "I saw Flossie and Charles Kennedy in town the other day. I've never seen a mother and son who are practically joined at the hip like those two are."

"What's their background?" Whenever he got the opportunity Alex was determined to learn more about the members of the community.

"Before they came to Horace Abel's so that Flossie could be his housekeeper, you mean?" Lauren thoughtfully sipped her coffee.

"Yes. Were they originally from Grassy Valley—or Wheatville?"

"No one knows," Mark said, interjecting himself into the conversation.

That was the answer he least expected. "What do you mean no one knows?"

Lauren put her cup down and twiddled with her paper napkin as she spoke. "Horace had advertised for household help in several papers. They appeared here one day when Charles was a child. Flossie said she'd come in answer to one of those ads and since she and her son were already on Horace's front step, he told them she could have a one week 'trial run.' They've been here ever since."

"She must have been a good housekeeper," Alex mused.

"She's a good cook, keeps a spotless house and knows how to drive a tractor if Horace is in a pinch. He thinks she's practically perfect."

"And he didn't mind the little boy?"

"Charles has always been bookish. When Horace bought him a computer, he disappeared into his room and has hardly come out since. Now he makes his living selling things on the Internet and pays Horace rent to stay in the house. It's worked out well for everyone."

"And no one from Flossie's past ever showed up? A friend or relative?"

"Not a soul." Lauren's expression was pensive. "Of course, it's been so long that now we assume there was no one."

The conversation hit a lull, and Alex took a sip of his coffee. It was good to hear about the people he would be living among. There were so many mysteries, so many unanswered questions.

"Hey, does anyone know that unmarked grave in the cemetery?" Alex asked, setting down his cup. "Should we be responsible for ordering something for it or . . . ?"

Dixon's and Lauren's eyes widened as they stared at him. "A grave? What are you talking about?"

Mark leaned forward in his chair. "Are you sure it was a grave?"

Alex looked from one face to the other and could see that they had no idea what he was talking about. He must be mistaken. Maybe he was just imagining things.

"I've got something in the pickup for you," Dixon said after Mark and Lauren had driven off in their separate directions. "I hope you don't mind."

"Why should I mind a gift?" Alex asked as they strolled toward Dixon's truck.

"It's not a traditional gift, just something I thought you needed." Dixon cleared his throat awkwardly. "It's something that also needs you. You can give it back, if you like, but I hope you don't. Give it a little time and see what you think before deciding."

"I have no idea what you're talking about." Alex looked at the truck for a clue. The truck bed was empty, and no box or package was poking up to reveal itself in the front seat.

He recoiled as Dixon gave an ear-splitting whistle. He flinched again when he saw a head pop up on the driver's side of the truck like a jack-in-the-box. It was a dog, its black-and-white head suggesting a Dalmatian somewhere in its ancestry.

"Dixon, I—"

"Don't say a word, and don't pass judgment. Just meet him first, okay? His name is Tripod." The dog bounced up and down inside the truck like a trampoline had replaced the passenger seat, his smooth head bumping against the top of the cab, his rosy red tongue lolling happily at the sight of them. "He's a good dog and he needs a home. I'd take him myself if push came to shove, but I think he'd be much happier with you and vice versa. When I open the door, just stand still. He has good manners and won't jump, but he might have to let off a little steam."

Slowly Dixon opened the door and a quivering black nose forced its way through the crack. Then, as if Dixon couldn't hold the dog back a moment longer, the door flew open and a thin, muscular dog with short black-and-white fur rocketed out of the cab and made a few happy circles around the men. He stopped directly in front of Alex and sat, his black rope of a tail thumping on the hard-packed ground. He gazed at Alex inquiringly.

"Dixon, I don't know what to say!" Alex could actually think of plenty of things, but none of them seemed prudent.

"Sure you can. You think I'm crazy, you don't want a dog, and he'll eat you out of house and home and make messes in your yard. You'll have to use masking tape on every one of your black suits because there will be dog hair on them; he'll bark, scare parishioners, and make a general nuisance of himself." Dixon looked at Alex. "Should I go on?"

"No, thank you. You've covered the major ones." The dog gently put a front paw on the tip of Alex's shoe.

"Then let me remind you of some of the positive things he'll do," Dixon offered.

"Do I have a choice?"

"No." Dixon didn't even smile, so intent was he on making his point. "He'll keep you company when no one's around, keep you warm in bed at night and think you're the greatest thing on earth since sliced bread."

Alex studied at the dog at his feet. He jumped up and began to wag his tail again. It was only than that Alex noticed that the dog stood with one hip higher in the air and the other lowered, as if he were standing on the side of a deep hill. "This poor thing only has three legs!"

"Of course. What did you expect of a dog named Tripod? But if you don't tell him something is missing, he'll never know. What do you think?"

"How is he able to run?" The dog obviously could, Alex had seen it for himself.

"A chair has four legs but a stool has three, and they're both sturdy enough to sit on. Tripod's like that stool. He creates balance with the remaining leg to make up for the one that's missing. It's second nature to him. He doesn't even know he's not exactly like other dogs."

Everything in Alex told him to reject this ridiculous idea with no further discussion, but something about the way Tripod held his gaze with an almost human look of adoration held him back.

"What about the parsonage? They surely won't allow a dog in such a lovely home."

"I cleared it with the board. They're fine with it. He's housebroken and kennel trained and sheds very little."

"What if he bites someone?"

"He has a very soft mouth. I gave him a raw egg to carry, and he did it without cracking the shell. I've been working with him ever since I rescued him, and he's the easiest dog I've ever trained."

Alex searched for more questions and came up empty.

"Like I said, I can keep him for myself," Dixon went on, "but I already have dogs and you don't. I think you'll be happier with him than without him, Alex. There may be times when you need someone to talk to about private things, and Tripod is an excellent listener. I guarantee he'll never reveal a word of what you tell him. Mum's the word with ol' Tripod here."

"Mutt is the word with Tripod."

Dixon grinned. "That too. So you'll take him?"

"I grew up in an apartment building in Chicago. I don't know what to do with a dog, especially a three-legged one." His arguments were feeble, Alex noticed. He wasn't trying very hard to convince Dixon to take the dog away.

"He'll teach you." Dixon dug behind the seat on the passenger side. "I brought his favorite food. Directions are on the bag. Let him out to run and do his business, and he'll be fine. The more you scratch him the better he'll like you." Dixon studied the dog, which had now lain down on Alex's shoes. "He appears to like you quite a bit already."

Dixon gave a leisurely but highly theatrical stretch and ambled to the driver's side of his vehicle. "I think I'll be going now. I know the two of you will be fine, but call me if there's any trouble."

He departed in a cloud of dust, leaving Alex and Tripod alone together in the middle of the yard.

He hoped what Dixon had said was true, Alex thought, as he stood with Tripod at his side. The dog, in order to survive life at the parsonage, would have to teach this preacher how to treat him. Suddenly laughter bubbled up inside Alex and he leaned down to scratch the black ears. "The Pastor and the Pooch, that's us, Tripod. What do you think of that?"

CHAPTER FOURTEEN

Alex and Tripod watched each other intently, neither moving a muscle. It was Alex who finally broke the stare-down. "Oh, come on then. We might as well get acquainted." Alex wasn't sure if it was proper etiquette to converse with a dog, but Dixon had told him Tripod was a good listener. "Would you like a dish of water? A bone?"

Tripod matched his pace to Alex's as they moved toward the house. The dog seemed completely unaware that it was missing a leg—and if Tripod didn't care, why should he?

Inside, he took an empty five-quart ice cream bucket he found under the sink, filled it half-full with cold water and set it on the floor. Tripod sniffed the bucket, found it to his liking and lapped up most of the water in record time. Then he stood looking up at his new master expectantly, waiting for his next cue.

This was more awkward than he'd expected it to be. A living being had just moved into his home and he knew nothing of its habits or personality. Maybe Tripod was a chewer or a barker or worse yet, a biter. But surely Dixon had better sense than to give a preacher a biting dog.

Alex moved into the living room and sat down on the couch just to see what the dog would do. It moved directly in front of him and sat stone still, big brown eyes gazing longingly at the cushion next to Alex's.

"Oh, all right," Alex sighed.

With a graceful leap, Tripod joined Alex on the couch and leaned into him, his warm, solid body resting against Alex's arm and shoulder. It was a surprisingly pleasant sensation.

"Now what do you plan to do?" Alex inquired of the dog, which seemed remarkably intelligent, at least to his inexperienced eye.

Tripod lay down on the cushion, curled himself into a tight spiral like a nautilus shell and closed his eyes.

"Very well, if you insist." Finally Alex allowed himself to do what he'd been longing for all day, particularly since the latest awkward venture to All Saints. Alex put his feet on the footstool, sank into the depths of the couch and closed his own eyes.

It was getting dark when he awoke. Tripod was still there next to him, motionless, his eyes open, watching for Alex's next move.

"This is a fine way to spend a Friday night," he commented to the dog. "Maybe I should make dinn . . . no, supper," he said out loud and Tripod's ears went up. "You're particularly bright for a dog, aren't you?" Tripod opened his mouth to yawn and Alex could have sworn he smiled at him.

The refrigerator was full of food; but Alex, already feeling like an overstuffed couch, decided that something light appealed to him tonight.

"Tomato soup and a grilled cheese sandwich," he told the dog who lay on the rug in front of the sink. "And I'm going to have to get over talking to you like you're human."

Out here he was forced to take full notice of the solo nature of his life. At one time, particularly before meeting Natalie, he'd relished his hours alone, away from students, classes, and the demands of both teaching and seminary; but tonight he felt a twinge of pure, unadulterated loneliness.

Dixon could read the future, apparently, for he'd brought Alex companionship even before Alex knew he would need it. Alex scratched Tripod's head and the dog's rope-like tail thumped happily on the black-and-white tiled floor. Now he would have a companion at supper.

A gas stove was something with which Alex had had little experience. His previous homes had always had electric ranges. How hard could it be? He buttered bread and peeled the wrapper off two slices of American cheese. *Turn it on, put the pan on the stove and grill the sandwich*—there couldn't be anything simpler than that. He'd put the bread and cheese on to grill just as the bell on the microwave rang, signaling that his tomato soup—made with milk, not water—was ready. He opened the door, grabbed for the bowl and sloshed steaming soup across the tops of his fingers.

"Ow!" Shaking his hand, he rushed to the sink, sending Tripod scrambling out of the way. He ran cold water on the burned spot, something he'd observed his mother doing for her own burned fingers when he was a child. *"Keep it there until it stops burning,"* she'd say. *"Put the fire out. Cool it off."*

The cool water did indeed ease the sting and he would have stood there longer if the smoke alarm hadn't begun to ring. Alex spun around to see flames licking up the sides of the frying pan, charring his grilled cheese sandwich. He was in such a rush to reach the stove he almost lost his balance on a wayward throw rug, but managed to turn off the gas and remove the pan from the burner without burning himself again.

The smoke alarm screamed in his ears until he found a step stool in a coat closet and hiked himself up to the alarm and dismantled it. When all was said done, the room smelled as if he'd had a campfire on the countertop, gray smoke hovered in the air and his supper was up in flames. Tripod, with a keen sense of self survival, had disappeared beneath the table to wait out the crisis.

He would reheat the spaghetti and meatballs tonight after all. If he dared chance the microwave again, that was. Alex made a decision then and there while still standing on the stepstool, hand stinging and ego more than a little bruised. He would learn to cook, even if it killed him. And if tonight were any indication, it just might.

Sunday morning dawned bright and clear; and Alex finally felt calm and relaxed about his initial sermon. He took a deep breath as he left the house and grew almost light-headed as a result. He'd grown so accustomed to fumes from automobiles, taxis and city buses that that air scented only with earth and its perfumes—flowers, loamy soil and cut hay—made him almost giddy.

What's more, he'd committed to running daily now that he had Tripod. The dog delighted in their early morning run and had kept pace with Alex unless he spotted a rabbit. Then he shifted into mach speed and left Alex eating his dust. When the dog tired of the chase, he returned to the relative sedateness of their jog.

It seemed amazing that he'd only been here a few days, Alex mused. The friends he'd already made—Dixon, Mark, Mike and Lauren—felt like they'd been in his life forever.

A whine behind him made Alex turn around. Tripod sat inside the house behind the screen door, head and ears drooping disconsolately.

"You can't come today. It's my first sermon, and I'm sure they don't want you lying underfoot in the pulpit. Don't worry, I'll be back soon."

Tripod slowly crumpled onto the rug in front of the door as if disappointment had dissolved his bones. Alex felt like he was leaving a child behind to fend for itself, but he knew better. The dog would be on his bed, head on a pillow, before the van left the driveway. Tripod just wanted a little sympathy first. Then he would make himself truly comfortable.

There was a single car at the church when he arrived. He could hear strains of the organ though the walls of the church. That would be the organist, Annie Henderson, whom he'd met only briefly to hand over the numbers of the hymns they would sing that day.

He rehearsed the morning in his mind as he mounted the front steps. First the service at Hilltop at nine, time for greeting the congregants and then off to All Saints for the eleven o'clock service. He had to be sure to leave Hilltop early enough in order to get to All Saints on time and without speeding.

Annie turned around the moment he set foot inside the church. "Good morning! Couldn't be any prettier out, could it?" She was a woman of rusty hues from the top of her red-brown hair to her sun-kissed skin, the generous smattering of freckles across the bridge of her nose, and the silky bronze blouse she wore. "I've been working on those new hymns. I hope you have a good, strong voice. Every time this congregation gets a new one to learn, they start to sing in whispers. I know God hears them, but it would be nice if they could hear each other too."

Alex put his sermon notes on the pulpit, opened the Bible, lit the candles and turned on the primitive sound system. Then he and Annie discussed the weather, the crops and the general topics that everyone out here seemed to feel necessary to cover before a real conversation could begin.

"You're early," he commented as he opened a couple windows to let the breeze freshen the room.

"I've got to be. Aggie and Leonard Lundqvist always come early, as do Brunhilda and Bessie Bruun. They're usually in their pews a half hour before the service starts. Bessie doesn't go out much due to her condition, but she loves to go to church and they come when they can. I'm surprised they aren't here already. Perhaps Bessie isn't up to it today."

"About that . . . "

"I don't know exactly what happened to Bessie," Annie said bluntly. "I've heard that she was always a little odd. Maybe it was shyness, I don't know. I haven't lived here all my life. I married into the Hilltop family. My husband says Bessie has been nervous in crowds for a very long time and the older she becomes, the more reclusive she is. Sorry I can't tell you more."

Alex tried to process this.

"Oh yes, and I forgot to mention Lila Mason, who always comes to church either an hour early or an hour late."

"Excuse me?"

"Lila's memory is good, but short. About a minute long, I'd say. She always forgets to set her clock forward for daylight savings in the spring and back again in the fall, so she keeps a clock set to each time 'Just in case.' That way she's always got the right time somewhere. Unfortunately, she usually can't remember which clock is which, so she comes when she feels like it."

"Is she...does she suffer from...is she safe at home alone?" He tried to frame the questions as tactfully as he could.

Annie smiled at the concern in his voice. "You mean, is something wrong with her? She's just forgetful. Sometimes she just doesn't *listen* when someone is telling her something, and she gets it all bollixed up. It used to be easier when she got most of her facts straight, but now..." Annie's friendly face creased with concern. "Too bad too, since Lila loves to gossip. Now there's a font of misinformation if I've ever known one!"

"Can she be helped? There are medications...."

"Oh, Lila doesn't believe in medications. Or doctors either, although she did go to the clinic once for stitches when she jammed her hand on the knife she'd put into her knitting bag."

Alex's eyebrows rose and Annie hurried to explain.

"She put it there because she couldn't find her scissors. If Lila takes anything, she's made it herself. She self-medicates."

Alex didn't like the sound of that.

Annie saw the expression on his face. "Nothing illegal or dangerous, mind you. Just concoctions she brews up. Her house usually smells like she's been cooking hay and old shoes, but she drinks the stuff and says it helps her memory. And she takes vitamins too. Her cupboards are just as full of vitamins as the Medi-Shop's pharmacy in Wheatville."

Annie began to ruffle through the pages of her music. "She's mostly harmless—as long as you don't try to get directions from her or ask her what happened on such-and-such a date. Lila's very 'in the moment,' like people say nowadays. LIVE IN THE MOMENT, her bumper sticker says. Unfortunately that's the only moment Lila has sometimes."

"That's very sad," Alex commented.

"Not for Lila. She's the happiest little camper on earth." Her hand flew to her mouth. "Oh, I hear a car driving in. Find your place, Reverend, the race is about to begin."

Alex was grateful for the familiar faces that walked through the door to greet him. Mike Carlsen arrived in a suit, and Lauren in a brightly colored jacket that highlighted the copper in her hair. Dixon Daniels and Mark Nash followed not long after. Dixon had forgone the Red's cap and even tamed his hair. Mark, of course, looked perfectly at home in a suit. They were early, no doubt, to give him moral support. Angels, that's what they were, Alex decided, sent to bear him up on their wings.

Ava and Ralph Johnson arrived with Ralph's mother Isabelle. Isabelle, according to Gandy, was a bit of a legend around Hilltop. Though she was remarkable in many ways, including her age, most knew her for her driving skills—or lack of them. Exceedingly independent, Isabelle refused to give up her car for fear of losing her autonomy. Others, including her son and daughter-in-law, were more in fear for her life—and their own—as long as Isabelle was behind the wheel. It was, rumor had it, a long-running battle.

Alex glanced through the door and was pleased to see a few teenagers gathering outside. Two were talking on cell phones and one was listening to an iPod. Typical teenagers in every way. Alex didn't recognize any faces, but there were a couple redheads in the bunch, and Will Packard came to mind. He hoped to see Will in church someday—if his father ever got over thinking the new pastor was crazy.

Other members of the call committee also came early. Stoddard Bloch stomped in, spine straight as if a steel rod ran up his back, wearing a gray wool jacket that looked hot and itchy on this beautiful day. His chins waggled as he walked. His wife Edith, in a pale blue, nondescript dress and bright cobalt blue shoes, scurried behind him like a little mother hen, clucking and chirping and agreeing with every word the man uttered.

Mattie Olsen followed, beaming happily because she'd met the new pastor *ages* ago and was pleased to tell that to anyone who would listen. She wore a hat with a veil, a fashion Alex hadn't seen since he was a young boy and then only on his grandmother.

Ole Swenson of Twinkle Toes fame arrived next. Wiry and thin, Ole wore a well-tailored navy blue suit that was shiny in the seat and at the elbows but still looked good on his sinewy frame. "You'll have to stop over and see the pigs," he told Alex as he shook his hand vigorously. His voice crackled with age but was laced with good humor. "I hear you were there when my truck tipped and Twinkle Toes made a run for it. I'd like you to meet her again, under better circumstances." His laugh, a hearty, infectious chortle, bubbled from him and he winked at Alex. "If you come at noon, we'll have a pork sandwich."

That juxtaposition nearly sent Alex's imagination into overload.

Mildred and Winchester Holmquist made a regal pair. Chester, attentive and solicitous, stood with impressive military posture by his wife's side. Mildred's hair was silver-white and her face surprisingly unlined. Her expression was serene.

Hans and Hilda Aadland, elderly Norwegian immigrants and Scandinavian to the core, entered the church holding hands. They were followed by Margaret and Dale Keller. Margaret's quick, bird-like movements and Dale's propensity not to raise his voice above a whisper made them a particularly odd pair.

A woman with platinum blonde hair tottered in on improbable but very stylish shoes. She was perfectly made up with smart, tasteful clothes. The man with her was equally well dressed. They made a striking couple.

"I'm Belle Wells, Pastor, and this is my husband Curtis. Welcome to the community. I hear you're from Chicago—how exciting! I'm from that area myself. We must have tea and talk about the city!" She turned with bright eyes to her husband, "Isn't that right, dear?"

"Oh yes," Curtis said absently, as if he'd quit listening to his wife quite some time ago.

As they walked away, Lauren sidled up to Alex and whispered, "Belle's never quite adjusted to being a country girl. She's always looking for someone who has been away from the farm. She and Curtis met while he was in the military and he swept her off her feet and carried her to Hilltop. I don't think she's ever gotten over it. Do you remember the old television show *Green Acres*? That's Curtis and Belle."

He was going to have to start a notebook, Alex decided as he greeted person after person, for keeping track of this wide and sometimes quirky flock. The buzz of conversation filled his ears, and young children gathered in the back pew to giggle and swing their legs.

Alex recognized the home-party lady by her perfume. Lilly Sumptner swished up to him in a stylish and puffy taffeta skirt and a cloud of Citrus Sunshine. She had her curly-haired husband Randy in tow. "My daughter in Minneapolis sent me this. Isn't it something?"

"It certainly is." It was something, all right, but Alex didn't know quite what. He'd never paid much attention to women's fashions. Apparently he should have.

A pleasant-looking young couple, Nancy and Ben Jenkins, introduced themselves and told Alex they lived on "the Hubbard place." Several people had mentioned it, but Alex still wasn't certain why.

"You'll have to stop by," Nancy said warmly, her brown eyes glowing. "We live in that old barn of a place, but someday soon we hope to have a home that doesn't have clanking radiators and drafty windows. It's better in the summer, so come soon. We love to entertain."

He'd be busy until a month from February, Alex realized, if he were to take everyone up on their offers of hospitality. He looked forward to it.

There were Clarence and Lydia Olson minus brother Jacob, downhearted Jonas Owens and his family, and so many others that Alex's brain threatened to implode. Even his study of the church directory hadn't prepared him for this.

A well-dressed and -coiffed couple, Katrinka and Harris Hanson, arrived, wondering out loud whether or not there would be food served after the service. Alex heard Matt and Martha Jacobson invite them over for a noon meal at their house to salve their disappointment at not having a free meal at church.

There were others, of course, some of whom stood out more in Alex's mind than others. Inga and Jim Sorenson were particularly memorable. Inga, the local artist, arrived in something she'd created out of what appeared to be white cotton dishcloths and tempera paints. Around her neck she wore a chunky, colorfully painted necklace made of clay beads. On her feet were slip-on white canvas shoes with faces painted on the toes so that they smiled out at all the other shoes. She was in her "youth and light" phase, she told Alex by way of introduction.

Her husband Jim made even Ole Swenson and Jonas Owens look obese. He was tall and beanpole thin, a skeleton with clothing. Alex heard him make a joke to Dixon about Inga's poor cooking. Alex made a mental note to himself avoid dinner at the Sorensons' home.

Then Annie Henderson began to play "What a Friend We Have in Jesus." That was Alex's cue to get to the front of the church. The Lord would take it from here.

He'd finished his sermon, one of his better ones, he hoped, and was shaking hands, when Dixon sidled up beside him and whispered in his ear. "You'd better get going or you won't get to All Saints on time for their service."

Alex glanced at his watch. "I know. I hope I haven't spent too much time visiting. Can I make it?"

"Depends on how heavy your foot is on the gas pedal," Dixon said with a grin.

Gravel roads were not meant for speeding, Alex decided on the way to All Saints. He gripped the wheel with both hands as the car shimmied, and he prayed he would stay on the road for the next nine miles. It would be a fine mess if the new preacher landed himself in the hospital the first Sunday out.

He winced as a small stones spit up from beneath his tires and made stone chips in the paint. He took his foot off the gas pedal and realized he was still stirring up a blinding cloud of dust behind him. He careened into the parking lot of All Saints and, legs still shaking from the adrenaline pumping in his system, grabbed his Bible and sermon notes and flew up the steps.

And all for fewer than twenty people.

They were clustered in the back pews like they wanted to leave as much space as possible between themselves and the new pastor. The organist hammered out "Beautiful Savior" on the piano, and a gaunt man with narrowed eyes, obviously the usher of the day, glared at him. The clock on the wall said 11:02.

Wherever two or more are gathered, he reminded himself. It didn't matter how many pews were filled. What mattered was who was in those pews. Whom did God want to speak to today?

He recognized Amy Clayborn and the elderly gray-haired woman from the quilting group. Amy smiled tentatively; and the older woman, to his surprise, gave him a thumbs-up. It wasn't much, but it was enough encouragement enough to carry on. He'd hoped to see Alf Nyborg in the pew, but apparently he'd chosen not to come today. It was discouraging, but Alex refused to allow himself to dwell on it. Alf would be able to hear him preach for many Sundays to come.

Afterward, Alex couldn't remember what he said, but he hoped he'd stuck to his notes to some extent. It was alarming and a little nerve-wracking to be late, ostracized and deemed an obvious disappointment on his first Sunday, but that was exactly how the experience had made him feel.

This was only his first Sunday, and Alex felt like he'd lived a few lifetimes during it. He was very glad to be able to go home and take a nap.

CHAPTER FIFTEEN

By Tuesday, a rainy spell had settled over Hilltop and, by the look of the weather report, much of the upper Midwest. The sky was overcast—a dreary gray that reminded Alex of the color of a tired old bathrobe his father had worn for years. Rain came in a soft, fine mist that the farmers referred to as a soaker. Some of them were even beginning to tire of the persistent mist, which they would have preferred in early June rather than now in late July. Alex felt soggy around the edges, and his shoes never seemed quite dry even though they sat on the rug overnight.

He opened a folder on his desk and found a note from the treasurer for both churches, Walter Englund, with information concerning the two new windows All Saints had purchased. Someone had left him a prayer request, and there was a jar of Lydia's strawberry-rhubarb jam.

Tripod had followed Alex to the church and lay by the front door on a rag rug Gandy had brought from home. A dog with manners, he knew enough to stay there until he'd dried off before making his way to Alex's desk, where he remained the rest of the day, encouraged by the occasional doggie treats his master slipped to him when Gandy wasn't looking.

A slamming door and boots stomping across the wooden floor announced Gandy's arrival. She breezed in with a jolt of chill, damp air, pulled off a rain hat and shook it wildly, much the way Tripod shook himself after a dip in a slough.

"M'rning," she mumbled. She didn't look in Alex's direction. Instead, she turned her back to him, hung up her raincoat, and scuttled backward to her desk, where she sat down, grabbed a folder, and held it up to her face.

This was odd behavior, even for Gandy who'd been very forthright about her quirks, which included chewing and snapping gum when she was nervous and an addiction to Milk Duds. He'd already come to rely on her to bring a ray of sunshine into the room. Especially on gloomy days, he welcomed her ever-ready smile.

"Gandy, are you okay?"

"Yup, yup. Fine. Never better." She pulled the folder closer to her nose. Her voice sounded nasal, like an old country western singer.

"Did you catch a cold?"

"Healthy as a horse." The folder never moved. "But thanks for asking."

"Is the material in that folder urgent?" Alex rose from his desk.

"Just some stuff I should have finished up weeks ago. I need to order new candles, the ones with the little fishes on them, and some pew Bibles because we're a few short. Oh yes, and Annie requested some new musical arrangements so she'd have some on hand when someone volunteers to sing a solo—
Eeeek!"

She squawked at Alex, who had stolen up beside her and lifted the folder from her hands. Her face was red and blotchy, puffy too, and her eyes looked boiled and bloodshot, like a pair of fake glasses Alex had once worn to a costume party.

"You've been crying."

"Now why'd you do that? I would have been just fine if you'd given me a few minutes to pull myself together." Her hands flapped inefficiently at her hair, which had turned into corkscrews in the rain. "I didn't want you to see me a mess but I didn't want to be late either. She reached for a tissue from the box on her desk and blew her nose. It was a honk to rival that of the geese in Mike and Lauren's yard.

"Would you like to talk about it?" he asked gently. "I'm a good listener."

"Not particularly, but it's going to be all over anyway so you might as well hear it from me."

"And what is that?" He pulled up a chair and sat down across the desk from Gandy. "Would you like a cup of coffee first?"

"Please."

He allowed her a few more moments to gather herself together and then handed her the coffee in the mug she'd told him was her favorite. It stated in bold black letters MOSES WAS A BASKET CASE.

She inhaled the fragrant steam and sighed.

"What is going to be all over soon?" he prodded gently.

"My brother Jonas has gone insane. It's all his worries. They've finally driven him out of his mind."

"Surely not."

"Really. His wife woke up from a deep sleep to find him screaming and pulling drawers out of the chests and pictures off the walls. He was crying and wailing and carrying on something frightful. He even pulled down the curtains! He was sleepwalking and having a fit. She finally got him to wake up by throwing a glass of water in his face. When he realized what he'd done, he sat down on the bed and cried like a baby. If that's not crazy, nothing is!"

Alex didn't think Jonas was crazy at all. The man was, however, in deep trouble.

"I don't know what we're going to do about him. Maybe we should have an intervention, or something." Gandy was pale and there was a small tic jumping beneath her right eye.

"Into what would you be intervening?"

"That's just it. There is nothing. My brother doesn't drink, smoke or gamble. He's faithful to his wife, God-fearing and family-loving." Gandy's eyes began to water and her lip to tremble. She looked at Alex with a pitiable expression. "And he's still crazy! Isn't it awful?"

"I think it's admirable that your brother is that fine a man, Gandy. He's distressed about the possibility of losing his farm. Anyone would be. Last night his anxieties and frustrations manifested themselves in his dreams. He's far from crazy. If he *weren't* upset, then I'd say you should worry."

"My sister-in-law told me she found a bunch of nasty letters he'd hidden from her—credit card collection agencies and the like. It's worse than even she knew. I know he's at his wit's end, and I have no idea what to do for him. We don't have any money to loan him, that's for sure. I'm afraid if he does sell the land to those people he will never forgive himself."

Alex recalled the meeting in the café with distaste.

"Selling the land to someone he knows would be hard enough, but these strangers . . . You saw them, you know they're hovering overhead like vultures waiting for Jonas to get so desperate that he calls them. He has good, productive land; and there's money to be made except, apparently, by Jonas." Gandy's face crumpled and she looked as if she would cry again. "I think he's close to doing it. And if he does, I don't know what will happen to him."

"When he asked the neighbors if they were interested in buying his land, did they all say no?"

Gandy looked askance. "He didn't even let on he was having problems. He was too ashamed to admit the trouble he'd gotten into. People suspected things were going badly, but no one knew how badly until recently. Things are tight for everyone right now, and no one has extra money lying around. Jonas wouldn't approach the neighbors because he'd never put anyone in the awkward position of having to turn him down." Her entire body drooped like a wilting flower. "His troubles would still be a secret if he could help it. Jonas thinks asking for help is the same as asking for handouts."

"Buying land outright is hardly a handout."

"You don't know my brother very well yet, Reverend Alex. He's a proud man. He certainly wouldn't grovel."

Alex had seen that for himself.

"'I hate pride and arrogance,'" Alex quoted softly, more to himself than to Gandy. "'Counsel and sound judgment are mine.' Proverbs 8."

"Jonas? He isn't arrogant."

"Not in the sense you mean. In this verse, arrogance is synonymous with pride. When we find ourselves wanting to do things our own way, to figure out our own answers, we're struggling with our pride, resisting God's leadership and refusing His help. God doesn't want us to do anything without Him. He wants to help. He's *waiting* to help—and we persistently thumb our noses at Him."

Gandy was silent as she pondered this.

"It would be insulting, wouldn't it? To have so much to give, yet to have those you want to help refuse it time and time again." She crossed her arms over her chest and frowned. "So by thinking his way is the only way, Jonas is refusing to let God into the picture?"

"It's something to consider."

"If Jonas were to let God handle it without any input from him, what do you think would happen?"

"I have no way of predicting God, Gandy. All I do know is that if Jonas were resting fully on God's wisdom he'd probably sleep better at night."

She looked Alex up and down with an appraising stare. "I'll talk to Jonas." She brightened, and her persistent optimism returned. "Maybe God's getting everything set up to help Jonas out of this mess and just waiting for the go-ahead from Jonas himself."

"Setting up? What do you mean?"

"We've been without a preacher for a long time. Now we've got one. Maybe God sent you to help Jonas through this." She smiled for the first time. "I'll bet you're it, the answer to my prayers and Jonas' too!"

"Gandy, I can't fix your brother's financial issues, all I'm saying is—"

"Pray about it, will you? See what God has to say about my brother."

"I'm really in for it now, Tripod," Alex groaned after he and the dog had taken a particularly long run that evening. "I can't fix problems with a snap of my fingers."

Tripod whined in commiseration and put his head dolefully on the floor.

"Or maybe I'm being as falsely humble as Jonas has been prideful," Alex murmured thoughtfully. He'd almost immediately taken to talking to the dog, who was, as Dixon had promised, an excellent listener. Of course he couldn't fix this. But God could. He would ask God to show him exactly what part he was to play in this unfolding drama.

Alex mounted the steps to his room two at a time and shed his running clothes in a pile on his bedroom floor. Before he stepped into the shower, he decided to do the deed he'd been dreading. He ventured onto the bathroom scale and watched the needle jump and flutter until it settled on a number.

It had to be broken. He backed off, made sure it was set properly and stepped on again. The number was the same. Surely it couldn't be—he was up eight pounds. In such a brief time? And he'd thought he'd shrunk his trousers in the wash! Horrified, he turned on the shower and stepped in even before the water had time to get warm. The cold, pelting droplets brought him to his senses. If he wasn't careful, he would turn into a round-faced, chubby caricature of himself. A six-foot-tall Tweedledum was what he'd be—pants hiked past his ample stomach to his armpits and held aloft by suspenders. He shuddered at the thought. Things would have to change around here. And quickly!

He approached the refrigerator warily when it was time to prepare his meal. There was a rasher of bacon and a quart of real cream in a Mason jar from Ole, who milked a few cows in addition to raising the pigs. Half of a to-die-for chocolate cake sat on the second shelf with a casserole of fresh garden vegetables swimming in butter and a half gallon of whole milk. In the cupboard were deep fried chips, chocolate chip cookies and a dozen boxes of items containing dreaded trans fats. He made himself a bowl of instant oatmeal and watered down the milk until it had the pale blue look of skim. He tried to feed his leftovers to Tripod but even the dog wouldn't eat them. It had to have been nasty for him to reject them.

Then he picked up the phone and dialed the Carlsens.

"You're sounding a little down," Lauren observed when she heard his voice. She could pick up nuances in a person's voice more quickly than anyone else Alex had ever met. "Something wrong?"

"Where's a place to buy vegetables? Fresh ones, I mean."

The long silence at her end of the line surprised him. He didn't think he'd asked a difficult question.

"What about your garden? If everything isn't ready yet it will be soon. Unless, of course, you want beets, cabbage, or melons. I didn't plant any of those this year. The grocery store has things, but mostly we don't *buy* vegetables. We *grow* them."

"What about people who don't have gardens? Where do they get fresh produce? Or do they settle for canned and frozen?" He heard the judgment in his question—suggesting that these options were second best. It was ironic, since the majority of the food his mother had ever served him was either frozen or canned. But at the moment he was on a mission. The waistband cutting into his midsection was reminder of that.

"I'll have Mike run over with a bag of tomatoes. And there's still some nice lettuce even though I've had a few cuttings. And green beans—I have them coming out my ears."

"You don't have to give me anything, Lauren. I'll have plenty soon, but it makes me wonder about the people who want to buy fresh things."

"It's a good question, Alex. It's just that around Hilltop we haven't needed an answer."

"What about Grassy Valley?"

"There are gardens there too, I suppose."

"How about a farmers' market?"

"There's one in Wheatville, but no one will drive forty or fifty miles to buy radishes or even corn when it's all right here. I doubt anyone around here has ever considered that there are people who actually need to buy that stuff."

"I see. Then how about organic foods?" He was going to improve his health even if it killed him, he decided.

"There are farmers around who don't use pesticides, if that's what you mean. Jonas Owens is one of them. And there is an organic food section in the grocery store. Unfortunately it's limited to soy milk, soy yogurt, and frozen gluten-free bread. There are a couple of kids in town with allergies. What is this all about, anyway?"

He told her about the number on the scale and his dreadful oatmeal, and she burst out laughing.

"Everyone who comes to Hilltop has the same problem at first. Don't worry, people will feed you less and less, and the busier you get the more quickly you'll see the pounds fade." She lowered her voice. "And if you don't tell anyone, I'll bring you vegetable lasagna that's out of this world but is absolutely healthy and low-cal. Don't worry; you'll be back in shape in no time flat."

He could only hope.

Gandy's face was long when Alex walked into the church office the next morning. She didn't even greet him with her usual cheer.

He pulled up a wooden chair in front of her desk and straddled it, his arms folded over the back of the chair. "What's wrong?"

"Jonas' telephone has been shut off."

"I'm sorry, Gandy."

"The lights were about to be shut off too, but I scraped up enough for the light bill."

Alex reached into his back pocket for his billfold. "Let me help." He pulled out a twenty dollar bill, all he had, and put it on Gandy's desk. "I can get more."

Gandy put her hand over his. "You've helped my brother so much already. It's Barbara who worries me. She's not handling this well. She told Jonas that if he couldn't figure this out, she'd take the kids and go to her mother's until he did."

"Is there anything we can do?"

"She's as bad as my brother about accepting help. Right now I think we have to wait this out."

So they settled into their work, for the day. Gandy busied herself at her desk while Alex puttered around the office.

"Somebody's bellowing like they're being hog tied and skinned out there," Gandy said, looking up from her desk where she was compiling the new church directory. She nodded toward the door.

Alex, who was on a ladder changing an overhead light bulb, carefully descended. Because he was agile and strong, climbing usually didn't frighten him, but a ladder with legs of mismatched lengths and a broken rung put the fear of falling into him. No use cracking his head open or breaking a leg if he could prevent it.

"I'll see what's wrong. By the way, see if you can find a space in next year's church budget for a new ladder, or at least put out a cry for help in Sunday's bulletin. Maybe someone has one they aren't using and would be willing to donate."

The front door flew open, and the source of the shrieking and bawling entered. It was Will Packard, being half-pulled and half-carried by a furious Clarence Olson. Will's hands and feet were churning like little windmills. Fortunately Clarence had been blessed with long arms and could dodge most of Will's flailing.

"I found this young hooligan in my pig sty with a pail full of garter snakes, a bird with a broken wing and that wretched skunk the Packards call a pet." Clarence's face turned the color of boiled beets. "And he said you gave him permission to be there!"

Garter snakes, Alex had observed in his back yard, had long colored stripes—mostly yellow in this region—and dark blotchy stripes between the yellow. They were harmless but snakes, nevertheless.

"Me? I . . . " Alex looked intently at Will, who'd quit thrashing and was now staring up at the pastor with a fearful expression. "Will, I did not tell you to take your . . . your . . . humane society to the Olsons'."

"Well, you said I had to take it out of the church shed. What was I supposed to do?" He scowled fiercely. "I thought you were going to help me find a new place!"

"The Carlsens took the cat and the chickens, and you gave the kittens away. I thought your shelter was closed down."

"Are you kidding?" Will looked at him, aghast. "There will always be animals to rescue, don't you know? 'If it's not one thing, it's another,' my mom always says. Right now the other thing is a bunch of garter snakes that Bucky was going after with a hoe and that bird I found. I think I can patch him up good as new. I've done it before."

"I didn't think you'd start collecting again after our little talk about using the shed."

"How could I stop?" Will's small face was intent and every freckle stood out. "Hurtin' animals are just like the poor, don't you know?"

Alex blinked. "What do you mean?"

"And you call yourself a preacher!" Will looked disgusted. "It's another verse my ma taught us. 'You always have the poor with you.' Well, we'll always have hurtin' critters too."

Out-quoted by a nine-year-old. Alex liked this child immensely. Despite the trouble he seemed determined to cause, he was clever and quick-witted. If that naughty energy could be channeled into something productive, he'd be a real dynamo.

"So did you or did you not tell him to use my pig sty?" Clarence finally let go of the boy. Will tumbled to the floor.

"I did not. Will thought that up by himself. The problem is, no matter how many times we kick him out of buildings, I believe he will find a new place and start collecting animals all over again."

"Not at my place." Clarence rumbled.

"No, definitely not there," Alex agreed, "but we're open to suggestions."

Pacified, Clarence's color was beginning to return to normal. "Why can't he use his own farm?"

"Are you serious?" Will chirruped. "My pa would kill me! Don't think he hasn't been tempted already."

Even Clarence's expression softened at that. Will's father was a real piece of work, Alex thought. Poor kid.

"Well, I'll leave him with you, Reverend. Just make sure he has that bucket of snakes and company out of my shed in the next hour." Clarence stormed out.

Gandy, who'd listened to the entire exchange with rapt interest, pretended to look at the directory, a smile playing at the corners of her mouth.

Will straightened himself indignantly. "I don't know why he's so persnickety. He wasn't using that old sty anyway. And he didn't have to be so crabby either. The snakes are already out of the bucket."

A warning bell sounded in Alex's head. "Then where are they?"

Will grinned at him. His front teeth were too big for the rest of him. "I kicked the bucket over when he wasn't looking. Now they're all over his yard."

"Will . . ."

The boy glanced over his shoulder and saw the organist Annie Henderson mounting the steps of the church with a sheaf of music in her hands. "Gotta go, Pastor Alex. Looks like you've got company." He darted out of Alex's grasp and headed for the door.

"We're going to discuss this, Will Packard. And you aren't going to get out of it!" he called after the boy.

Will never turned around, but he waved his hand over his shoulder and disappeared from sight.

"What are you going to do?" Gandy asked. She'd cheered up considerably now that her mind was on things other than her brother.

"I'm not sure. I'm afraid that Will's father will punish him more severely than the infraction calls for, but I really can't ignore it."

"Will's mama is a good woman. Maybe you could talk to her." Gandy picked up the phone. "I'll see if she answers the phone."

Almost before Alex could gather his wits, she handed him the phone.

"Hello, Mrs. Packard, my name is—"

"Gandy told me. How nice of you to call." Her voice was sweet and mild, and Alex immediately understood why it was difficult for her to stand up to her husband.

"I'm afraid this is a bit of a business call. It's about Will."

Her sigh came across the line loud and clear. "Now what's that child done?"

Alex told her about Will's animal rescue and the bucket of snakes.

She was silent for a long time. When she spoke, there was amusement in her voice. "You know, it might even be funny if I didn't know Will's daddy would punish him terribly if he knew."

"About that—"

"My husband loses his way sometimes, mostly when he's been drinking. I keep praying that God will pick him up and shake some sense into him and scare him sober, but I don't know when that will be."

"So I should leave the conversation with Will to you?"

"I'll take care of it, Reverend, although I can't promise how much it will help. My Will has a big heart for hurting things, and I really don't want to punish that out of him."

"I know you'll do your best."

"I'll try. And by the way, I'd appreciate it if you'd pray for my husband. I can't think of anyone who needs it more."

Humbled by the woman's faith and endurance, Alex hung up the phone.

At the end of the day Alex was relieved to hear Mark Nash's calm, refined voice on the other end of the phone line. "Have you got plans for supper?"

"Not really." He had a freezer full of rich desserts and casseroles, but nothing that was going to help him shed a few pounds.

"Tonight is meatloaf night at the Cozy Corner Cafe."

"Does that place serve salads?" He looked longingly at the candy dish on his desk. Gandy had filled it with miniature chocolate bars.

"Definitely."

"Then I'll come."

"Good. I'll pick you up in ten minutes."

The café was busy; meatloaf was apparently a popular item. Despite the plates of mashed potatoes and glistening brown gravy going by, Alex ordered a chef's salad with oil and vinegar on the side. Then he told Mark about getting on the scale and the too-tight trousers.

Instead of getting sympathy or the least little bit of commiseration, Mark, like Lauren, burst out laughing. "I could have told you that would happen. Just be glad you caught it before it turned into twenty or thirty pounds. That happened to a pastor many years back. He looked like a walking heart attack before the ladies started feeding him roasted turkey breast and fruit salads instead of fried chicken and ambrosia."

Alex said nothing for a long while. His mind had wandered to something far more important than his waistband. "Have you heard how Jonas is doing?"

"Like I said before, I knew Jonas was in trouble," Mark said softly. "I'd have to be blind not to, but even I had no idea how deep it was." He looked troubled. "Maybe on some level I didn't *want* to know. There have been Owenses on that land since the 1800s."

"Isn't there any other way? Could he grow something that would bring in more cash?"

"Only thing I can think of is wind."

"Grow wind? I know you can do wonderful things out here, but isn't that a little over the top?"

"I mean wind farms. There are several in the state, big windmills that turn wind into energy, but those things cost a pretty penny. No, this has to be something quick, something that would help Jonas immediately."

"If you can think of any way I can help him other than moral support and prayer, let me know, will you?"

Mark looked at him with sympathy in his eyes. "You got thrown into the deep end of the pool here, didn't you, Alex?"

CHAPTER SIXTEEN

Mark's words resonated in Alex's head. Actually, he'd been swimming in the deep end of things for some time now.

To his relief, thoughts of Natalie and curiosity about what might have happened had they stayed together came less often now. Because he was occupied with other things, the sting was not quite so sharp. For this he was grateful. He couldn't have borne that original agony for very long. Still, he felt emotionally bruised. The wound was still tender.

He said that very thing to his sister when she called Friday afternoon.

"Are there any interesting ladies in Grassy Valley?" she'd asked hopefully.

"I have no idea, Carol. I'm not looking."

"You can't hide out there, Alex, and avoid relationships altogether. You deserve a good wife by your side."

How like Carol to worry about his heart.

"I didn't say I'm against marrying someday, Sis. But I'm hardly good husband material. I advise people all the time not to marry on the rebound. Besides, I'm not even sure what all led up to her decision. She refused to talk about it."

That bothered Alex more than anything, leaving things so open and unfinished. In his position as a pastor, the reconciliation of divided parties was practically part of his job description; yet in his own important relationship, there had been no settlement, no feeling of completion. But that was too difficult for him to attempt to explain to Carol, so he changed the subject. Carol always loved a party.

"The people here are planning an open house for me."

"How nice! When Jared got home from North Dakota, he immediately told me how nice the people were there."

"How *is* Jared? I really enjoyed having him travel with me."

"Impossible. Crabby. Angry. Irritable. Surly. Shall I go on?"

"Are we talking about the same kid?"

"I don't know what's with him. I told him he should take a preparatory class in August in order to be ready for college testing, and he hit the roof. He roared that he *wasn't* going to college and that his dad and I couldn't make him. He's hardly spoken to us since."

"Something is going on, Sis. He's never been like that."

"I wish you were here, Alex. He's always been close to you. Maybe he'd tell you something."

"Maybe," Alex said vaguely. He'd worked with college kids long enough to know that if they didn't want to talk, dynamite wouldn't get it out of them. "Tell him to call me when he's ready to discuss it."

After the call, he decided to make some calls of his own— of the face-to-face variety.

He climbed into his van. As soon as Alex was settled, Tripod leaped from the ground like a horse jumping a fence.

He soared past Alex's lap and landed on the passenger seat. He sat there looking expectant, as if this maneuver should earn him praise or at least a scratch behind the ear.

Although Alex didn't want to reward the dog for bad behavior, Tripod's strength and agility were admirable. The dog had become his personal shadow, and Alex had to admit he liked it.

Until he'd moved to Hilltop, there had been so much noise in his life—students, peers, traffic, televisions, radios, complaining staff—that it was a little *too* quiet here. But there was also more time to spend in study and prayer. And the more he did, the more he wanted. He was always hungry for the Word, and there was much more silence here with which to sate it. He was beginning to like it. Who could have predicted that Alex Armstrong would become a country boy?

But not all silence was golden. All Saints was an active volcano rumbling and churning beneath the surface, and Alex was steeling himself for an explosion. So far, however, they'd been absorbed with the installation of two stained glass windows, gifts from two families in memory of loved ones.

Alex was eager to see them in place. It would certainly warm up the church's interior. Even that was a step in the right direction. The thaw had to start somewhere.

He'd been back to the church to visit with the quilting ladies, but never run into Alf Nyborg. Was that intentional? If so, he'd have to be the one to seek Nyborg out.

But first he wanted to visit with Mildred and Chester Holmquist. Dixon had told him that Chester understood Alf about as well as anyone could, since over the years he and Chester had occasionally driven to meetings together at the VFW in Wheatville.

"Are you ready for the open house at the parsonage this afternoon?" Gandy asked when he walked into the church on Wednesday morning. She was busying digging plastic flowers out of a large rubber tub. She held up a cluster of crimson roses. "Do you want the fancy decorations for the table, or do you prefer fresh cut flowers?"

"Fresh cut, I think."

"I've got five dozen cookies in the car I'd like to put in your kitchen, if you don't mind. I'll check your flowers then."

"You are a treasure, Gandy. I don't tell you that nearly often enough."

"I hope you still thank me when this thing is over. I haven't heard if anyone from All Saints is attending."

"Don't worry. We've extended the invitation. Now the ball is in their court."

The ball might be in All Saint's court, Alex mused as people began to arrive at the parsonage, but evidently they weren't interested in returning the serve. There wasn't an All Saints member in the bunch.

He found the Holmquists in his backyard, though, beneath a lawn umbrella, and he headed toward them.

It was no wonder Mildred's beauty was legendary, Alex thought. Her cheekbones were high and her face an attractive oval. Though she was deep into her eighties, her face was remarkably unlined. There'd been no long days in the sun for her. Her white hair was of a silvery cast and framed her placid face in soft wisps. Mildred's delicate, pale pink dress swirled around her ethereally, as if it were part chiffon and part cotton candy.

"My girl is lovely, isn't she?" Chester looked at her with adoring eyes. "She won a beauty pageant, you know, Miss

Midwest Heartland in 1949. I'm a lucky man. Do you know how many suitors she had? Why . . . "

Before Alex could respond, a blushing Mildred put a hand on Chester's arm. "Now, don't go talking like a besotted teenager, dear. The reverend will think we're a silly old couple reliving our youth. Chat about something substantial. Tell him about that antique musket you just purchased for your gun collection."

That wasn't exactly what Alex had hoped to discuss, but he smiled and nodded.

Chester looked at Alex with an appraising eye. "You might think it's strange, keeping all these old guns around and enjoying them the way I do, but I've got my reasons. These guns remind me of all that has been sacrificed over the years. I spent my entire career as a military man, but now I'm a man of peace, not war."

"Me too," Alex said softly.

They stood silently, side by side, watching children playing tag on the lawn for a long while before Alex spoke. "I understand that Alf Nyborg was in the military as well. Mark Nash told me that the two of you sometimes rode together to the VFW in Wheatville. He suggested that you might be able to tell me a little more about him. I know he's very influential at All Saints."

"Alf is a funny guy," Chester murmured more to himself than to Alex. "He's probably avoiding you."

"He doesn't even know me."

"Alf holds things inside and lets them build up. He is, rightly or wrongly, upset with Hilltop. Alf carries grudges like a mule carries pack bags. Mildred compares him to a pressure cooker. When he has to, he lets off just enough steam so that he doesn't explode, but he's hot and angry inside all the time anyway. If he ever blows, he'll scald everyone around him."

"Has he always been this way?"

"No. He was a different person before the fire that took his first wife and child." Chester's expression saddened. "Always laughing, telling jokes. Cheerful as could be. Of course, I can't blame him. After a tragedy like that, I'd quit smiling too."

"How did it happen?" Alex felt a desperate need to understand this man who was so actively standing between him and one of his parishes.

"An accident, pure and simple. It started near a propane furnace in his basement. Bad luck. Propane is volatile around sparks. The furnace exploded, taking the house with it. Alf's wife and five-year-old son were inside. He was out in the barn, milking cows. He never had a chance to save them. When the fire truck arrived, he was trying to get inside and his clothes were on fire. They got to him before the burns went too deep, but he was scarred for life, inside and out."

Life had run roughshod over him, that much was clear.

"He's been angry ever since. Alf remarried—a nice woman with a heart of compassion. They had another son and a daughter who are both grown. They don't come home very often, and I can't blame them. They were able to escape." Chester shook his gray head mournfully.

"All Saints wasn't so lucky. Alf emptied himself and his suffering into work for the church. It was as if he tried to fill the hole inside himself, the one left by his first wife and son. It's my theory that Alf does all he does at All Saints to help himself forget.

"It didn't sweeten him up, unfortunately, but it did make All Saints dependent upon him. He's held every office and been on every committee. He works tirelessly on the building and grounds. It's thanks to him that they have new cupboards in the kitchen. He made them by hand. And he's the one who recently started to buy and plant trees around the cemetery. When All Saints needs funds, Alf chips in. He alone likely pays half of the salary you get from All Saints."

That made Alex particularly uncomfortable.

"He's treasurer, custodian, and permanent church board member. All Saints has been relying on him for so long—and their numbers have shrunk in the past few years—that they are afraid to be without him."

"So he's the primary spokesperson for the church?" The unfortunate picture was growing clearer.

"Yes. And just about everything else. In his effort to move past his pain, he's trained those people to depend on him."

"Where does God fit into this picture?" Alex inquired softly. The noise and clatter of the party receded as they spoke.

"Alf would like to boss Him around too." The old man's expression was grieved. "I think he still blames Him for that fire. Of course, that's a lot easier than blaming himself."

A sense of foreboding spread in Alex. "What do you mean?"

"A couple days before the fire, Alf had run a new piece of copper tubing to the furnace from the outside propane tank. Every day of his life he's wondered if he missed something when he checked the connection to the furnace for a proper seal. If he did, he was responsible for the fire. He couldn't bear that. Of course many other things could have happened. A spark inside the furnace when it kicked in, for instance. Alf's little boy was found downstairs, with the remains of the family dog. They could have set something off by accident. Who knows? It's been killing Alf slowly for years."

A shudder ran though Alex, followed by a surge of compassion. No wonder Nyborg was a difficult man, considering the pain he'd carried around inside him all these years.

Even though Gandy seemed determined to keep him busy every minute of the workdays, Alex couldn't get his mind off Alf. Neither, it seemed, could anyone else.

Although the open house was a rip-roaring success as far as Hilltop's congregation was concerned—the ladies particularly loved the new kitchen—All Saints members' notable absence cast a pall over the otherwise delightful party.

"Can you believe it?" Lilly Sumptner said, waving a spatula in the air. "Not a soul showed up from All Saints. I'll bet Alf Nyborg is behind it. How rude!" She went back to dishing up the marble cake, which was being eaten almost as fast as she could get it out of the pan.

The women in the kitchen nodded dolefully as if they'd all thought the same thing.

"More for us," Katrinka Hanson said brightly. "May I take home some leftovers?"

Katrinka, or Trinka, as most people called her, enjoyed free food, Alex had observed. It was, Lauren had told him, a money-saving measure. The Hansons were quite wealthy, but they'd never gotten over squeezing everything they could out of a penny.

In the yard, Alf wasn't faring much better.

Alex pulled Dixon aside. "Why is everyone so sure Alf is behind All Saints' absence today?"

"Because he usually is."

It was a puzzle, Alex thought, one he'd have to solve—soon.

No time like the present, Alex told himself the next morning as he drove out of his yard. It was now or never. He was going to talk with Alf about the enmity he had toward Hilltop. Love, he thought, was the only antidote for what ailed this man. Ignoring the situation was out of the question, and expecting him to be rational about something that would cause anyone to become irrational was naïve. He'd depend on God for orders on this one.

His cell phone rang, startling him so much that he might have driven into the ditch had he not been crawling along at a snail's pace.

It was Gandy. "The Ladies Aid wants to know what they should serve next Sunday. We're going to have a fund-raiser for missions. Do you have any favorites?"

"Favorite missions or favorite foods?"

"Very funny. Food, of course."

"I've never been in a place that fuels everything they do with food. Tell them to surprise me."

"That could be dangerous. Last time the ladies surprised someone, they'd gotten a line on a hundred pounds of lutefisk. I'm not sure you're ready for that."

"Lutefisk?"

"Like I said, you're not ready yet."

"Gandy, you started this. The least you can do is tell me what lutefisk is."

"It's cod fish soaked in lye. Around here they serve it with boiled potatoes, peas, and lefse. My mother likes it with mashed rutabagas. When you cook it, it becomes translucent and stinks like crazy. Then you pour butter all over it and . . . "

"You're right. I'm not ready for that." His stomach roiled at the thought of stinky fish and mashed rutabagas.

"I thought so. I'll tell them, but you aren't going to get out of eating it forever, you know. Around here some people compare it to eating lobster."

"Gandy, pouring butter on overshoes would make them taste better too, but I'm still not interested."

"Consider yourself warned. Lutefisk is in your future."

Perhaps the future was bleaker than he'd anticipated. "Anything new at church?"

"Brunie called to say Bessie was having a bad day and asked that we pray for her. Bessie's obsessive compulsive disorder is kicking up, and she has been washing her hands all day. Walter Englund called to let you know that he'd be happy to go over the church books with you any time. Sam Waters, who owns the hardware store behind the grocery store, heard our ladder was bad and offered to give us a new one. Oh, yes, and Porkchop Smith has a lot more soup bones than he can sell. He wanted to know if we want some for a soup dinner or something. I told him yes. I hope that's okay with you."

"Sure, I suppose so." No one in seminary told him he'd have to decide about soup bones. "How's Jonas? Have you heard from him lately?"

"No, but my sister-in-law called this morning. She said he prowled the house half the night." Gandy hesitated and Alex heard a catch in her voice. "She asked me if I knew of anyone who might rent them a house—cheap. I think it would break my sister-in-law's heart if she had to give up her house."

Gandy cleared her throat. "She also asked if I knew if the grocery store threw away expired produce."

"They're that hard up for food?"

"I told Lauren about it, and she's going to see what she can do."

"There should be a food shelf in Grassy Valley," Alex commented.

"Lauren said the same thing. Maybe she can get one up and running, but I doubt it will be in time to help Jonas' family."

CHAPTER SEVENTEEN

Alex's mind whirled with what he'd learned about Alf's heart-break and with his concern for Jonas. He'd wanted to be a pastor of a small church where he could serve people and love them. And God, in His generosity, had given him exactly what he'd asked for.

Alex's heart felt bigger out here, like it had grown as expansive as the prairie he'd come to. That old cliché was true. God did not call the qualified to serve Him; instead He qualified the called.

Still, when All Saints Church appeared on the horizon, Alex's gut clenched.

There were cars parked around the church—the quilting ladies, no doubt, because they often met more than once a week. One of them would steer him toward Alf if he was not already somewhere in the church.

Alex walked into the sanctuary to look at the newly in-stalled windows and found it fascinating which two scenes had been chosen—the stoning of Stephen and Daniel in the lion's den. They had been chosen, Dixon had told him, by Alf. Had he selected them because of the dark, hard places he'd been in his own life? Is that how he felt—like he was being pelted to death by grief or in mortal danger of being eaten alive by his own feelings? It was one more thing to think about.

He walked down the stairs, dodging the beam that threatened to behead anyone who walked under it and emerged in the dining area.

The ladies were all standing around a table, a large piece of freezer paper with pencil sketches lying before them. Seven heads turned and seven pairs of eyes seemed to pierce right through him.

Ignoring the welcome, Alex strode to the table. "Good morning, ladies. Hard at work, already? Between you and the quilters at Hilltop, I don't believe I've ever seen such industrious workers."

They didn't seem to know whether to take this as a compliment or not, Alex noted. Never mind. It was his plan to put All Saints and Hilltop into the same sentence as often as possible.

"We're planning a new quilt," Amy said. She pointed to the drawing. It was divided into squares, and on each of them was the name of the family who attended All Saints. The Nyborg name was squarely in the middle.

"Each of us is going to make a quilt block depicting something important to the history of our family. When we put it together, it will be a history book made of fabric. We plan to hang it right here." She pointed to an empty wall that was crying out for decoration.

"That's a great idea," Alex said, genuinely meaning it. "Then I can look at the quilt and know more about you. It's a perfect tool to introduce a green preacher to his congregation."

Smiles spread across the ladies' faces, and one woman stepped forward. "My name is Emma Bright. I'm glad you like our idea. We never thought about it that way, but you're right. It's not just for us but for everyone who comes to All Saints."

It's not just for us.

"Exactly! No church is just for its members. If a church isn't reaching out, it is dying from within." A glimmer of hope fluttered within him. "I wish Hilltop would do something similar." Then he paused. Maybe they didn't want to hear about Hilltop.

"You mean they haven't done anything like this?" Emma said.

"Not that I know of. I can ask Gandy, of course, but there's nothing on display."

"So we're the first?" Her eyes brightened and a small, Mona Lisa smile graced her features.

Alex could see that the women liked this idea. The little sister had finally come up with a new idea, one that deserved some attention. "You are. If you don't mind, I'd like to suggest that the Hilltop quilters do something similar. I'm sure they'd be pleased to hear of it. Maybe you ladies could advise them as to how to go about it."

The smiles were a little wider now and the tension in the room had been erased by something close to conviviality. "In fact," Alex continued, building on the small opening that had occurred. "I'd love to visit your group sometimes and hear the family stories while you work. Would you mind?"

"Not at all," Emma said, "and plan to stay for coffee."

"I'll do that. I hope you won't get sick of me. I'm very anxious to know you all better."

"You really mean it, don't you?" There was a bit of wonder in Amy's voice. "Alf always said . . . "

Alex decided to pretend he hadn't heard her last words. "Of course I mean it! What's more, Gandy told me that someone in this group makes something called a Sally Ann molasses cookie. Is there any chance of me tasting one of those during coffee hour some day?"

A woman in the back blushed a furious red. The maker of the Sally Anns no doubt.

He stayed a half hour more, relishing the relaxed laughter and the chatty discussion of molasses cookie recipes. At least one door at All Saints had been opened.

When he left, it was with a sack of cookies, directions to the Nyborg farm and, at least for the moment, a lighter heart.

It seemed that the closer he got to the Nyborg farm, the rougher and narrower the road became. He thought it was rather appropriate as his tire sank into a pothole and threatened to stay there. If Alf had wanted to deter guests, he couldn't have picked a better method.

The farm itself was nice enough, tidy and well kept. There were few trees and fewer flowers. The house was large but simple, a rambler with gray shutters and pale blue siding. Most of the windows were closed, the drapes drawn tight. Maybe Alf had even expelled sunlight from his life.

"You're making things up, Armstrong," Alex muttered to himself. In his anxiety, he'd built this meeting up to be something painful and ominous. It didn't have to be that way. Still, he prayed for wisdom for the meeting ahead.

The large door was open to the machine shed. Through it, Alex could see a large green combine. A shadow moved, and a man jumped down from the cab and walked out into the sunlight wiping his hands on a greasy rag.

He was in his midsixties, a little round at the middle as if his once substantial chest had migrated southward. His legs, clad in denim, were thin, bordering on spindly, and his shoulders slightly rounded. He wore a checked cotton shirt and an old vest from which tools sprouted. On his head was a cotton bucket hat with a down-sloping brim to shield the sun from his eyes. There were harsh lines in his face, the kind that come with suffering.

"Yeah? What do you want?" was the not-so-friendly greeting. "If you're selling something, I don't want it."

That, despite the fact that Alf knew full well who he was. Nyborg wasn't going to make this easy.

"Hi. I'm Alex Armstrong, your . . . " He held out a hand, which Alf didn't take.

"What are you doing here?"

"Just visiting." Alex allowed his hand to drop to his side. "I'd like to get to know the members of All Saints better, and since you are currently president of the congregation, I thought that we should—"

"I've been president of our church council for years. Nobody else seems to want it."

Alex decided not to touch that.

Alf looked at him from beneath furrowed brows. "Just so you know, we're not Hilltop, and Hilltop's not us."

"That's been obvious to me since I got here. You are your own special entity. Every church has a personality, Mr. Nyborg. I wouldn't dream of trying to take that away from you."

"No?" Alf looked surprised. "Well . . . good."

At that moment, a woman with mouse-brown hair exited the house and came toward them carrying a large thermos and paper cups. "You aren't much of a host, Alf. Who do we have here?" She had pleasant features and an air of kindness about her that Alex sensed immediately.

"Mrs. Nyborg? I'm Alex Armstrong."

She glanced sharply at her husband and then back at Alex. "Welcome. It's good to have a new face in the pulpit. I like fresh starts, don't you?" Her choice of words seemed directed at her husband, who ignored them completely. "My name is Betty." She reached out her hand and gave Alex's a shake with a firm, warm grip.

"I understand you were on the call committee from All Saints, Mr. Nyborg, but I didn't get the opportunity to talk to you during the interview."

"What was the point?" Nyborg didn't mince words. "Those people were going to do what they were going to do whether I liked you or not."

"Would you like to come inside and have some of this lemonade? That way we'd be out of the sun," Mrs. Nyborg suggested in an attempt to diffuse the awkward situation.

"I can't stop working to be lollygagging around the house," Alf said shortly. "Go ahead, Reverend, if you want, but you'll have to excuse me." With that, he turned and headed back to the shop.

Betty smiled apologetically and gestured Alex toward the house. "Just because he's cranky, it doesn't mean that we can't enjoy ourselves. Come on."

The interior of the house was like that of so many ramblers built in the late 1950s and early 1960s: kitchen, living, and dining areas across the front, and a row of bedrooms and baths behind, running down a long hall. It was meticulously neat.

"Sit down. I'll get you a real glass to drink from." She set the paper cups aside and went to the cupboard. Then she sat down across from Alex, folded her hands and beamed at him. "I am *so* glad you're here."

"Tell me a little about yourself," Alex encouraged. "I'm on a mission to learn a little something about everyone in the community." He tapped his head with this forefinger. "And to keep their names and faces straight."

"Good luck with that. The older I get, the leakier my brain becomes. Some days my memory is like a sieve." She sipped her lemonade. "You want to learn a little about me? There's not that much to tell. I have lived on this farm my entire married life and have two children—Jessica and Jerome. They both work in the Twin Cities. Jessica teaches kindergarten, and Jerome is a realtor."

"And before that?"

Betty smiled sweetly, as if he'd struck a happy nerve. "I was a missionary in South America for a number of years. I worked with an orphanage in Lima, Peru. Those were some of the best days of my life. It was difficult work and there were so many in need, but every day was gratifying. Good physical and spiritual things happened for the children. It was easy, in a sense, because we could witness the changes in them. It's harder to be in a mission field where you wonder if your voice is even heard."

Like Alf? He almost said out loud but stopped himself.

Betty looked directly into his eyes. It was if she were reading his mind. "You're thinking that if Alf is my current mission field, I've probably bitten off more than I can chew, right?" She sighed. "It's true. Alf can be a hard man to get along with but he has many fine qualities as well. He's generous to a fault, hardworking and a good, faithful husband." Betty smiled and soft dimples nicked her cheeks.

Then her expression grew serious. "You've heard about the fire and Alf's son and first wife?"

"Yes. How tragic." He ventured onward. "I understand that it was about that time that Alf and Hilltop had a parting of the ways."

Betty nodded thoughtfully. "From what I've pieced together from what Alf and others have said, people from both All Saints and Hilltop surrounded him, but no one could comfort him. Hilltop church worked hard to console Alf, but he wouldn't accept it. The pastor at the time was on sick leave and his fill-in was an inexperienced student. He said some misguided and badly chosen things while trying to comfort Alf. That verse from Ecclesiastes really set him off."

Alex searched his mind for what that might be.

"It's one of my favorites but it certainly hit Alf the wrong way. 'For everything there is a season, and a time for every matter under heaven. . . . ' "

The light bulb came on in Alex's brain. "'A time to be born and a time to die; a time to plant, and a time to pluck up what is planted.'"

"Exactly. Alf said there was *no time* that a little boy should die. He kicked that young man out of his house, said Hilltop had done wrong by sending him over and closed his heart tight as if he'd put a lock on it." Betty put her hands behind her and kneaded her lower back.

"Of course that pastor didn't mean to say a child had to die. I believe that passage is all about timing."

Alex waited for her to continue.

"God's timing, that is. The only way to have peace is to accept that God's timing is perfect, no matter what time schedule we'd prefer for ourselves. And if we can't accept that, and discover and even appreciate His divine timing then, like Alf, we either doubt God or resent Him."

Betty's face glowed with a peace and serenity that Alex found beautiful. "One thing I learned early is that if I move ahead before God's ready or if I resist Him, things don't work out very well."

Alex knew the feeling. "No wonder Alf feels such despair and discontent. He's disillusioned with God and God's people."

"We're complicated folk, aren't we? My husband probably can't even tell you why he behaves the way he does, at least not any more. He's made a habit of being contrary. It stuck, and it made him a bitter man. And somehow Hilltop got mixed up in his head with that. Alf's never gotten over it."

"Pastors aren't perfect," Alex said slowly, feeling exceedingly unqualified himself. "Nothing this side of heaven can make a man faultless." How many times had his own words been taken in ways they were not intended?

"Of course not, but Alf in his grief and guilt couldn't sort that out. Everyone says he's been a different man since that awful day."

Betty studied Alex's face carefully. "Maybe you're the one who can bring him around. He's done his best to convince the people of All Saints that they can't do without him and that Hilltop is not to be trusted. It doesn't make sense, but after all these years, it's just the way it is. Seeking relief from his pain, he's made himself a one-man show around that church, and All Saints accepted what he offered. Frankly, there are those who'd like to have better relations with Hilltop but have no idea how to accomplish it without causing Alf more pain. It's touchy business."

That, Alex thought, his gut in a knot, was an understatement.

"Thank you for your honesty," he said, meaning it with his whole heart. "But how can you . . . ?" He let the question drift away.

"Are you familiar with termites, Reverend?"

"I've never had them in my home, if that's what you mean, but I know what destruction they can do."

"My husband is like a house with termites."

She smiled at Alex's quizzical look. "From the outside, he looks sturdy and strong, but inside he's being eaten away by termites, these thoughts that just gnaw at him. His memories are eating him up inside; and when it happens, there is no way for me to reach him or to get inside his pain.

"The guilt, loss and fear are with him as much today as they were with him the day of the fire. It made him a driven man. He needs to do something to assuage the guilt he feels. In his need to do something, he's managed to take everything about All Saints onto his own shoulders and, in the process, taught its people to depend on him for everything.

"He's tried to replace his son with All Saints and thinks if he can be busy enough, he won't hurt. It doesn't work that way, of course. He needs to forgive himself and to trust that God can forgive him. He's a man of the church who doesn't know God, Pastor, at least not the loving, gentle God we know."

"What does that leave for you and your children?"

"Not much, sometimes. Jessica and Jerome avoid him if they can. It's very sad. He has a new son in Jerome, a living, breathing, healthy son that he sometimes ignores to think about the one he lost. Alf just can't let go, and he's too stubborn to believe that God can handle this without his help. I'm afraid that at the end of his life, Alf is going to have a wagonload of guilt about both the son he has and the one he lost."

"And what about you?" Alex asked gently.

Betty shrugged lightly, her eyes warm and sad. "I understand him and I love him. He can be wonderful, too, you know. I'll just keep on keeping on." Then she smiled, and it lit up her face. "I suppose I do view Alf as my personal mission field. I have more hope now than I've had for some time. I've been praying for someone who can get through to Alf. Now you're here. Maybe you are my answer."

When Alex drove away, Alf didn't even come out of the shed to say good-bye.

He drove slowly down the rutted path, dodging holes and large rocks, but his mind was not on the road. Instead it was on the heavy cloak of responsibility he felt settling on his shoulders. Jonas, Will, Alf and who knew how many others? He asked again the question that had stalked him since the first time he saw Hilltop church in the distance: *Now what?*

CHAPTER EIGHTEEN

Alex was so deep in thought that he almost didn't realize he was out of gas. He had no idea how long the aging van's fuel light indicator had been on. Hoping vapors could carry him as far as Grassy Valley, he headed for Red's.

The vehicle limped into the gas station and died with a sputter in front of the pump. Alex glanced around, hoping no one had seen this inauspicious arrival.

He was about to jump out of the vehicle to fuel up when a grizzled-looking man with a chin full of stubble and four prominent teeth in his upper gum line stuck his head in the window. "Fillerup?"

"Fill it up with gas, you mean?"

"You betcha. Fill 'er up?" The man grinned and the four teeth looked gargantuan in his mouth.

There were no self-serve signs on these pumps. It had been a long time since he'd been to a gas station with an actual attendant. "Yes, thank you. That would be very nice."

"You betcha." The man busied himself opening the gas cap. He started the pump and then hurried to the hood to check the oil.

Alex was unaccustomed to such attention. He felt a little useless. Alex got out of the van and headed toward the station itself.

"Check the tires?" called a voice from behind him.

"Please!" City folk considered themselves civilized, Alex thought, but the finer things of life—like not having to gas up your own car—happened here, at what urbanites consider the end of the earth.

The large, rambling building that was Red's appeared to have once been several smaller structures that were now joined together by halls and walkways. It was barn red with white trim. Shutters had been added, and a wooden porch ran the entire jagged front of the building. The porch rail was made to look like a hitching post, and wooden rockers, benches and tables littered the area. A soda and juice machine hummed near the front door, as did a freezer chest with ICE inscribed on the lid. Alex was sorely tempted to sit down in one of the rockers, put his feet up and watch the world go by.

Instead, he walked inside and was met by an eye-catching array that was part gas station, part fast-food restaurant, part clothing store, part gift shop and part hardware supply. To his right was a bank of coffee and soda dispensers; a rotisserie with bratwursts and hot dogs warming; a bakery case full of doughnuts, bear claws and maple bars; and a display of chips and candy that would rival any grocery store in Chicago. In the center of this were four small tables with benches, all occupied by workingmen on their breaks and a small woman behind a counter frying burgers.

The clothing portion of the arrangement included sweaters and shirts sized six-months to XXXL, billed caps, rain slickers, and dreadful-looking matched scarf and mitten sets leftover from the winter stock. Fuzzy yellow work gloves, sunglasses and T-shirts with various sayings emblazoned on them filled other shelves.

There were tacky gifts—plastic horses with clocks surgically inserted into their bellies, lava lamps, stuffed animals—as well as WD-40, de-icer for gas tanks, windshield washer fluid, motor oil, belts and wrenches. One could rent movies, play in the video arcade, shower in the trucker's shower room, do laundry in the tiny Laundromat, do one's Christmas shopping and buy enough glazed doughnuts for a large brunch, all under one roof. A sign hung suspended from the ceiling with arrows pointing in opposite directions. Under one arrow were the words INSURANCE, THE AGENT IS *IN*. The arrow pointing in the other direction said TV REPAIR.

Red's was a veritable feast for the eyes and took the place of at least seven or eight separate businesses in the city.

Then he heard something smash to the floor and an eruption in the direction of the small kitchen. He moved to check it out. Two of the men he'd noticed at the tables were now on their feet, glaring at each other, fists raised. On the floor was a shattered glass plate. Parts of a hamburger and a bevy of french fries were strewn across the floor.

The woman behind the counter scooted out of the tiny kitchen carrying a spatula, waving it in the air. "Break it up, you two. Break it up! Bucky Chadwick, you know better!"

"He knocked my food on the floor." The speaker was a fellow in his late twenties. His nose was bulbous, his coloring ruddy, and acne scars ran deep across his face. His already narrow eyes slanted even further as he curled back his lips, ready for a fight. In his mouth were a set of very large teeth that appeared to have had nowhere to grow except out.

Bucky Chadwick. Will Packard's nemesis. The one who was unkind to animals and people alike.

The little woman swatted at him with the spatula, and hamburger grease splattered across his already oil-spattered clothing. "Bucky, you behave yourself. I won't have anyone picking fights in here, you understand? I'll pack you a burger and fries and bring it out to your pickup truck. You can come back when you decide to behave like a gentleman."

"Ah, Ma."

"Go!" The little woman roared. And Bucky did as he was told.

"Sorry about that," the woman said to the other diner. "Your food is on the house today." And she turned around calmly and returned to her kitchen.

Not knowing what to make of what he'd just seen, Alex turned toward the check-out and nearly ran into another man, one with flame red hair, freckles so thick that they overlapped and a big grin. A well-chewed toothpick dangled from his mouth.

"You are a quart low on oil in your van." the big redhead said politely. "We can put in some 5W30 for you."

"Thanks. That would be great."

"Good, 'cause we already did it." The man studied Alex. "New in town, aren't you?"

"I'm the new pastor at Hilltop Community Church." Alex thrust out his hand. "Alex Armstrong."

The other took the proffered hand and shook it vigorously, like a pump handle. "I'm Red O'Grady. Welcome to our part of the world. And don't worry about that little dust-up back there. Bucky is a troublemaker, but his mother is spitfire enough to keep him under control in here. Too bad she can't follow him around like a tick on a dog and make sure he behaves everywhere."

"Red, come here and look at this carburetor," a mechanic called from the doorway.

"Excuse me. Again, welcome." Red disappeared into the garage part of his minikingdom, leaving Alex to pay his bill.

On the way out, between the inside and outside doors, was a small vestibule with huge bulletin boards covered with sheets of paper advertising everything from Labrador retriever puppies to babysitting, housecleaning and livestock sales. He stopped to look at them and noticed he could buy an antique tractor or a prize bull. Then his eyes fell on a flyer that announced WHEATVILLE FARMERS' MARKET—EVERY SATURDAY 8–NOON. Listed were an assortment of vegetables, pastries and jams. There were even homemade quilts available.

He was still studying the flyer when a tall, sturdily built woman with white-blonde hair entered the outer door and stopped beside him. "Are you looking for fresh vegetables?" she asked, seeing where his gaze was fixed.

"I just noticed the flyer for the farmers' market. Is there anything like that around Grassy Valley?"

The blonde, whose shoulders were nearly as wide as Alex's, reached up, took a stray tack off the board and posted a sign of her own. HOME GROWN VEGGIES—CALL LOLLY ROSCOE. "There isn't, but I wish there were. It would be a lot easier for me to bring my garden produce to one location and sell it. People have mentioned it over the years but no one has ever taken the bull by the horns and organized it. In the past I suppose it was unnecessary since most everyone planted a garden, but times have changed. What's more, this gas station has become pretty famous for its burgers and good service. People stop here a lot. I'll bet a few tables of vegetables would sell well if they were in Red's outlot."

"Surely it couldn't be too hard, could it?"

"I wouldn't think so. In fact, I'd help whoever started it. I just don't want to have all the responsibility." She smiled at him and he noticed her white, even teeth and bright blue eyes. "You're the new pastor at Hilltop, aren't you?"

"I am."

"I go to Hilltop sometimes. I'm Lolly Roscoe, by the way, if you haven't already guessed."

"And I'm Alex Armstrong."

She shook his hand and her fingers were warm and strong. What's more, her eyes were sharp and appraising.

"Maybe you would be interested in helping me start a farmers' market," she said lightly. "What do you think?" There was a flirtiness in her smile that set off warning flares in Alex's mind. Obviously he wasn't ready yet, not open to a relationship. When would memories of Natalie quit stalking him?

He swallowed thickly. "Not at the moment, but if I find someone who can, I'll let you know." Suddenly he felt the urge to escape her appraising stare.

He excused himself as quickly and politely as he could and headed for the food counter, which held soda dispensers and a variety of fast foods.

Carrying the foot-long hot dog and bag of potato chips he'd purchased at Red's, Alex entered the house to find Tripod standing on the area rug in the entry, tail wagging so hard it shook the whole dog. At the first whiff of the hot dog, his tail began to pound on the floor.

"Don't worry, I got you one too," Alex said, reaching into the depths of a sack and pulling out a regular hot dog with no mustard and ketchup. "But you get it only if you promise not to beg while I'm eating."

Tripod gave a sharp whine and tipped his head to one side but followed Alex into the kitchen and lay down on the floor beside his master's feet as he ate. When the foot-long was gone, however, Tripod jumped up and gazed longingly at the other hot dog.

The dog was more disciplined than he would have been, Alex thought as he tossed bits of frankfurter and bun to Tripod, who caught them midair. When he was done, Alex threw away the paper wrappings, wiped the counter and walked into the living room. He stood in front of the large picture windows and stared out at the serene scene before him as the sun lowered in the sky. The days were long here on the prairie so far north on the continent. In the summer it was still light out at nine or even ten o'clock.

Alex rambled through the house trying to shake the feelings of isolation and restiveness he was experiencing. Finally he picked up the phone and dialed his sister Carol's number.

Jared answered. "Hi, Unc. What's up? Do you miss me?"

"I certainly do. Do you want to move out here with me and go to school in Grassy Valley?" Alex asked.

Alex was joking, but Jared answered somberly, as if it were the most reasonable question in the world. "I wish I could, but it probably wouldn't help. I *hate* school."

They were both silent. Alex tried to digest the venom in Jared's voice.

He decided to change the subject. "I have news. I got a dog."

"No kidding?"

"None whatsoever. His name is Tripod."

"That's a weird name for a dog."

"Not if it only has three legs."

"A three-legged dog? Are you crazy?" It was Carol. She had picked up another phone extension and was now on the line.

"No more so than usual, I don't think."

"I suppose it's nice to have company out there in the country all alone, but if you were—"

Alex closed his eyes and groaned inwardly, knowing exactly where this was going.

"—married and had a nice wife to keep you company . . . "

"I hear you, but let's not go into it tonight."

"If you guys are going to talk about Uncle Alex getting married, I'm hanging up."

"I'll call again and we'll leave your mother out of it," Alex promised.

"Cool." A click signaled that Jared had hung up.

"How are things going? Any more outbursts?"

"The only thing I can really connect it to is school—or the mention of it. He's never loved school, but this year he's counting down the days until it starts and getting more miserable with each one that passes. He scares me sometimes, Alex."

"Maybe once it starts things will be better."

"I hope so," Carol said without much confidence, "but I doubt it. I've never seen him as agitated as this."

They engaged in desultory chatter for a few more minutes before they hung up.

The conversation hadn't eased his mind whatsoever. Now Alex's mind was whirling even faster. He felt the need to do something, to make something positive happen. He got out the slim phone book that held the numbers of everyone in the communities around Grassy Valley, found what he was looking for, and dialed. An answering machine picked up.

"Hello, Jonas? Gandy said you have a green thumb and that your garden is huge. She also said you grow everything naturally, no pesticides or the like. Is that true? Because if it is, I have an idea I'd like to run past you."

Late that afternoon, Alex and Tripod were sleeping on the living room floor and being warmed by the sun when they awoke to the sound of the church bells clanging.

"Whaaa—?" Alex jumped to his feet and shook his head to clear out the cobwebs that had lodged there during his nap. The telephone began to ring. He stumbled toward the table and picked up the receiver. "Hello?"

"Reverend Alex!" It was Gandy and her voice was even higher pitched than usual. "There's a grass fire by All Saints and the wind is blowing it right toward the church! The fire department is on its way. Mac just drove over there. Some of the men are trying to get the pews and altar out in case the building burns, but they need help."

"I'm on my way." He didn't even pause to consider that he was still wearing the dress trousers, white shirt and slip-on loafers he'd donned before the Ladies Aid meeting this afternoon. He left Tripod whimpering inside the house and raced to his van.

He was growing accustomed to taking these gravel roads at high speeds, Alex thought grimly as his white-knuckled hands gripped the steering wheel. If he were going to stay in the Hilltop and All Saints communities, his next car would have to be something heavy like an all-terrain SUV—or a souped-up tractor.

He could see smoke rolling skyward. A chill shivered through him. It had been a dry summer, Dixon had explained.

There was not much ground moisture and the last rain had done little to allay the aridness. He saw the large pasture, parched and brittle from the heat, on fire. The flames were spreading outward and moving rapidly toward the little country church. Yellow and orange tongues of fire hungrily gobbled up everything in front of them.

There were several vehicles in the churchyard and out in the pasture, a bright red fire truck. Its crew labored to hold back the flames. Alex recognized the vehicle driven by the All Saints janitor in the mix, as well as the pickup truck he'd seen in the Nyborg yard.

Dixon loped toward the van. He was traveling faster than Alex had ever seen him. "We're moving things out. A lot of it is on Mark's flatbed trailer, which he's pulled out of harm's way. There are still a few pews left, and the pulpit."

"We can't let that burn!" Alex was horrified at the thought of the beautiful piece of art created by Alf's grandfather being reduced to dust and ashes.

"It's pretty solidly installed." Dixon glanced at the rolling flames inching their way toward them. "I don't know if we can get it out in time. Alf is inside working on it. He's determined to get it out or die trying." Dixon paused and gave Alex an intense look. "Literally."

Another chill spread through Alex although he felt sweat pouring down his sides beneath his shirt. "I'm going inside." He was surprised to hear the strength of his own voice.

It was startling how much noise a fire made. There were yells of the men from All Saints and Hilltop, for once working side by side, moving the rest of the pews and the piano out the front door. But more remarkable to Alex was the crackle and snap of dry grass and the rush of water from fire hoses dousing the flames. The scene was chaotic.

Inside the church, men were grabbing sections of altar. Someone yelled "If they don't get it stopped soon, this place is going to go up like a tinder box. We need to get out of here."

Alex found Mark trying to gather candlesticks and collection plates into his arms. Mark turned to Alf, who was frantically working to unscrew the bolts that held the hand-carved pulpit in place. "You'll have to leave it, Alf. It's not worth risking your life over."

"No!" was the strangled response. Alf looked up and Alex was shocked to see the tortured expression, the sheer terror, on his features. There were tears streaming down his face. "Someone's got to help me!"

In this moment, Alex realized, Alf wasn't fighting for this pulpit or even this church. Alf was reliving another place and time, fighting to change history, to somehow redeem himself for not saving his wife and son.

Without thinking, Alex dodged behind the old-fashioned altar and picked up a piece of microphone stand that was stored there and attacked the planks around the platform, prying them loose. Alf, realizing what Alex was doing, began to use his screwdriver to help Alex pry at the planks. If they couldn't get the pulpit off the floor, they'd take the floor with them.

Together they worked like mad men, chopping, prying and weeping. Somewhere in the distance Alex heard the sound of another fire truck approaching, its siren wailing.

When Mark realized what they were trying to do, he added his muscle to the job, working the massive piece forward and back until the wood creaked and snapped.

It was almost loose when a fireman appeared in the building, his thick yellow and black gear making him appear large and alien. "Out! Now!"

It was as though Alf hadn't heard him. He continued to work frantically, sweat soaking his shirt and hair, oblivious to the warning.

Alex and Mark exchanged glances; and, as if of one mind, they approached Alf. Each slipped a forearm beneath one of the man's armpits and lifted him off the floor and half-dragged, half-carried him through the now-empty sanctuary as Alf kicked, fought, and screamed.

They emerged from the church and deposited him on the ground by Mark's truck. "They want us all to move. We saved most of the furniture. You have to let it go, Alf," Mark said. "It's not worth it, not for a piece of wood."

"It's not just wood!"

Alf's scream pierced a hole in Alex's spirit.

Silently, they lifted him into the truck and drove him to safety.

The men of the church stood helplessly by, staring at the scene before them. Minutes passed like hours.

It was Dixon who noticed the change first. "The wind is dying down," he said. "Feel it?"

"And I think it's turning," Alf added. "They'll be able to stop it now. Thank God."

"Let's pray," Alex said and bowed his head in prayer. "Lord, You control not only the wind but our hearts. Thank You today for a double dose of Your generosity. Thank You for sparing most of the church, Lord, and odd as this might sound, thank You for allowing us the opportunity to work together as one. Thank You for the men of All Saints and for those of Hilltop who were united in a single purpose today. You are able to bring blessing out of tragedy, Lord, as You have proved once again. You are a good and gracious God. Amen.

A chorus of amens erupted behind him. When Alex looked up he noticed that Alf had slipped away. He heard him start his pickup and watched him drive away. The fire must have brought every painful memory back.

One by one, the men drifted over to stare at the site, at the small miracle that had transpired.

Guided by the changing wind, the line of fire had stopped at the southwest corner of the church before burning off in another direction. The church lawn and the pasture beyond was charred black, and some of the church's siding was slightly charred; but for the most part, the little country church sat unscathed, ringed by burnt grass.

"Quite something, isn't it?" Tim Clayborn, husband of Amy, murmured as he stood next to Alex. The men of both churches had gathered together and were talking softly among themselves. "The fire somehow went all the way around the church. The siding is blistered and some sparks burned holes in the roof, but it's still here. It's as if God directed the wind to blow right around All Saints." Tim, a strong, athletic looking man, glanced at Alex. "Do you think He can do that?"

"He can do anything He wants, Tim," Alex murmured. "I think He's done something much bigger than directing the wind."

"Huh?" Tim looked at him blankly.

Alex nodded to the cluster of people nearby. The men of the two disparate and conflicted congregations were smiling with relief and clapping each other on the shoulders in celebration, both overjoyed that the little church was safe. "The wind is nothing compared to blowing these two groups into the same place and after the same goal."

Tim took off his cap and scratched his blond head. "It was nice to see us working together for a common cause."

CHAPTER NINETEEN

The Ladies Aid is still waiting to hear what they should serve for the missions fund-raiser," Gandy said when Alex and Tripod entered the church office.

"It all sounds like a lot of work. This church must have as many meals as it has services." He thought back to the casseroles, baked goods, venison and dozens of other kind acts involving food that he'd experienced in the few short weeks he'd been at Hilltop.

"Don't try to stop a Ladies Aid member from cooking a meal they've already made their minds up about. It would be like trying to stop the Amtrak with a pile of bean bags. Like I said, I told them to hold off on the lutefisk, but you aren't out of the woods yet. You'd better be specific—meatballs, ham, tuna casserole, pot roast . . . "

"No tuna casserole, please."

"Okay, I'll tell them to pick one of the others." A smile played on Gandy's lips. "You're pretty popular from what I hear. No one's complained about anything you've done so far. Congratulations."

"Is that unexpected?"

"This place doesn't have a critical spirit, if that's what you mean, but to go this long without doing *anything* wrong, well, I'd say it's remarkable."

More likely miraculous, Alex thought, but didn't verbalize it. "By the way," he said, recalling the thought he'd had during his morning run, "I think it would be a nice gesture for Hilltop to invite the people from All Saints for this dinner."

"I think there goes your winning streak."

"You don't think Hilltop would like that?"

"Not after they stood us up at the open house." Gandy shook her head. "Of course things have softened up between us considerably since the fire. I've even been invited to All Saints to learn how they're putting together their history quilt. But invite them to the Ladies Aid? I don't know. "

Alex moved toward his desk, which was stacked with hymnals, Bibles, sermon notes and bags of red licorice The licorice was Gandy's big downfall but he'd discovered for himself that it was almost as addictive as chocolate and started his own stash of the candy. He decided to move to a more neutral subject. "How's Jonas' garden this year?"

"Huge. He loves to put seed in the ground. He's Hilltop's Johnny Appleseed. Jonas subscribes to the old way, even with his crops. He rotates crops to put nutrients back into the soil and doesn't depend on fertilizer. He lets land lie fallow to rebuild itself, and he plants a variety of crops on the land so that no one crop drains the soil of its nutrients. What some crops take out of the soil, others put back in. Maybe that's part of his problem. He's *too* good a steward of the soil. He could make a lot more money dumping fertilizer, pesticides and who knows what other chemicals on his land, like everyone else does." She paused to study him. "What is this about?"

"I'm sure there is a place for both kinds of farmers, Gandy. I'm just trying to figure out the place where Jonas fits in."

She harrumphed loudly. "Jonas doesn't fit in anywhere these days."

"I'm not so sure about that. I think that Jonas just hasn't found his niche yet."

"*Neesch*? What's that?"

"It's an area that is particularly suited to someone's gifts, talents or personality. In business, it can mean a specialized market."

"I don't get it," Gandy said bluntly. "What does that have to do with my brother?"

"Niche markets specialize in a certain type of product or service."

"Like what?" Gandy was interested but unconvinced.

"Snowblowers, for example, or tree removal."

She stared at him, confusion written all over her face. Alex thought he'd lost her so he hurried to explain.

"Say that you like to fix lawn and garden tractors and lawn mowers, but you especially enjoy fixing snowblowers. In fact, you're really *good* at fixing them, better than anyone else in a hundred and fifty mile radius. People begin to hear about your work and start to bring you their snowblowers to repair. Word spreads and soon you are the most prominent and popular snowblower repairman around. Snowblower repair becomes your niche, your specialty, the thing that sets you apart from everyone else. It's the same way with tree removal. My father had to have several sick elms taken down around his apartment building, but he wouldn't let just anyone come in and start chopping. He made an appointment with the best company in town, one that had taken down more elms than any other. That was their niche."

"And Jonas' niche is . . . ?" She cocked her head, waiting for an answer.

"Pesticide free, organically grown crops and vegetables."

Her eyes narrowed as she thought about it. "That's true, but what of it?"

"You might take that for granted out here. I'm sure Jonas has been making a practice of it so long that he thinks of it as completely normal, but it's not. Organically grown produce, grown with no synthetic fertilizers and no pesticides, needs to meet standards set by the government. If Jonas' crops meet those standards, he can label and sell his produce as organically grown."

"So what?" Gandy was a hard sell, that was for sure.

"If Jonas could meet the qualifications and find a market for what he grows, he'd earn some decent money. Until then, he should bill himself as a chemical-free producer and consider participating in farmers' markets in the area—or start one himself."

"What's the big deal with that?" Gandy was losing interest. She started to shuffle papers around on her desk.

"People are willing to pay much more for food that is organically grown."

That caught her attention. "Here? I'm not so sure about that."

"But where I come from they do."

"But he's here and they're there."

"Then he will have to find a way to sell his product to a wider market. It would take some research and some solid business advice."

Then Alex told her about the woman he'd met in Red's, and the conversation they'd had about a farmers' market and the message he'd left for her brother.

She stirred the cup of tea on her desk. "Jonas really respects Mark Nash. Mark's got a good business head. Maybe he could talk to Mark and get some advice."

"Perfect!"

She studied him intently, her pale eyes filling with tears. "You really care, don't you?"

"Yes, Gandy, I really do. I want your brother and every other person in this community to thrive. In my business, their souls will always come first, but their success and happiness is a close second."

Her eyes narrowed again, and Alex could almost hear the wheels turning under that mop of blonde hair. "Who did you say you met at Red's? The woman who was interested in a farmers' market?"

"I'm not sure if I remember her name correctly, Lolly something, but she was tall and had white-blonde hair. She looked very Scandinavian."

"Lolly Roscoe?"

"Probably. I knew hers was an unusual name, but I must admit I had my mind on Jonas at the moment."

"Lolly is hard to miss," Gandy said dryly. "A lot of people think she's beautiful."

"She's very nice looking, I'm sure, but I had my mind on other things."

"She's single, you know." Gandy appeared to think this was monumental information.

Alex didn't know quite how to respond. "I see."

"And she's been single a long time. She's been engaged a time or two, but it didn't work out."

"I see."

"What is it you see, Reverend? That you just stumbled upon a beautiful single woman who wants you to help her start a farmers' market? Seems to me that you don't see at all. In fact, you're plumb blind to what's right in front of you!"

He didn't like the direction this was going, so he decided to change it. "Lolly is a very unusual name. Where did it come from?"

"There's a story about that."

"There's a story about everything around here." Alex poured coffee into a mug and prepared to listen.

"Lolly's mother wanted to name her something pretty. She read in a book that another name for Charlotte was Loleta. The trouble is, the nurse misspelled the name on the birth certificate and it came out as Lolita."

"How unfortunate."

"Exactly. Her mother was upset, but decided to make lemonade out of this particular lemon, and she's been Lolly every since."

Alex was at a loss for words.

"Word has it that she'd like to get married. She's not getting any younger, you know." She looked him up and down in that disconcerting way she had. "Neither are you."

"I don't exactly have one foot in the grave!" he protested.

"No, not yet. But you'd better watch out. One day you'll wake up and realize you're old and alone and wonder where the time went." Gandy tapped her temple with her forefinger. "You have to watch out for these things, you know. It happened to Walter Englund and it will happen to you."

Here it was, another of Gandy's mercurial leaps from one subject to another. Alex was going to be a mental gymnast by the time she got done with him. He had to admit, however, that he enjoyed talking with Gandy immensely. She didn't mind saying exactly what was on her mind even if he was her pastor. It was enormously refreshing.

"Walter is a good man, but terribly shy. He would have made a wonderful father, but he was too bashful to ask a woman out on a date. And now he's in his sixties and alone, without anybody in the world." She furrowed her brows. "Don't you go doing the same thing."

"I'll remember that." He had an uncomfortable vision of being whisked down the aisle to the altar with Gandy on one side and Lolly on the other. "It just might be, however, that what I'm looking for in a wife is different from what you imagine for me."

"Just don't get too fussy." She waggled a finger at him. "Remember, 'he who hesitates is lost.' Is that quotation from Scripture? Proverbs, maybe?"

"It's an American proverb. Or maybe it originated on the front of a T-shirt."

"Oh," Gandy was undaunted. "All I'm saying is, if love slams you in the face, don't slap it away." She smiled proudly. "And that is a Gandy Dunn quote. Feel free to use it whenever you wish."

Alex was relieved to hear footsteps outside. It was Mattie Olsen, marching in with the same determination she'd had the first time he'd met her when she was on her mission to destroy the ant population of Hilltop Township. Her square jaw was set, her beady eyes flashed with fire and her footsteps sounded like a soldier marching in heavy boots. What had she run into this time? Wasps?

"I have just heard the worst possible news! I don't know what those two young people are thinking. It's practically a historical monument, at least around Hilltop. Desecration! That's what it is, defilement!"

She was certainly given toward melodramatics, Alex mused. What had happened now? The way she was talking, someone might have just torn down the Statue of Liberty. But there was hardly an equivalent to that in Hilltop. Was there?

"What are you jabbering about, Mattie?" Gandy got up and poured the little woman a cup of coffee. Then she dug in her drawer for a Nut Goodie, a candy, Alex had discovered, that was available primarily in the Midwest.

"Ben and Nancy Jenkins, that's who. I was in town today for a new perm"—she patted the tight ringlets haloing her head—"and I heard from the beauty operator who'd heard from one of her clients who'd been at the lumberyard and overheard the young Jenkins couple discussing tearing down the Hubbard house and building a *rambler* in its place! A plain old ranch-style house in place of that mansion? My source also said they'd visited the bank, possibly to discuss a *loan*."

Her source? Mattie was obviously well connected in the grapevine.

"Can you imagine?" Mattie was warming up to enjoy her rant. "That house is homage to the people who settled here, a tribute to show what people can do. The Hubbards came here penniless, worked the land, made good, and built that lovely home; and now some great-great-grandchild wants to tear it down? Sacrilege, I say, disrespect!" She spun on her toes and faced Alex. "What are we going to do about it?"

He must have looked like a trout out of water, working his lips and trying to catch a breath, Alex thought. *We?* When had saving houses become his responsibility?

"Tear the house down?" Mattie snorted. "Why, that house has been a landmark here for decades. What could those children be thinking?"

Who knew, Alex thought; but he put Nancy and Ben at the top of his visitation list. Next time Mattie asked that question, perhaps he'd have an answer.

CHAPTER TWENTY

The scream nearly curled his hair.

Gandy leaped to her feet and knocked her chair backward so that it rolled across the office's sloping wooden floor and slammed into the metal file cabinet. This sent up a racket as the mug rack on top tipped over and the cups went rolling. "Is somebody being scalped out there?" she said, as she hurried to retrieve the errant mugs.

"I don't know, but I plan to find out." Alex strode out of the church and paused on the top step to stare at what was unfolding before him.

Will Packard had arrived in the church parking lot with his bicycle and an old red wagon that had seen better days and probably a dozen children before Will. In the wagon was a wire cage, with a printed cardboard sign hanging off the door that said *Rose*. But the wire door on the pen was open, and the person who opened it—Bucky Chadwick—still had his hand on the wire. Rose, meanwhile, was meandering off at a surprising pace, her wide, squat body waddling from side to side as she moved.

"You get away from her, Bucky!" Will's voice was hoarse from screaming.

"Skunks should be dead, all of them," Bucky retorted in a flat voice as he raised the shotgun he was carrying to his shoulder and took aim. "I haven't got any time for skunks."

"Drop it. Right now. No guns on church property." Alex wondered for a moment if that commanding voice was actually his. Of course, he'd never before been quite this furious with someone.

From the corner of his eye he watched Will scramble to catch up with his skunk. "I could call the police if I thought that you were trying to kill someone's pet."

"It's only a dumb skunk," Bucky growled. His face flushed an ugly red that did nothing for his complexion. "Dragging that thing around in a cage like it was a prize rabbit from the fair, that's just plain stupid."

"And what would you call trying to shoot someone's pet, even if it is a skunk?"

"I was just kidding. I wanted to give the little twerp a scare."

If there was one thing Alex hated, it was bullies who hid behind the line "just kidding" when they got caught. "That's not kidding, that's cruel."

Bucky scowled and thrust a bill into Alex's hand. "I didn't follow him out here to do it, if that's what you mean. Red told me to drive out here and deliver the water softener salt you ordered. I always carry my gun, so I thought I'd do the world a favor and get rid of that rodent. I never thought a guy like you would try to protect a nasty critter like that. Those Packards are crazy, you know."

So he hadn't been kidding at all. He would have shot Will's pet, given half a chance.

Bucky slunk to his pickup and unloaded the forty-pound bags from the pickup bed, his sullen expression never changing. When he was done, he got into the pickup and drove off without an apology to either Alex or Will, who'd corralled Rose and was hugging her tightly to his chest. He stuck as closely as possible to Alex until Bucky was out of sight.

"He'd have killed Rosie if you hadn't come along," Will said bitterly. "Shot her dead. Bucky is the meanest dude in five counties, I'll bet."

"You didn't try to set up a humane society at his place, did you?"

Will looked shocked. "Of course not! That's where I *get* a lot of my rescue animals. Bucky is always picking on something."

"I recommend that in the future you leave Rose at home— for her own safety."

The boy's thin shoulders drooped disconsolately. "But she's my best friend!"

That struck Alex as terribly, terribly sad. "Will, have you or any of your family been to Sunday school?"

"Nah. My dad says that's for sissies and nerds." Will stroked the skunk gently before placing her back in her cage.

"He does, does he?" Alex made a mental note to visit with Will's parents before Sunday school started again in the fall.

"Gotta go," Will said suddenly. He darted to his bike and got on.

"Where?"

"I just thought of a great place for my hoomain society. Me and Rose are going to check it out." And before Alex could give him the third degree, Will pushed off, pedaling as hard as he could. The wagon and its load swayed and bounced behind him.

Alex pinched the bridge of his nose between his thumb and forefinger and sighed. Who would be the next to call and complain about a *hoomain* society in one of their outbuildings?

"It's a good thing that boy has you to protect him," Gandy said. She'd come up beside him so quietly that Alex had not realized she was there. "That Bucky is a mean one, through and through."

"You talk as if Will doesn't have another soul in the world to turn to."

"That's a pretty accurate statement if you ask me. His mama is timid, his daddy is rough and it's hard to make oneself heard in a rowdy group of siblings like his."

Alex expelled a long sigh. "There's need everywhere, isn't there?"

"Yup. And it's been building up since we haven't had a preacher for so long. You walked right into a backlog of need." Gandy might not be eloquent but she certainly knew how to get a point across.

She scowled. "And speaking of need, I called over to All Saints and invited them to our fund-raiser."

"Excellent! Do you think anyone will come?" Alex couldn't keep the hope from his voice.

"Who knows? If word gets to Alf Nyborg and he says he isn't attending, it might be pretty sparse. But if Alf does attend, we can expect a houseful."

"How will the cooks prepare for that?"

"I'm not sure how they do it, but they make a lot of food and know how to spread it a long way. It's not like the loaves and fishes, of course, but meatballs do seem to come out of thin air sometimes."

"There's a vision," Alex said with a chuckle, "meatballs flying through the air like badminton birdies."

"By the way, Nancy Jenkins just called. She and her husband are going to be away on Sunday, so she asked if you could come for coffee today."

Alex glanced at his watch. "I don't know if I should be off drinking coffee when there's church work to be done."

"Reverend Alex, around here, drinking coffee *is* church work."

Alex was getting more adept at driving in the country. At first he'd thought he'd never catch on.

No one used real directions around here. He was hoping for something simple, like *"Take the Twenty-Eighth Street exit and follow it to Twenty-Third Avenue. Travel on Twenty-Third until you come to a four-way stop. Turn right onto Harrison Lane."* Here, everyone used landmarks that had been heretofore invisible to Alex.

Gandy insisted on giving him directions to the Jenkins' home. "Go about two miles, maybe three, as if you were going away from Grassy Valley. Go past the shelterbelt that will be on your right side. It's all pine trees, you can't miss it. Then the farm is on the first road to your right after that . . . or is it the second? Anyway, it's marked with a huge stone that has HUBBARD engraved on it. If you go too far, you'll run into a dead end. There are two separate drives into the yard. You can use either road into the yard since it's summer, but you can only use the one on the left during the winter."

If people gave directions like that in Chicago, everyone would be lost.

When he'd inquired about the two roads leading to the Jenkins' home, he'd received another mysterious explanation.

"The summer road is quicker because it follows the tree line and so it's shorter. The problem is that in the winter, the trees catch too much snow for the road to be useable. That makes it only a summer road. The winter road is the one they plow and keep open in the winter, but of course you could figure that out for yourself."

Not likely, Alex thought. He was learning to "speak Hilltop," but he wasn't very adept at the language yet.

The Hubbard house, Alex realized, was even more spectacular up close than from a distance. It was a grand three-story structure with a wide porch that ran around three sides of the house. Ionic columns separated the first-floor porch from the second. Large windows overlooked a sloping horse pasture. To reach the front entry, Alex mounted six steps. The double doors that greeted him were made of mahogany and intricately carved.

Nancy Jenkins threw open the door and welcomed him inside. "I'm so glad you could come today. Ben and I feel terrible about missing the fund-raiser. I made a plate of sandwiches and a cake. I hope you can join us for lunch."

"Why, yes, thank you. I'd like that." Alex was so engrossed with studying the intricate wood carvings that graced the open staircase and the massive ceiling moldings that he could barely get the words out of his mouth. There were old, elegant rugs on the maple flooring, and much of the furniture appeared to be of the same vintage of the house. "What a lovely home you have."

"*Hmm* . . . I suppose it is," Nancy agreed. "If you like this sort of thing."

"And your great-great-grandfather built it?"

"Yes. Would you like to take a tour before we sit down to eat?"

"It would be wonderful . . . if you don't mind, that is. I don't believe I've ever been in a house quite this grand before—at least not one that hasn't been turned into a museum."

"That's what this place is," Nancy said, sweeping her hand around, "an old museum. It creaks and clanks in the night, and the rooms are drafty. You can't imagine how difficult this is to heat. I've forgotten how pretty it is because of all the upkeep and high fuel bills."

He followed her through the hall to peer in at several bedrooms, each uniquely decorated around a theme quilt on each bed.

"This is amazing. You have an eye for decorating."

"Thank you. I enjoy it. I had a wonderful time when we first moved here, making quilts and choosing accessories. But now we practically live in the kitchen area for most of the winter so we don't have to heat the whole house." She paused thoughtfully. "I wish it were fun again, but it's not."

He followed her to a closed door. She paused. "My ancestors loved parties," she said. "The bigger the better. Everyone in Hilltop wanted to come to my grandmother's shindigs, which were usually held in the ballroom."

"Ballroom?" Alex asked. Surely he hadn't heard her correctly.

"Yes. Up here, where most people have attics. We have a ballroom. It was built for my great-grandmother who also loved to give parties. Come upstairs and you'll see what I mean."

They ascended the steps, and when Nancy moved aside at the top, Alex gasped. It *was* a ballroom. And not just any ballroom either. The ceiling was arched and painted a soft blue, with puffy white clouds through which sunlight seemed to shoot. An occasional bluebird dotted the sky and hummingbirds hovered overhead. Even on a cold winter's night, it would be like standing in the sun on a summer day up here. The floor underneath their feet was parquet and Alex could imagine what it might look like if it were polished to a high gleam. In its heyday, this must have been a wondrous place indeed.

"I've never seen anything quite like this in a private home," Alex admitted. "It's fantastic."

"Yes, I suppose it is," Nancy sighed. She sounded torn, as if she believed his statement to be true yet somehow resented it.

"What's wrong?" The words slipped out of his mouth a little too abruptly. "You don't have to answer that, I mean . . . "

"I don't mind. Let's talk about it over lunch."

He followed her downstairs, rather sorry to leave the fantasy world on the top floor of the house. When they entered the kitchen Ben Jenkins was waiting there. He was quick to offer Alex a cup of coffee.

"We heard about the fire," Nancy said. "It's a miracle that the church didn't burn. Ben said that Alf Nyborg took it pretty hard."

"His wife says he's doing better," Alex commented. He and Betty had talked on the telephone a number of times since the incident. He didn't, however, have time to dwell on Alf as Nancy led him into the kitchen.

The kitchen of the old house was big and sunny. There were cupboards everywhere, and they sat at a large wood table in the middle of the room, which Nancy loaded with food while her husband poured pink lemonade into tall, chilled glasses. After Alex said grace, they dug into the food and didn't speak for some moments.

"Delicious!" Alex said. "Even a sandwich out here tastes like ambrosia. I've never met so many good cooks in one place."

Nancy laughed. "I couldn't help but learn. The two things all the Hubbard women did well were food and parties." Her eyes held a faraway expression. "But it's different now."

"How so?"

"There's no extra cash for parties anymore, especially not the kind my family used to give." Her expression hardened. "This house eats up our money. It will be good when it's gone and we are living in something that isn't impossible to heat."

Alex recalled Mattie's dramatic announcement of the other day. "What exactly do you mean *gone*?"

Ben and Nancy exchanged a look.

"We've decided to raze this house and build something smaller. We might take it down ourselves. If we moved out I'm not sure I could bear to see it slowly crumbling before my eyes." A cloud of melancholy seemed to overcome her.

"Surely there's another way."

Nancy rubbed her stomach. "We've tried to think of one, but considering the circumstances . . . "

Alex raised his eyebrows.

"You're the very first to know, Pastor. Ben and I are going to have twins."

"Congratulations!"

"So you see we're pretty desperate to do something as soon as possible. The heating bills for this house nearly broke us last winter and now, with two babies . . . "

"I wish I could suggest another way."

"If you can think of one, let us know," Ben responded. "This is breaking Nancy's heart, but we can't go through another winter heating this place. It has so many leaks that we heat more of the outside of the house than in. I really wish there were some other way."

Another way... another way... The litany rang through Alex's head as he drove back to the church. Who was he to cruise into this place and start telling people what to do? This was his time to listen and learn, wasn't it?

Or was it? The light-bulb moment occurred as he pulled into the parking lot.

He hurried inside, glad Gandy had gone home for lunch. If he was going to stick his nose into someone else's business, he preferred to do it alone.

It took him only a moment to find his cousin Dan's phone number. He dialed quickly and then waited impatiently for someone to pick up on the other end of the line.

"Armstrong, Lerner and Cooper Architects, may I help you?"

"May I speak to Dan Armstrong?" Alex tapped the toe of his shoe on the floor.

"Who may I say is calling?"

"His cousin Alex."

"Certainly." Her tone became obsequious. "I'll put you right through."

"Yo, Cousin Alex! What's up?" Dan's cheerful voice greeted him. "How's living in Timbuktu working out?"

"It's not quite as remote as you might think it is. And it's lovely here. I had no idea what I was getting into, but so far I'm glad I'm here."

"Good, good. Then why the call? Are you going to build yourself a parsonage?"

"I have a very good one, thank you." And he told Dan about the old Hubbard house and Nancy Jenkins' grief about having to move out. "Your firm does a lot of home restoration, what would you recommend?"

"Without seeing it with my own eyes, it's hard to say, but usually there are some basic things that can seal up a building like that without destroying the integrity of the house or breaking the bank."

"Like what?"

Dan rattled off a list of suggestions.

"That still sounds expensive."

"Too bad the house couldn't be turned into a money-maker. It would pay for itself in no time. We've restored several old homes that were then turned into B and Bs. It's a perfect combination, really. The work can be paid for and written off as a business expense."

"I can't pay you for this so I can't make you do it, but if you'd be willing to write a letter telling this young couple what you've told me, I'll pass it on to them. Whatever advice you can give would be helpful, and I know they can't afford an architect. It will give them something to think about, at least."

"Consider it done. In fact, I'll overnight one to them directly."

"You don't have to do it that quickly. I am, after all, meddling in someone else's affairs, and I haven't yet got a plan as to how to present this."

"Don't waste time. If they decide to tear down the house, all is lost. If the house is the gem you say it is, you don't want it disappearing from the landscape."

Suddenly Alex was infused with a sense of urgency. "Thanks, Dan. You don't know how much I appreciate this."

CHAPTER TWENTY-ONE

Alex looked down upon a sea of faces as he gave the congregation a final blessing. He was shocked to feel himself close to tears.

The Hilltop congregation was out in full force. The cooks, who'd taken up the last pew in the back, had disappeared immediately after the sermon to check the roasters and coffeepots in the basement. Everything was ready to show their welcome to their new pastor.

The members of All Saints had come to the morning's combined service held at Hilltop, with Alf and Betty Nyborg leading the procession.

Alex was glad to see him. It had to make Alf feel good to be greeted here with such enthusiasm and compassion.

"Now, before we go downstairs to eat, let's sing the table prayer." Alex closed his eyes and listened to the warbling tones of older voices, Winchester's rumbling baritone, Lauren's perfect pitch, a sweet section of sopranos and a few pleasantly off-key voices rusty with disuse. It was heavenly music to his ears.

There was a bottleneck at the back of the church as people had to go single file down the narrow staircase. Already warnings of "Watch your head" and "Be sure to duck" chorused. Alex wondered anew why the two churches had been designed with such hazardous staircases.

Then Dixon Daniels cleared his throat and bellowed, "We should let the pastor go first!"

"That's quite all right. You know us pastors, we like to feed our flocks first," Alex rejoined.

"You at least have to get ahead of Dixon," Mike Carlsen advised, "or you might not get any food at all. He's got a hole in one leg, you know, and he tries to fill it every time there's a church dinner."

Mark, who'd been quiet until now, spoke up. "I think it would be nice if our guests from All Saints were the first to eat. We're glad to have you here."

Gandy was right about the ladies' meatballs having some of the loaves and fishes qualities. They seemed to come out of nowhere in endless supply, along with accompanying gravy, creamy mashed potatoes, string beans with almonds, hot and fluffy rolls, and strawberry shortcake with berries fresh from Jonas Owens's garden.

Several people stopped at Alex and Dixon's table to talk, but it was Tillie Tanner, her brightly dyed red hair clashing fashionably with her even brighter yellow sweater, who touched Alex's heart when she handed him a pint jar filled with flowers clipped from her garden.

Then the elderly woman Alex remembered from All Saints—the one with her thinning white hair worn in a bun, blue eyes, and a pleasant but wrinkled face—appeared by his side. "My name is Althea Dawson. We first met at our quilting group." Before Alex could reply she continued, "It's a blessing to have our churches sharing a meal once again. Thank you."

"Don't thank me," Alex said softly. "It's Him," and he pointed heavenward with his forefinger, "you ought to thank."

"There was a time when our two churches were very close, but we drifted apart," Althea said. "Hardly anyone remembers that now. It's ironic that it took almost losing one of the churches to bring us back together. Perhaps we can retrieve some of what's been lost over the years. Today is a start." She squeezed his hand and he felt her bony fingers and warm, fragile skin.

Alex was savoring a second cup of coffee and his strawberry shortcake when Dixon waved three people to their table. One was a bull of a man in his seventies with a dark, leathery skin and dark hair with surprisingly little gray. Despite his age, his strength was apparent. When he smiled, his teeth flashed white and even.

The other man was taller and much younger but soft looking, as if he rarely saw the light of day. His hair was light brown with a reddish cast, his eyes big behind thick glasses. His movements were choppy and awkward. The woman with them was at least five-foot-nine and looked as though she too was accustomed to heavy farm work. With her nondescript brown hair, a pleasant smile and simple cotton dress, she could almost certainly blend into any crowd of middle-aged women. Her hands were rough and reddened, the knuckles thick, the nails chewed so short that no white above the nail bed could be seen. Working hands, Alex deduced, and nervous ones.

"I'd like you to meet Horace Abel and his housekeeper Flossie Kennedy and her son Charles," Dixon said. He was forever the social director around Hilltop, and took his job very seriously.

Alex jumped to his feet. "I'm pleased to meet all of you."

Horace's handshake was painfully strong, and Alex was glad he didn't have arthritis in his knuckles. Charles's grip was just the opposite, damp and limp. It reminded Alex of a rubber glove filled with tepid water.

"I think these are the hardest-working people in the township," Dixon commented amiably. "Horace keeps his place as tidy as the Queen's gardens, and Flossie does the same for his house. Charles, on the other hand, sits at the computer twenty-four/seven."

Charles's lip twitched, amused by Dixon's exaggeration.

Before Alex could say more, Mattie Olsen bustled over, coffee carafe in hand. "More?" She lifted the carafe and began to pour as Horace Abel and the Kennedys slipped away.

"This is some of the best coffee I've ever tasted." Alex looked into the bottom of his white cup. "It's so," he searched for the word, "clear." That was the first time he'd ever described coffee that way.

"Egg coffee." Mattie chuckled at the pastor's expression. "Mix an egg into the coffee grounds before you make the coffee. We do it in those big white coffeepots you see on the stove. Best in the world, egg coffee. No bitterness, no acidity. It's Scandinavian, you know. The diehards mix not only the egg but also the crushed shell into the coffee before they cook it."

"It looks like wet potting soil," Dixon offered, "but it works."

So this was the egg coffee Dixon had mentioned. That would teach him to turn up his nose at things before he'd tasted them.

Eggs in coffee, fish soaked in lye—and yet these were some of the best cooks he'd ever come across. And there were all the foreign-sounding foods he'd heard bantered about for the last few weeks—rommegrot lefse, krumkake, egg and anchovy sandwiches, and perhaps the oddest of all, fish balls—made like meatballs—in a can. From now on it might be wise to just eat and not ask too much about the sources of these delicious flavors.

He picked up his cup and walked to the back of the room, where Jonas Owens was standing.

"My sister Gandy told me what you said, about the organic farming," Jonas said without prelude.

"I hope you don't think I was meddling." The difficulty with being a preacher and mentor as well as friend was how to draw the line between being interfering and simply caring enough to take action.

"Meddling? Hardly. I appreciate that you care." Jonas looked down at his feet. "I've been trying to go it single-handedly, and it's been mighty lonesome these past months. I especially left God out of the equation. I've been so ashamed of myself and of what a bad steward I've been for the blessings He gave me, that, frankly, I thought He'd given up on me. Remember what He did to the guys with those talents."

It took Alex a moment to realize what Jonas was talking about. "In Matthew 25, you mean?"

"That's the one. How does it go again?"

"A master was going away so he divided money among his servants. Each was given the amount the master knew they were able to handle. Everyone got an amount that was right for his particular abilities. Each was to care for that money and use it well. All found ways to make even more for their employer by the time he returned except the one who, instead of using his money, buried it in the ground. We all have other gifts too—time, resources, skill—and He expects us to use them wisely until He returns, not let them lie stagnant."

Jonas' gloomy face grew longer still. "See? I didn't use what God gave me well. I had a farm, and now I'm about to lose it. God isn't rating us on what we have, but what we *do* with it. I'm sunk."

"Is that it? You're giving up so easily?"

Jonas smiled faintly. "Not *easily*, exactly. I did get on the computer and do a little research on organic farming." He snorted. "That's just a big fancy name for what I've been doing all along."

"That's exactly what I was thinking." Alex hoped against hope that Jonas had taken it another step.

"So I called a friend of mine. We went to grade school together before his family moved away. Now he's a county agent and he got really excited when I told him that I only used natural pesticides and the like on my farm. He said there were lots of places looking to buy organically grown stuff and that I should get approved by an office inside the Department of Agriculture. There are accredited certifying agents that see if the food you grow meets certain standards.

"There are a lot of hoops to jump through but I'm going to try—if I can find a way to hang onto the land long enough. My buddy is going to look into it for me. He says that because organics cost more, I'd earn more money on the farm."

"That's great, Jonas." Alex paused, "But what will you do for money in the meantime?"

"There's the rub, Reverend. There's the rub."

Alex had greeted several more people when a robust blonde woman walked up to him. "Remember me? I'm Lolly Roscoe. We met at the gas station. I'm the one who was talking about starting a farmers' market. Gandy Dunn encouraged me to come today."

Alex reminded himself to strangle the meddling Gandy as soon as he could get his fingers around her neck.

"I'm still interested in that farmers' market concept. I've done a lot of research." She fluttered her lashes. "Could we get together one day and talk about it?"

Warning flags popped up all over his brain. Alex found himself almost relieved to hear an angry, angry voice on the other side of the room, a reason to excuse himself from Lolly's rapt attention.

Will Packard, who he'd only realized was in church during the final hymn, was having a food fight with another, slightly older redheaded boy. A lump of mashed potatoes had just landed on Dixon's lapel.

Will was a lucky boy, Alex decided. If anyone but good-natured Dixon had taken the potatoes all over the front of his suit, Will might have been sent packing. Dixon, however, was handling it with aplomb as Alex strode up to stand next to him.

"Are you boys hungry?" Dixon asked as he scraped the potatoes, which were fortunately gravy-free, onto an empty plate.

"Yes, sir," the replied in unison.

Alex noted that the pair was definitely cut of the same cloth—red hair, freckles, high cheekbones and rascally expressions that virtually screamed *trouble*.

"Then maybe you two should grab a couple of spoons and eat these potatoes you launched at me. I wouldn't want you to go away from a church dinner hungry."

"Gross!" Will squeaked.

"Double gross!" Both boys stuck out their tongues. "Is this how you'd behave in your own home . . . ?" Dixon's voice trailed away, obviously realizing that it probably *was* familiar behavior to the Packards, and he changed tactics.

"If you aren't inclined to eat them—and potatoes are made for eating—then think how disinclined I am about wearing them."

"I was aiming them at Ricky," Will explained. "If he hadn't ducked, they never would have hit you. Make *him* eat them. It's his fault."

"That's flawed logic if I've ever heard it. If you'd never thrown them, they wouldn't have hit me either."

Will looked dismayed. "We're sorry, Mr. Daniels. Really."

"Then your punishment is to go tell your parents what you've done and apologize to them as well as me." Dixon wiped the last remnants off his jacket.

The boys' faces went as white as sheets, and Will made a strangled sound in his throat. Alex and Dixon simultaneously saw their reactions, and Dixon smoothly interjected, "Or better yet, tell Pastor Alex about it and apologize to him."

The relief in the boys' faces was obvious. They nearly fell over themselves to get to Alex.

"We're sorry. We really are."

"We didn't mean to cause trouble, honest."

"If you let us come back, we'll be good."

Were those tears in Will's eyes? Alex wondered. Was he afraid that this little episode would get him banished from church altogether?"

"Of course you can come back. That's what church is, a place for people who do wrong things to come and to be forgiven."

"Sinners, you mean?" Ricky straightened up and leaned forward, suddenly interested. "My ma told us about sinners."

Bless Mrs. Packard's heart. The woman was trying to teach her children spiritual things against what, Alex was beginning to suspect, were nearly insurmountable odds.

"Exactly."

"My pa calls me a little sinner all the time," Will admitted, cheering up. "And that's the best of the names he calls me."

Alex exchanged a glance with Dixon who was listening with interest. "Is he here today?"

Ricky pointed to the far corner of the church basement. "Over there, with our ma."

Alex followed the direction of the grubby little finger. A hulking man with a mop of black hair, a surly expression, and a suit straining at the seams sat next to a petite red-haired woman with a carefully blank expression on her face. There were other children with them, including a baby, all redheads.

"It was nice of them to come."

"It wasn't out of nice that Pa did it," Will informed Alex. "They had a big fight over it, and for once, Ma won. Besides, he was curious."

Ricky, seeing an opening, scampered off.

"He said he wanted to see someone 'stupid enough to come out here in this forsaken place.'"

"I see." Was that what he was? Stupid?

"I told him you weren't stupid at all, but he didn't believe me. He's not much for ministers and church. He leaves that up to Ma. She's crazy about it. She probably wouldn't have gotten him here if you hadn't had food." His eyes grew wide. "He had *three* helpings."

Alex put another notation on his mental list. Spend some time with Mrs. Packard. The woman, he had a hunch, would welcome some support and encouragement.

Out of the corner of his eye, Alex saw a tall man in jeans and a chambray shirt dart out of the kitchen and through the back door carrying a package. "Who was that?" he asked Lauren who was collecting used water glasses from the tables.

"Oh, that was Jacob Olson. He must have come to pick up his dinner. I'm surprised too. Usually Lydia or Clarence takes it home to him."

"Why didn't he simply join us for dinner here?" He was finally getting accustomed to calling the noon meal by its locally acceptable name.

"Jacob? He doesn't socialize." Lauren said that as if it were a commonly known fact. Before Alex could inquire further, she added. "I talked to those from All Saints as they were leaving. They were thankful to be included. Alf was very quiet, however."

"Alf's wounds go deep."

"Thankfully he has a wonderful wife who encourages him to let go of the past."

"I don't get the impression she's had much success as of yet."

"Betty's a prayer warrior and she has faith. How else could she have stayed with Alf all these years?"

How indeed? He could learn a thing or two from that woman, Alex realized, particularly about refusing to give up and about honoring God's timing, no matter how impatient he was for results.

As the crowd shrank, Alex found his way toward Mark Nash. He was sitting at the end of a table with Dixon, sharing a carafe of coffee. He sank down beside them with a sigh. "You're both look pretty serious. Is something wrong?"

"I was just asking Dixon what he thought of my plan." Mark reached out and poured coffee into a cup for Alex.

"For what?" He savored the coffee as it tracked across his lips and down his tongue to the back of his throat. Mildred Holmquist had shown Alex how to make egg coffee on one of his trips to the kitchen, and he'd already decided to make it a tradition at his house. He could hardly wait to show this off to his sister Carol.

"To help Jonas out of the hole he's dug himself into."

That made Alex sit up. "Do you have an idea?"

"He told me he's looking into the organic business," Mark said. "It's a great idea. He also told me Lolly Roscoe had asked him if he'd be interested in taking part in a farmers' market. He's going to need capital long before that falls into place, if it ever does. That's why I was just asking Dixon if he thought Jonas would sell me a quarter of his land."

A quarter, Alex had learned, was one hundred and sixty acres. That was large in a city, but not so very much land out here.

"There's a quarter of his land that abuts some land I farm. I don't mind offering him top dollar. It's good land, flat and with no sloughs. If he'd take it, he could use the money to pay off his bills and get his feet back on the ground."

"It would give him time to look into this organic farming thing," Dixon added. "He'd lose one quarter of land but not the whole farm. What do you think, Alex?"

"I think it's a great idea . . . if Jonas will go for it."

"Pride runs deep around here," Mark observed mildly.

"And pride goes before the fall," Dixon added.

"This is very generous of you, Mark."

The lanky man shrugged. "I'd like more land. Jonas needs help. It doesn't seem generous at all, just practical. I only wish he'd come to me months ago or that I'd known how big the problem was earlier."

"Practical, then. When are you going to talk to him?"

"I thought I'd drive over there this evening."

"I'll start praying for both of you." Praying, Alex thought, that Jonas' pride wouldn't stand in the way.

"You do that."

Dixon walked upstairs with Alex after Mark left. His expression was troubled. "What did you think of that little Packard boy's reaction when I mentioned his father?"

"Those kids turned white as sheets. Do you think something is going on in that home? Something bad, I mean."

"If Earl Packard could be thrown in jail for being mean, nasty, callous, irritable, cantankerous, belligerent, ornery and spoiling for a fight, then he'd be there already. I've never heard of him lifting a hand to those kids, but who knows? His wife is as sweet as a woman can be."

"I think I'll keep an eye out for those children."

"That shouldn't be hard," Dixon said. "They're constantly in trouble. You'd have a hard time not seeing them."

CHAPTER TWENTY-TWO

A day off. Alex hardly remembered the concept; and now that he had one, he didn't know what to do with it. He'd awakened at his usual time, six o'clock this Monday morning, despite his plans to the contrary.

He picked up the phone and set it down again. He wanted to talk to Carol and Jared, but the last two times they'd spoken, his nephew had been gloomy and negative, and his mother, frustrated.

"It's all because of school," she complained, "and it hasn't even started yet!"

"Maybe things will be better than he expects."

"You tell him that. I certainly can't get it through to him. He won't even talk to me about it anymore."

"Carol, is Jared depressed?" It was difficult even to ask the question about his easygoing, cheerful nephew. "Maybe this isn't about school at all, but something else."

But he'd wondered what could that something else be as he returned the receiver to its cradle.

Alex grew restless thinking about it and decided that only physical activity would shake the cobwebs from his brain.

"Want to go for a run, Tripod?" he asked the dog who was sleeping in the early morning sun that filtered through the eastern-facing windows.

Tripod's ears twitched; and even though he was in a deep doggie sleep, he roused himself, sat up, and his tail began to pound rhythmically on the floor. *Run* had become his favorite word and he literally jumped with joy when he saw his master's running shoes come out of the closet.

"Come on, then. Let's check on the neighborhood."

They exited through the screen door and headed east, where the sun was rising rapidly. Alex veered northward, turned east to take a loop past the Carlsens' farm, and then turned south and finally west until he had gone what Dixon called "around the block."

As he passed the Jenkins's house—the old Hubbard place—he slowed to study it in the morning sunlight. The windows sparkled, and the flecks in the granite block foundation twinkled in the sun. It made Alex sick in the pit of his stomach to think of it being torn down. But he'd meddled enough already by talking to his cousin last week. He'd heard nothing back from Dan, either. Maybe he'd asked too much of a very busy man. Now it was time to back off and let life take its course.

"Hey, Rev!"

Alex's gaze followed the path of the voice and Tripod's ears went on alert. Ben Jenkins was heading toward them, wearing jeans, a white T-shirt and slippers. His hair was still rumpled from sleep. "You're out early," Ben said as he stopped at the mailbox. He opened it to reveal the previous day's mail, which included the weekly *Grassy Valley Gazette*. "Or I slept in. Nancy's making breakfast. Want a cup of coffee?"

He was about to make his apologies when Alex realized it was his day off. If he wanted to have coffee with a neighbor, there was no reason not to. Besides, both he and Tripod could use a break.

They followed Ben to the house, where he produced a dried pig's ear snack for the dog. "I keep them on hand." Ben grinned boyishly. "You never know when one of your visitors might have four feet . . . or three."

"You're a fine host, Ben." Alex took the treat and made Tripod sit before he gave it to him.

"Nancy and I both like having company. It fills this big old house and makes it feel lived in."

Nancy greeted them at the door. "Did you come for breakfast?" she asked hopefully. "I'm making Dutch babies and I'd love for you to try one."

"Babies for breakfast? I don't believe they're on my diet."

"Not that kind! They're puffy pancakes I fill with apples, butter and cinnamon."

"Then how can I say no?"

Nancy set the table with lovely old china—her grandmother's, she said. She also put out linen napkins and sterling silverware before placing her centerpiece, a small bowl of fresh flowers. "In my family, we have a policy. We don't save the good dishes for guests. We enjoy them every day. It's that old adage about treating your family like they were guests and your guests like they were family, I guess."

She disappeared into the kitchen and soon reappeared with a puffy pancake in a large cast iron pan. "Voila! Do you want syrup or powdered sugar?"

She returned again to the kitchen and came out with a platter of thick cut, crisply fried bacon and a fruit compote. She poured the men mugs of rich, dark coffee before joining them.

"Do you cook like this every morning?" Alex couldn't help but ask.

"When Ben encourages me." Nancy spooned fruit onto everyone's plate. "I would cook like this every day if I could, but he says I'll have to open a restaurant and feed someone besides him or he'll weigh four hundred pounds."

"Nancy loves to cook and to sew. She gardens and paints too," Ben said proudly. "Miss Domesticity, that's my wife. She'd be happy if she could do that all day, every day."

Nancy blushed prettily.

"By the way, we got a letter from an architect in Chicago who said he knew you."

Alex felt his own neck redden. "I stuck my nose into somewhere it probably didn't belong. Feel free to tell me to mind my own business. It's just that I've heard so many people concerned about losing this house that I decided to ask an expert about it."

Alex explained the telephone call to his cousin Dan. "I did it without asking your permission. It was impulsive and I'm sorry."

"Don't be. It's nice of you to be concerned," Nancy said. "His letter made a lot of sense. He listed some of the most inexpensive things he recommends to people who are restoring old houses. Unfortunately I'm not sure we can afford even that."

"We spent most of January and February with temperatures in minus double digits last year. All we really know is that we can't afford another heating bill like that," Ben said bluntly.

Nancy touched her belly. "With two babies on the way we'll have lots of extra expenses, and I don't intend to keep them in a cold, drafty house either.

"We'll have to study it, I suppose." She looked at Alex. "Who knows? But thanks for caring."

"It would be hard *not* to care about the people here," Alex admitted, relieved that they'd taken his help in the spirit it had been given. At least he'd tried.

Alex collected Tripod, thanked his hosts, and resumed his run at a much slower pace now that his stomach was full. He was on the main road that ran past the church when Lauren caught up to him in Mike's pickup.

"You're out early on your day off," she commented as she rolled down the window. "Do you need something to do?"

"Not really, but what do you have in mind?"

"I've got apples that need to be used up. You can have them if you want them. To make a pie or something."

"Me?"

"Don't sound so shocked. Some of the best cooks I know are men."

"Let me think about that for a while, but thanks for the offer."

"No problem." Lauren waved cheerily and pulled the truck away.

It wasn't long after he'd showered and shaved that Alex *was* wondering what to do with himself. Then he remembered the trove of calendars and trunks Jared had found in the old garage.

The building smelled of diesel fuel. Over the years, oil had soaked into the rough wooden floorboards, leaving them with a permanent blue-black sheen. The windows were small and caked and crusty with years of grime, as if this narrow, nondescript building had been overlooked time and time again.

The old calendars on the walls beckoned invitingly, but today it was the trunks that held Alex's interest. Aged as some of them were, they could have come west with the settlers of this area on prairie schooners or sailed the Atlantic from the old country. What could be stored in here that no one had ever come to retrieve?

He pulled a flat-topped trunk that looked like it had come from the early 1900s into the middle of the space. He found a small milking stool, which he placed so that he could view into the depths of the trunk. It opened with a loud creak, as if the leather straps and metal hinges had been untouched for decades.

The inside seemed a disappointment at first. A few old books, a felt dress hat, a moth-eaten wool suit, and a strange, collapsible basket made of wire. Alex didn't know what to make of it.

He was thumbing through one of the books—a volume of Shakespeare—when he heard footsteps behind him.

"Hey, preacher man, what's up?" a cheerful and upbeat voice said.

"Dixon, I'm glad you're here."

"I just wanted to see if you were entertaining yourself properly on your day off. Otherwise I'd invite you to go with me to pick up a used garden tractor I purchased."

Alex waved him over. "I saw these trunks in here when I first arrived, and my curiosity got the best of me—who left them here? Why?"

Dixon squatted down beside him, resting on the tips of his toes. "I doubt I can explain all of them, but I do know what that one is about." He picked up the odd little basket and collapsed it in upon itself and then pulled it into shape again.

"When you looked around the cemetery did you notice a few graves at the back that had only small, flat headstones or plaques?"

"I did. I meant to ask someone why they were so different from the rest of the headstones."

"Most of those graves are those of hired men." Dixon played with the basket thoughtfully. "Men who used to work on the farms, live in the bunkhouses and sometimes die there. Usually when a hired man died, his employer would provide a small funeral and a burial plot. Very few shelled out a lot for a regular headstone and they were buried together in that section of the cemetery. Lots of times they didn't have families or their relatives couldn't be reached, so there was no one to take the belongings. One of the former pastors started storing those things in this little garage."

"Do you think that unmarked grave is one of those men?" Alex couldn't get it out of his mind.

"I doubt it. No one like that has been buried here in many years."

A wave of sadness broke over Alex as he imagined those alone and lonely men, buried in a mass plot, their life possessions limited enough to fit into a small trunk.

"Ashes to ashes, dust to dust," he murmured.

"It that in the Bible?"

"No. It's from the Book of Common Prayer, but it expresses beautifully the fleeting nature of life and the eternal nature of God."

They sat side by side, silently and companionably considering the transitory qualities of life on earth, until they heard the crunch of tires on gravel.

Shaking off the somber mood, Alex and Dixon rose to check on the new guest.

It was Lolly Roscoe with a plate of macaroons in her hands. Her smile was wide and engaging but it faltered when she noticed Dixon emerging from the shed with Alex.

"Oh, *you're* here," she said to Dixon.

"Yep. Sure am." He made no offer to leave. In fact, he seemed to plant his work-booted feet more firmly on the earth.

"What have we here?" Alex asked, uneasy with the odd conversation.

Lolly bestowed her high-wattage smile on him. "Jonas and Barbara Owens and I spent a little time together this morning to discuss the idea of a farmers' market. We set a date to try it and made a call to Red to see if we could set up in his parking lot. He said it was fine with him as long as we paid him in strawberries and peppers." She thrust the papers into Alex's hands. "Here's a sample of the flyer we want to make up."

The paper depicted a quaint-looking market with striped awnings and carts overflowing with fruits, vegetables, and flowers. There were happy vendors beside each cart. All in all, a very inviting scene. The date and time was listed.

"We're calling around. Lydia Olson said she'd bring pint jars of jam to sell. Nancy Jenkins is bringing quilted potholders. I told her she should bring her larger quilts as well. You never know what could sell. We want to have more stuff than just produce. I think it will be wonderful!"

Then she frowned. Even that didn't mar her Scandinavian beauty. "There is some hang-up about a permit. I'm going to check into it this afternoon. I hope it doesn't cost a lot of money or prevent us from moving ahead."

"I'm sure you'll figure it out," Dixon said cheerfully.

Lolly scowled at him. She seemed to want to say some-thing, but hesitated, glanced at Dixon, and closed her lips tightly.

"Thank you, Alex. I . . . " her voice trailed away and she seemed at a loss as to what to do next. "I'd better get going."

Reluctantly, she headed for her car.

When she'd driven out of the yard and onto the main thor-oughfare, Dixon chuckled.

"What was that about?" Alex scratched his head, puzzled. "Why did I just feel so uncomfortable?"

"Other than the fact that Lolly's set her eyes on you for her next romance, you mean? Lolly's upset with me." Dixon appeared impish and unrepentant.

"Why?"

"Because I didn't marry her."

Alex's jaw dropped.

"She's upset with Mark too. He didn't marry her either. She's looking for a man who wants a permanent relationship. Mark and I were terrible disappointments to her." Dixon eyed Alex. "You'd be wise to remember that before you get too involved with Lolly Roscoe."

"Don't worry about that," Alex said vehemently. "There's no danger of my getting involved."

"Methinks you doth protest too much," Dixon quipped, approximately quoting Shakespeare.

"Maybe, but I've got my reasons."

Dixon crossed his arms across his chest and studied Alex. "So you either had a close call or a total wreck in the romance department."

"Let's just say I was engaged once, and she found someone else." His voice sounded terse in his own ears.

"Ouch."

"You could say that." It actually felt good to tell someone his story. He'd kept his breakup mostly to himself until now.

"Are you over it?"

Alex hesitated. "I think I'm more 'over it' every day since I've come to Hilltop. I don't think of Natalie as much. It's a healing place, Hilltop."

"So you aren't interested in getting involved again?"

"Involved? Not now. I have no intention of getting caught up in another relationship."

"No? Then keep that in mind around Lolly. Otherwise you might find yourself in a marriage trap before you know it."

There were land mines everywhere, Alex thought with alarm. What would he step into next?

Chapter Twenty-Three

Alex walked his company out, and on his way back inside, he noticed a brown paper grocery bag containing apples on the porch. Lauren, he thought, determined to see him learn to cook.

He showered, made coffee, ate one of the apples out of the bag and settled at the kitchen table with a stack of catalogs that had come in his mailbox. There were a million things to be done but he didn't feel like doing any of them. He was going to have to get some new hobbies. He couldn't go out and pick up a game of basketball here, nor could he walk three blocks to see a movie or go to the library. Lauren had once told him that in the country people learned to entertain themselves, not have others do it for them. He was beginning to understand exactly what that meant.

Alex was relieved to hear a rapping on his front door, glad for a diversion from his own little pity party. He opened it to find Lydia Olson on the porch.

"Lydia, to what do I owe this pleasure?" He swung the door wide to allow her to enter.

She tittered like a young girl and walked in. "You have such a way with words, Pastor. Clarence came to work on the well. There's something that needs to be replaced in the pump, I believe. I rode over with him to weed your flower beds. I'm sure you haven't had time, especially with all that's been going on."

"That's very kind of you, but not necessary. You have work of your own to do. You people of Hilltop are too good to me. Besides, Tripod and I have been pulling intruders every time we come back from a run. I think you'll find the place surprisingly weed-free."

Lydia frowned. "Oh dear. I'm sure Clarence will be here at least an hour or two. He'd be very provoked with me if I asked him to give me a ride home now. Do you have anything else I could help you with—windows to wash? Laundry to hang on the line?"

Alex was about to offer to take her home himself when an idea struck him. "Lydia, could you teach me to cook? I've got a bag of apples crying out for a pie, and I've never made one."

The little woman's face lit up like the night sky on a Fourth of July. "I'd love to help you. How about an apple crisp instead? That might be a little easier to start with."

"Excellent." Alex ushered her into his beautiful kitchen. "Show me what to do first."

It was peaceful, he realized, and comfortable, working side by side with Lydia. She bustled about humming as she set him to washing, peeling and coring the apples while she placed oatmeal, flour, brown sugar, butter, cinnamon, nutmeg, measuring utensils and a large bowl on the counter.

He was reminded of Miss Merrill, his high school chemistry teacher, a plump, meticulous woman, laying out beakers and setting up Bunsen burners and microscopes in the lab for the day's experiments.

"I've laid out everything you'll need and jotted down the recipe for you to follow. Just put the ingredients in this bowl in the order I've listed them. You'd better take the butter out of the refrigerator so it softens."

As Alex did so, Lydia picked up a paring knife and began to work on the apples, her fingers swift. The red peel went flying.

"So, Lydia, tell me more about yourself." It seemed perfectly natural to ask the question in this convivial atmosphere.

"There isn't much, I'm afraid," she said wistfully as she rested her forearms on the sink. "Hilltop has always been my home but, wonderful as it is, I've always wanted to get away for a time and see the world. I've often had the feeling that there is something out there for me, but there's always too much work to do. Clarence and Jacob depend on me, you see. I even dreamed of marrying, but once our parents died, I became responsible for our house, and after that . . . "

The longing in her voice struck Alex as particularly sad. Lydia must have been a pretty young woman. She had a good sense of humor and a charming laugh—both of which were more obvious when her brother wasn't around to quash them.

"Maybe it's not too late." Alex kept his eyes on the apple he was peeling. "You could travel. Take a cruise. Find a friend and drive cross-country. Lots of things."

"Me? Without the boys?"

It always astounded Alex that out here any man who was single, no matter the age, might be called a "boy." Clarence had passed boyhood several decades ago.

"I've never even considered that." Lydia fingers slowed as she peeled. She looked up at Alex with bright eyes. "It's something to think about. I've always wanted . . . " Then, deftly, she changed the subject. "Do you have a bladed dough blender for cutting the butter into the dry ingredients for the topping?"

Alex peered helplessly into the drawer that held small kitchen gadgets. He wouldn't know a dough blender if it jumped up and bit him. Lydia, however, plucked the bladed device out immediately.

He hoped he hadn't started something by encouraging Lydia to exhibit some independence. Surely she wouldn't go too far with it. Otherwise he'd have to deal with Clarence and the mysterious Jacob.

He wanted to inquire about Jacob, to unravel the puzzle of why he was so reclusive and what had caused him to be that way, but he had a feeling in his gut that it might shatter the pleasant camaraderie that he and Lydia currently shared. Instead, he picked up the recipe and pretended to be interested in reading it.

Lydia Olson's Apple Crisp

- 2 cups flour
- 2 cups rolled oats (I prefer the old-fashioned kind)
- I tsp. cinnamon
- I/2 tsp. nutmeg
- I I/2 cups brown sugar, packed
- I I/2 cups butter
- 2 quarts peeled, cored apples (Whatever type you have will work. Delicious makes a more mushy crisp but it still tastes wonderful.)
- Combine dry ingredients. Cut butter into mixture until it's crumbly.
- Pat half of mixture into bottom of 9 × 13 pan. Top with apples.
- Cover apples with the rest of the crumble and bake at 350 degrees.
- It will take 45–50 minutes or until apples are tender.

Delicious served with whipped cream or ice cream (vanilla or cinnamon).

Alex chuckled to himself. How could this *not* be delicious? His mouth began to water. Lydia paused to look out the window, her expression wistful. "It's funny, isn't it, how life works out. What you dream of and what you actually do are sometimes very far apart."

What were Lydia's dreams? Alex mused. And how far afield had they gone?

"It was wonderful to see Alf Nyborg at the church dinner," Lydia said. "That fire may have been a blessing in disguise. And Earl Packard and his family! I don't know that he's darkened the door of the church much since he was a teenager, and I can't imagine a man who needs it more. He's got the sweetest, meekest wife and those darling children."

Alex didn't quite know how to formulate his next question. "Is he . . . good . . . to them?"

Lydia looked at him sharply, and he saw the keen intelligence in her eyes. "Does he abuse them, you mean? Nobody has ever come out and said that, although the children are careful to stay on his good side. Earl is a bully, and in his mind the glass is never half-full, only half-empty. It's amazing, really, how bright and charming—if mischievous—the children are."

"I have a lot of unanswered questions about that family," he admitted as he measured out two cups of flour and two of rolled oats.

"It will take a while to understand everyone here," Lydia said sympathetically. "But give it time." She tossed a cup and a half of packed brown sugar into the bowl while Alex measured the cinnamon and nutmeg.

"My nephew Jared said something to that effect—that I'm surrounded by stories and I've only read the first page of each."

"You wouldn't expect to read a hundred books all at once and finish them immediately, would you?"

"Of course not."

"Then you can't learn everything about Hilltop in one sitting either. And just like books, some of the people of Hilltop are easier to read than others."

"Have patience, you mean?"

Lydia smiled at him. "You said it yourself."

"I believe I will learn a lot from you, Lydia."

"And I've already learned a lot from you," she said.

The crisp was out of the oven and they started a fresh pot of coffee brewing just about the time Clarence finished repairing the pump and came to the house.

"So my sister is teaching you to cook. You picked a good teacher, Reverend Alex. A mighty good teacher."

Lydia blushed at the compliment and gave Clarence an extra large square of the crisp and a mound of vanilla ice cream to go with it.

Alex brought his own plate to the table, but a pounding at his door forced him to set it down and check to see what the commotion was all about.

As he opened the door, Will Packard darted inside and grabbed Alex's legs. The boy was trembling.

"You've got to hide me, Pastor. I'm going to get killed!"

And Alex had thought dramatic announcements were Mattie Olsen's domain.

"Surely not, you're . . . " Then he got a good look at the boy's face. It was filled with genuine terror.

"Bucky Chadwick spotted me trying to unleash a dog he's had tied up for days. It got its foot caught in a trap and Bucky left it there to suffer. If it doesn't get help, it's going to be just like Tripod!" Will's tear-stained face was enough to wrench Alex's heart. And the thought of what had happened to Tripod . . .

"He yelled that he was going to go back inside and get his gun and shoot both me and the dog." Will's body was shivering slightly less as he clung to Alex. "I got the dog loose and carried him as far as I could. I hid him in a spot where me and my brother have a fort and then took off running for here. I've got some other animals there too. If he shoots that dog . . . "

Clarence was on his feet with a roar. "That outlaw has got to be stopped! He's been causing trouble since he was six years old, but this is ridiculous. He can't just pull out a gun and threaten to shoot people."

"Maybe we should call the police," Alex ordered, seeing red himself.

"I'll take care of this," Clarence stormed "and I know something that scares Bucky more than the law."

"What's that?"

"His mother."

"Will, you stay here with Lydia. I'm going with Clarence."

Will didn't argue.

By the time they got to the Chadwicks', Bucky was already traversing the field near his house in the direction Will said he'd taken the dog. True to his word, he had a shotgun in his hand.

Clarence, driving his four-wheel drive pickup, ignored the *Keep Out* signs in the driveway. He drove right across the field of wheat that was not yet ripe. He pulled up next to Bucky, who stopped to glare at him, his eyes narrowing to slits.

"Just what do you think you're doing?" Clarence boomed.

"Going hunting. What's it to you?"

"Dogs aren't in season, Bucky."

The fellow looked surprised, and then suspicious.

"Who says I'm hunting dogs?"

"Will Packard, that's who."

"That little weasel has been trespassing on my land and now he's stolen my dog," Bucky snarled. "I won't let him have that dog. I'll kill it myself if I have to."

"No, you won't."

Alex marveled at Clarence's turnabout. It wasn't long ago that he'd been furious with Will and his animal rescue project. Suddenly they were on the same team.

"You're trespassing too, you know. I oughta call the police."

"Do that, please. Will you? I have quite a bit to say to Grassy Valley's finest."

Bucky, realizing that tactic wouldn't work, turned on Clarence with a snarl. "There's nobody on this green earth that's going to stop me from finding and killing that dog. And I'm going to give that kid a whupping too, once I catch him."

Clarence reached for something in his pocket. "I can think of someone who'll put a stop to this."

Bucky laughed a grating, rusty laugh. Then his expression changed as he noticed that Clarence had pulled out a cell phone. "Who are you calling?"

"The one person who knows how to put you in your place." Clarence pushed a button and a call started to go through. "Your mother."

It was gratifying to see Bucky turn ashen.

"Myrtle? It's Clarence. How are you doing? Is it busy at Red's? No? Good. Then maybe you could come home and solve a little problem for us. Your son threatened one of the Packard children and he has a gun. He wants to shoot your dog."

"Is he with you?" They could all hear Myrtle Chadwick's voice through the mouthpiece.

"Yes. Do you want to speak to—"

"Bucky, you get yourself into the house!" Myrtle yelled so loudly that Alex wondered if she actually needed the telephone.

Clarence winced and pulled the phone away from his ear. "I'm on my way home right now, and if you think you're going to hurt anything, then you've got another think coming!"

Her voice calmed as she said to Clarence, "I'll be right there. Have him leave that gun with you. Take it home and get rid of it. And watch him until he goes into the house. I don't want him slipping off before I get there." Her voice raised and she was addressing Bucky again. "If you're gone when I get there, don't bother to come home again."

Bucky flung the gun into the bed of the pickup and stormed off toward the ramshackle two-story without another word. The screen door slammed behind him, and they could hear the sound of the television being turned to high volume.

"He should stay there. He doesn't mess with his mother." They got into the pickup and Clarence backed down the driveway to return to the parsonage. "He's a difficult person, but the one person who can handle him is Myrtle. We'd better get Will and see if we can find that dog."

When they got back to Alex's, Lydia was feeding the boy apple crisp and ice cream. The tears had dried into dirty little tracks on his grubby face. Alex couldn't remember ever seeing anyone more pitiful—or worried.

"Did he get the dog?" the child asked, his voice wavering.

"No, Clarence got to Bucky before he had a chance."

The relief on the boy's face was palpable.

"We'll go look for it, if you want," Alex offered.

Will jumped to his feet. "I'll call Ricky. He knows where our secret hiding place is. He can hide the dog in our barn until I find a new place for my hoomain society."

"Will, about that . . . "

Three pairs of eyes watched him expectantly, Alex noted, as he scrambled for something more to say.

CHAPTER TWENTY-FOUR

Alex sighed deeply, wondering what he was getting himself into. "Maybe you'd better use one of the outbuildings here at the parsonage for your 'hoomain' society until I can figure out something better—and before you get in trouble with every person around Hilltop. If, that is," he cautioned, "I can get permission from the church council."

"Consider it done," Clarence said relief apparent in his voice. At least he would not have to deal with any more critters. "I'll speak to them myself. There's the little well-house that's not used for anything. It will hold a couple cages and maybe a bed or two for cats or dogs. But, Will, you had better figure out how to stay out of trouble with those animals, or this opportunity will disappear."

"You mean it? You both mean it?" Will bounded up from his chair and flung himself at Alex and then at Clarence. "This is great! Wait until I tell Ricky and the others. They'll find me lots of animals, I'll bet."

"Whoa," Alex said. "There's only room for a few. Don't go overboard. And we'll probably have to think of an alternate solution sooner or later."

Will turned shining eyes on Alex, who was struck with affection for this dirty, red-haired boy. "And I can be at your house every day!"

Alex hadn't thought of that, but he was surprised to find that the idea didn't upset him. In fact, he rather liked it. Having a little boy and his pets around might be just the remedy for some of that restlessness of his.

"You'll have to behave."

A halo practically sprang out of the top of Will's head, so innocent and sweet was his expression. "You can count on me, Pastor Alex."

Alex already knew he could count on Will. He just wasn't sure for what.

⬛▪️⬛ ▪️⬛ ▪️⬛

"So what do you think of Hilltop so far?" Lauren asked as she, Mike and Alex shared a pizza on the picnic table outside her home. A bee buzzed in the distance, no doubt romancing a sweet-smelling flower nearby. Occasionally a hummingbird dipped close, interested in the pitcher of red Kool-Aid on the table. Tripod's tail thumped happily as he lay with the Carlsens' dog on a lawn with grass so soft and thick it must have felt like a cool, plush bed.

"In many ways it's like something out of a dream. A step into the past." Then he thought about Clarence whipping out his cell phone to report Bucky to his mother. "And yet it is totally contemporary and relevant. I feel welcomed like a family member, and yet I have so much yet to learn."

He thought of the problem of Bucky and his mother and wondered how long the little woman would be able to manage the young man before he tipped over into real criminal activities. He recalled Alf Nyborg's suffering and the toxic drift that had settled over All Saints because of it. There were the mysteries too. Why did Jacob Olson never come out in public? What made Flossie and Charles Kennedy so reclusive? What exactly were Bessie Bruun's mental problems, and was there any way to help her? He thought of Jonas, Gandy, and the Packards, particularly the belligerent Earl and the effect he was having on his children. There was Lolly Roscoe, who made him as skittish as a deer in the forest. He wanted to know more about Matt and Martha Jacobson and their movie star daughter Amelia Jacobs, and to spend time with the delightful Ole Swenson and to hear stories about Twinkle Toes.

What's more, he hadn't yet seen Inga Sorensen's artwork or visited the Aadlands or the Hansons. He wanted to spend time with the cheerful, if slightly addled, Lila Mason and to have coffee with Tillie Tanner, who brought him a little gift nearly every Sunday—wildflowers, a cookie, a colorful stone—and thanked him for becoming their pastor. And he still needed answers about that grave.

He'd barely scratched the surface, just as Lydia had pointed out.

"Happy enough to stay around for a long while?" Lauren asked. "I know you're a fish out of water here. I'm just hoping that you're figuring out how to breathe here at Hilltop and not itching to go back to the ocean." Her expression was somber. "I know that we're not the biggest, fanciest place you could have gone. . . ."

He hadn't even considered what a concern that might be to his parishioners. "No chance, Lauren. For the first time in my life I feel . . . right. As if I'm in the place God wants me to be.

I won't run away from that. Until I get word from Him that I should move on, I'll stay."

She heaved a sigh of relief and held up the pizza pan between them. "More pepperoni?"

Even though Lolly had managed to acquire the needed permits for the farmers' market, she hadn't been able to control the weather. It had rained all night, flooding the lot at Red's and forcing the participants—a small but determined few—to make do on the school playground.

It wasn't an auspicious beginning, Alex thought as he turned off his alarm clock. He'd set it because Jonas had warned him that the best produce was likely to be gone by eight thirty; and if he wanted any of Jonas' famous sweet peppers or burpless, seedless cucumbers, he'd better come early. What's more, Mildred had harvested lavender and was selling fragrant potpourri. Most exciting of all, according to Gandy, Lilly Sumptner had decided to have a rummage sale right there at the market and sell out all her leftover makeup, not that Alex would be interested, but Gandy predicted it would draw a big crowd.

It was already difficult to find a parking spot, Alex discovered when he arrived at the school. But why should he be surprised? People around here got up so early that they had to wake the birds. The ball field had been designated as a parking lot, so he parked on third base and walked toward the hubbub.

Red was in the middle of the crowd, waving his hat and directing traffic, his toothpick clenched in his teeth, a smile on his face.

Jonas was in his booth, bagging vegetables, while Gandy counted out change to the customers. The worry lines in her face had softened somewhat, taking several years off her features.

"By the way," Gandy said to Alex, "I'm planning to up my tithing next month. From now on I'll be in the church office a half hour more each day."

Surprise must have shown on his face because Gandy added, "We'd give more if we could. God's good, you know."

Touched and humbled, Alex could only nod.

Dixon, of course, was already meandering through the booths when Alex arrived. He was carrying a thermal mug of hazelnut-flavored coffee and shelling green peas and popping them into his mouth.

"I picked green peas for my mother every summer for eighteen years and never got one into the house to cook," he admitted cheerfully. "My mother said I'd turn green and round one day, but it hasn't happened yet."

"You're chipper." Alex sat down next to him on the bench on which Dixon had taken root.

"What's not to be happy about?" Dixon took a sip of coffee and sat down the mug. "Little Will Packard has a place for his animals, Bucky's afraid to go anywhere near him, and Nancy Jenkins told me this morning that they aren't going to tear the old house down this fall like they'd planned. Her doctor told her he didn't want her messing with anything like that during her pregnancy. Instead they're going to spend a little money to seal it up like your cousin told them to. The house might still be on death row, but it has a temporary reprieve.

"Nancy also told me she'd gotten a good price for one of her quilts. Somebody from back East was passing through and saw the signs. She said it would be enough to get a new storm door for the house."

"That's good news." Alex eyed Dixon, who was grinning and waving at everyone who passed by. "You seem in high spirits."

"You're sharp, I'll give you that." Dixon sat back on the bench, stretched and removed his cap to scratch his head. "I got a letter from my twin sister Emmy yesterday. She's coming for a visit."

"I'll look forward to meeting her."

A faraway look filled Dixon's eyes. "Emmy and I used to be inseparable, like that." He crossed his fingers. "But she left the farm and I stayed. Emmy is a nurse and she was able to go anywhere she wanted to work. The time between our visits has gotten longer and longer. Lately it's been once or twice a year. I'd give anything if Emmy would decide to come back to Hilltop. It's funny, but twins do somehow feel more complete when they're together."

"What would bring her back?"

"Nothing I can think of except a miracle. There's barely a clinic in Grassy Valley, and she loves her work. Now she's become a nurse practitioner. There would have to be something pretty tantalizing here for her to stay around. Unless a hospital springs up on Main Street, I think I'll have to settle for our yearly visits."

"There's just something special about family," Alex commented, thinking about Jared. "When is she arriving?"

"She wants to be here for harvest. Says it's the best time of the year on a farm. I have to agree with her."

"Never having experienced that, I have to ask, why?"

"Even the air changes during harvest. It's dry, crisp, fresh and dusty all at once. The nights are often spectacularly clear. And it's exhilarating. The combines and trucks roll day and night. It's the time of year that farmers are finally rewarded for their hard work. It's thrilling when they can finally bring their crops in. It's like nothing else."

Alex tried to imagine the anticipation. A year's work paying out, collecting the bounty from the fields into the bins, knowing at long last if the winter rations would be sparse or plentiful. No wonder it was electrifying.

"This is the time of year you'll see the church coffers increase," Dixon added. "After harvest, people know how much of their year's income can be put in the offering plate. When I was a kid, the church set aside a Sunday after harvest to show appreciation for the preacher and the organist."

"How so?"

"There were two offering plates, one for the preacher, the other for the organist. People dropped checks or cash in each plate, giving as much as they could or as much as they thought the two should receive."

"I hope that's stopped by now. I don't need one more thing." Alex surprised himself with his own words. Back in Chicago, he'd worried how he'd make ends meet once he took the salary Hilltop had offered, but he'd rarely thought of money since he arrived. The parsonage was everything he needed and more, he had food coming out his ears, and offers for help with everything he might ever have had to hire done in the city. He felt downright rich on half the salary he'd had in Chicago.

Jonas strode over to join them, his shoulders back, and his chin high. "How do you like it? I think it's going pretty well in spite of last night's rain. It should help that the Cozy Corner is going to have its meatloaf special today. That usually draws more people into town."

"It's a good start."

The man's gaze flickered. "I'm more grateful than I can say, to all of you for your help and support." He pointed upward, "And to Him."

Gandy fluttered over to them eating fluffy cotton candy that vaguely resembled her hairdo. "There are more people asking about those burpless cukes, Jonas. You'd better get back to your stand." She looked at Dixon and Alex on the bench and popped a clump of spun sugar into her mouth. "Best day I've had in months!"

As they sat there, Alex and Dixon saw most of Hilltop and of Grassy Valley amble by, and many stopped to talk. At noon, they stood in line at the Cozy Corner to eat meatloaf and fresh green beans, and afterward they stopped at Licks and Peppermint Sticks for an ice cream cone. Dixon got his hair trimmed while they were there.

When Alex arrived at home in the late afternoon, Tripod greeted him with such wild abandon that he nearly knocked Alex flat. Alex finally managed to divert him by throwing a ball across the gentle green slope of the lawn. They played the game until even Tripod was tired, and then sat together on the front steps watching a fat, improbable bumble bee hover in the flower bed. Bees defied logic and physics by being able to fly with those large bodies and tiny wings, Alex knew, but nevertheless, they flew. He wasn't much different. He seemed an unlikely candidate for helping others. And on his own, he was. But he wasn't alone.

Whatever came next, whoever stirred the pot and caused the trouble, Alex refused to worry about it today. This was the day the Lord had made. He would rejoice and be glad in it.

JUDY BAER is the author of more than seventy-five books. She won the Romance Writers of America Bronze Medallion and was a RITA finalist twice. Judy is a North Dakota native and lives in Elk River, Minnesota, with her husband.